SCHOOLED: CONFESSIONS OF A ROOKIE VICE PRINCIPAL

by Lenore Hirsch

Copyright 2021 Lenore Hirsch
All rights reserved

ISBN: 979-8-9850746-0-4

No part of this book may be reproduced in any form, except brief excerpts for the purpose of review, without written permission of the publisher.

DISCLAIMER: Events in this book are based on author experience at eight or more schools (the author has lost count). Characters have been combined and changed to no longer bear resemblance to reality. In fact, the author no longer recalls what really happened. Fiction is definitely easier than life.

ALSO BY LENORE HIRSCH

My Leash on Life: Foxy's View of the World from a Foot Off the Ground

Leavings

Laugh and Live, Advice for Aging Boomers

CREDITS: Cover art by Aaniyah Ahmed, 99designs.com
Book design by Lorinda Ruddiman, L2napa.com

Laughing Oak
Napa, California

Dedication

For the students and teachers who provided the challenges, humor, and personal impact that inspired me to write this book.

CHAPTER ONE
OUT OF THE CLASSROOM...

"Education is not preparation for life; education is life itself." —John Dewey

HAVE YOU EVER JUMPED FROM A ROCKY CLIFF into a deep pool far below? Sure, you've been told it's safe, you'll be fine, but as the soles of your feet taste the breeze, you wonder if you've made a terrible mistake. That's how I feel walking through the front door of Hamilton Middle School on this warm June afternoon. I've apparently passed the screening interview with the district team, and now I'm going to meet the principal, who will be my boss if I get the job. Sweaty, but on time, after rushing from my classroom a half hour away, I wait for the secretary to show me into John Carlson's office.

I've had other vice principal interviews. Quite a few, actually. Times I thought it went well, only to be told they hired someone else. Someone they knew. Or a male. But I'm optimistic—maybe this time it will be me. Finally, the gal with the too-red lipstick puts down her phone and opens the door to the inner sanctum. John Carlson doesn't rise from his chair, but from the table where he is sitting, holds out his hand.

"Ms. Walker, I'm happy to meet you."

He grasps my hand in his—pudgy and moist—and squeezes. I take the seat across the round table from the equally rotund man. He sports a mustache that needs a trim, hairs sprouting every which way. His smile reveals crooked, yellowing teeth. The scent of tobacco is in the air, despite the fact that California outlawed smoking on school campuses years ago.

"So, Cynthia—may I call you Cynthia? —why middle school?"

"I've taught this age group for ten years and I love it. I can influence their character development, help them to see their positive attributes at an awkward time of life…and they get my jokes."

"Good. This is one of the finest middle schools in the country. I hope you know it's a big deal to be considered for this position."

I smile and nod. Finest in the country?

"I've been here eight years and have turned this place around. Test scores are up. The teachers are awesome. And the parents—well, the parents are my partners. We work together."

Did he forget someone? "And the students?"

"The kids? They love me, of course. You'll see. Our last VP learned so much from me that he's now a principal in the district. I'm looking for someone new to train, to back me up in this important work."

I want this job, even if the guy in charge isn't inspiring me with his dedication to curriculum or students. Plus, I've done my homework; Hamilton's test scores are not bad, but they're inconsistent. Maybe he's not a data guy, but has other endearing qualities?

"So why should I hire you?" he asks.

"I care about the kids and the curriculum. I'm detail-oriented and organized. My special education background will make a difference for your special needs students. I'm all about improving instruction. Oh, and I'm a hard worker.…"

"I'll make sure you work hard." He gives me a sly grin.

Chapter 1

"What are your weaknesses?"

My response, from a repertoire of previous answers: "I'm an overachiever. I like to finish every task. And I don't give up on people."

"That's great. And you're OK handling student discipline for all the grades?"

"Sure," I answer. *All* of it? What will *he* be doing?

He grins and rises. "Shall we go for a walk?"

John Carlson's failure to talk about programs for students gives me qualms, but I take a deep breath and follow him out the door for a tour of the campus. Teachers are still at work after hours.

He intercepts a man walking into a science lab. "Bert Sheldon, meet Cynthia Walker. She's a VP candidate." Sheldon shifts his armful of books to shake my hand.

"What do you teach?" I ask.

"All science, all the time," he says, with a grin. He's tall with a round face and an extra chin. Small bald spot. "Got to go," he says and he's off. I appreciate his enthusiasm.

"Sheldon is good, a very charismatic guy," says Carlson.

We approach another classroom, its door standing open. "Let's meet Mr. Simons," says Carlson. The teacher rises from his desk to greet us.

"Derek, I'd like you to meet Cynthia Walker, maybe our new VP. Cynthia, Derek Simons." I like the sound of "our new VP." Hope springs eternal.

Derek Simons extends his hand and dazzles me. Slim and at least six feet tall, his dark hair curls over his collar. When he smiles, I feel a bit of rock star magnetism. I can almost hear a ding off his sparkly teeth. Soft lines grace the corners of his green eyes. He's one good-looking guy. The pre-teen girls must be mesmerized.

"Pleased to meet you," he says. His handshake is firm and

3

warm, with a tender squeeze before he releases my hand.

"You too," I manage to get out. I've noticed the posters in his room. "Social studies?"

"Yes, seventh grade. You're welcome to visit soon."

I smile as Carlson leads me away. We continue past the cafeteria, gym and athletic fields. He talks non-stop about the great staff he has hired, the wonderful parents who are his friends, and the students who love him.

Circling back to the parking lot, he says, "Thanks for coming," shaking my hand again and grasping my forearm, like the handshake isn't enough contact. "We'll be in touch."

Shortly after I get home, I get the call from the district—I'm the new VP. I put down the phone and do a happy dance. "I did it! All right!"

After catching my breath, I phone my parents and my best friend, Erica, with whom I've worked for years. And I leave a message for my current principal. She'll need to hire a new teacher.

I pour a glass of wine and settle into the sofa, giving my doubts free rein. Am I tough enough to tackle the behavior problems? The long days and evening events? Will the teachers accept me as a leader? I'm giving up the security of tenure. After years of teaching English and math to learning disabled middle schoolers, if they don't like me at Hamilton, I'll be out on my ass. I push away thoughts about the egotistical principal, who thinks he's the center of the universe. I'll find a way to make it work.

AFTER SCHOOL on one of my last teaching days, my friends give me a warm send-off in a classy bar. Wine and good wishes abound, and the gifts make me laugh. A whistle on a fancy neck chain. Band-Aids for "the wounds to follow." A nice bottle of wine for "the end of a trying day—there will be many." When the party ends and I say my goodbyes, I'm filled with bittersweet

Chapter 1

emotion—I'm going to miss these guys. Erica gives me a parting hug and a "Go get 'em, girl."

Driving home, I recall the two years of night classes to get my administrative credential. Too many applications and unsuccessful interviews. My car is filled with boxes of teaching materials accumulated over many years. Getting to this point in my career has not been a cakewalk. However, I've got my shot now and there's nowhere to go but forward. Alone.

My summer vacation is short, as I must report for work a week before the kids show up. I make time for a week in Florida with my parents. Dad, a newly retired corporate manager, has always wanted to see me take on more responsibility. We've had many conversations about my job, the lack of recognition, and low pay.

"I'm glad to see you advancing out of the classroom," he says.

"I'll miss teaching English, but I'll still be working with kids, helping them with their problems. I hope I'll have solutions."

Back at home, I buy a new wardrobe of more professional clothes—skirts, suits, and little heels. In early August, before I report to Hamilton, I'm like a child anticipating the first day of kindergarten. What will they think of me? How will I handle my new duties? Misbehaving students. Teachers at all ages and stages, needing encouragement or help. I want to find out if Bert, the science guy, and Derek, the cute social studies teacher, are good at their jobs. And then there's the boss. My first impression of John Carlson is that he's all talk. I hope I'm mistaken, because every administrative task at this school will be up to him...and me.

What is that saying? "Fake it until you make it." That's me. My plan is to look and act the part and hope I know what I'm doing. Maybe it will work.

CHAPTER TWO
FIRST DAYS

AFTER YEARS OF COMMUTING MOST OF AN HOUR in traffic, it's magical that my new job is just two miles from the house I purchased last year. Living and working in the same community sounds like a dream, until it occurs to me I may not enjoy seeing students and parents at the supermarket when I run out in sweats, without makeup, to pick up milk. Or when I'm at the bar in my favorite restaurant. My mind wanders to other fears. What if the kids I'm destined to suspend from school find out where I live? Enough, Cynthia. Let the future unfold.

A few days before I must report for work, I visit Hamilton to pick up a key and check out my new office. I stop in the staff room to put drinks in the fridge.

"Hi, I'm Cynthia," I say to two women at the copy machine, which is running full blast.

"The new VP," says one. "I'm Gloria Burrows, PE." Gloria looks the part. Her shorts and tee shirt reveal a muscled body. She looks like she could sprint out of the room on a moment's notice.

"Laura Gonzaga, special ed," says the other, holding out her hand. "I've heard you have a special ed background." Laura is around my age, a willowy blonde.

"Yes, ten years in the classroom with learning disabled kids."

"We've got a couple of challenging Special Day classes," says Laura. "But the staff is really good with the kids."

I'm aware of the challenges that students who need full-day special education can have: autism, severe learning disability, emotional disturbance. I've never taught these students; now I'll be expected to handle them on their worst days. The thought makes my jaw clench, but I force a smile.

"Glad to hear it," I say and continue on my way to my new office. A postage stamp, about eighty square feet, it has a desk, a couple of straight-backed chairs, and a bookshelf. But it's mine. The glass door and windows face an open area of the office, so I'll be able to see what's going on. The only wall decoration is a Hamilton Tigers gold and black pennant. I'm a Tiger now. Not since high school have I been a person to yell encouragement from the bleachers for my team. And I'm no sports fan. I need to work at becoming a cheerleader for Hamilton and its athletic teams.

BEFORE SCHOOL STARTS, managers must attend a two-day retreat. In my previous district, the administrators gathered at resorts near the ocean or Lake Tahoe for days of wining and dining and talking about their jobs—all in the name of team building. Just my luck, due to budget constraints, the first retreat for this newbie takes place in town at district facilities, with boxed lunches.

The first morning we gather in the old high school. Would you believe that because it's not earthquake-safe, it serves as an administration building? If the building collapses on managers, no big deal! About thirty administrators sit in groups around small tables in a former classroom. The long agenda includes contract negotiations, construction projects, and new state curriculum standards.

Not sure which parts are most relevant, I take notes on my yellow pad, sitting with the principal, John Carlson. He occasionally whispers something in my ear, like, "Don't worry about that; we'll talk about it later." His breath suggests he recently

Chapter 2

smoked a cigar. Gross.

Over my box lunch, I chat with the vice principal of the other middle school in town. "How do you like Hamilton so far?" she asks.

"Well, I'm just getting set up. Haven't spent much time there."

She continues, "Call me any time you have questions. I'm sure you will." And she winks.

While we talk, a few others come over to introduce themselves. I meet Bruce Milburn, fiftyish, short, and stocky, who tells me he was the VP at Hamilton until he got promoted in the spring. Now he's an elementary school principal.

"Congratulations," I say.

"Thanks, and good luck at Hamilton. You're going to need it." He laughs and continues, "Call me if I can help." The lunch break ends and there's no time to ask what he means. What is it about Hamilton that I don't know? Will I need to call on Bruce for help?

On the second afternoon, we board a school bus for a short ride to the county ropes course. The staff there divides us into teams. I'm the youngest and most agile in my group. I help the others to stay upbeat as we manage the "alligator crossing," a series of square platforms, each one smaller than the last, spaced apart and a couple of feet off the ground. We have to get six of us from one location to the next using only a six-foot board. The alligators are imaginary, but some older teammates hesitate, fearing injury if they fall off the board.

"Go Margaret, you can do it!" She walks too slow, trembling, but makes it to the next platform.

I wait for the others, then skip across with nary a concern. Late in the afternoon, I stop by the school to leave my notes and pick up my laptop. Carlson's office door is open. I poke my head in. He's wearing a blue golf shirt and his glasses rest at the bottom of his nose as he studies a newspaper article in front of him—or is it the sports page?

"Hi, John. I didn't see you today."

"I had more important things to do," he says. "The parents are my number one priority. You'll learn that, if you want to succeed. I had a couple of meetings with parents whose kids need some special attention."

"Anything I need to know about?" If it involves students, I surely do.

His ample forehead reflects the afternoon light as he puts down his pen. "Not today, no. But I got a $1,000 check towards the computer lab upgrades we need. What do you think of that?" He grins in his self-aggrandizing way.

I mutter something and leave. Does he expect me to kiss up to parents? To ask for donations? I have no training or interest in either.

BEFORE THE FIRST DAY OF SCHOOL, the teachers have a workday without students. It will begin with a staff meeting. It's a perfect time to meet the teachers and support staff in a more relaxed setting than we'll have once the kids show up. On the other hand, what kind of impression will I make? I can't come on board like I know everything already—I don't. It's important for me to hear their wishes and concerns. But I don't want to look too green either. Sleep comes very late the night before as I try to strategize. In the end, I can only be myself and hope it will all work out.

I'm awake early, full of nervous energy. If I were still a teacher, I'd wear jeans and a tee shirt for setting up my room. But I want to look professional from day one, so I go through my new outfits and select a skirt and blouse. The speedy two-mile drive feels like a fun ride at Disneyland. It's barely 7:30 when I meet Sharon, the principal's secretary. Her auburn hair in a pinned-up do suggests lots of hair spray. She puts down her

10

Chapter 2

giant, red-lipstick-marked coffee cup.

"Welcome," she says. "Come with me and I'll introduce you to Gaby."

I follow the powerful scent of Shalimar down the short hall, praying I won't sneeze, to the open area opposite my office. It holds desks for the attendance clerk, Roxanne, and Gaby, whose official duties include overseeing the schedule and clerical work for me. After all those years alone in my classroom, I'm actually going to have an assistant. I wipe my hands on my skirt and struggle to stand still.

"Gaby," Sharon says. Gaby doesn't look up but continues mumbling to herself. She's sorting through a stack of sheets, maybe the computerized list of classes and teachers to which students have been assigned. Sharon taps her long ruby-red nails on Gaby's desk and raises her voice a notch. "Gaby..."

Gaby finally looks up at Sharon, then at me, and breaks into a grin.

"Ah, Ms. Walker. So sorry. I'm happy to meet you."

I will learn a lot about Gabriela de la Luz Rodriguez Vazquez in the months ahead. Just five feet tall, she's shorter than many students. My guess is late forties. With her hair in a bleach-streaked bob and flashing brown eyes, she exudes energy. Born in northern California to a large Mexican family—six brothers and sisters—she's sharp, funny, and talks all the time. She's about to become my portal to the student body. When I need to see students, she'll track them down and summon them to my office. She handles the paperwork that goes with student discipline, my new *raison d'être*.

Gaby gets back to her work, and I gather my materials for the staff meeting. The school has twenty-six teachers, a part-time counselor, and a few support staff. We'll be in the school library, where the custodian has pushed tables together so everyone can sit around one big work surface. I offered to lead an opening icebreaker. Carlson wants me to talk about duty sign ups, including Curriculum Council, which requires one representative from each subject area.

A coffee machine emits my favorite morning scent, while teachers munch on pastries from a platter provided by food services. I would ordinarily be delighted to have a bear claw after breakfast, but not today. I introduce myself to as many people as possible before Carlson strolls in. He says, "I'm sure you've all met our new VP, Cynthia." Some introduction!

I break the teachers up into teams and give them kazoos, asking each group to move to a corner of the room, agree on a song and practice to perform. After the noise subsides, they come back to the table and each team plays their song for the crowd. Laughter abounds, as there is a lot of off-key squeaking, and "Yellow Submarine" is barely recognizable. I take a deep breath and lean back in my seat. Maybe this is going to be OK.

I pass out the duty schedule and sign-up sheets and ask them to talk in subject area groups about who is going to do what. When they pass the sheets back to me, I see the social studies department has picked Derek Simons for the Curriculum Council. That's one familiar—and handsome—face in the group I'll be meeting with monthly.

After an hour, the teachers return to their rooms to prepare for class tomorrow. I head back to the office to check in with Gaby.

"So, you've met with Mr. Carlson?" she asks.

"Yes, but I haven't seen him much."

Gaby giggles and shields her mouth with her hand. She whispers, "Nobody knows where he goes—the invisible man... well, maybe Sharon knows." I don't ask for more, as my plan is to have big ears these first weeks. Invisible?

The next day, I'm on campus early again. Learning the school map—who is in which room—will take time. Hamilton

Chapter 2

has six hundred kids in grades six through eight. There are three separate buildings and I intend to introduce myself to all of the students, one room at a time. If I visit every English class, I'll encounter each student just once. I'll be on my feet all day, but I want them all to know the new VP on day one.

I drop my things off in the office. No Carlson in sight. Returning to the front of the school, I say good morning to arriving students and parents. The district has given me a plastic name tag that makes me official. The kids pay me little notice, but parents come up and introduce themselves. I thank them and marvel at the good vibe of this school community.

The bell rings and I start my visits to English classes. Here goes! My spiel includes a bit about myself and time for questions.

In the first classroom, from a pretty blonde girl: "Are you married?"

The best response to this line of questioning is short. "No, I'm not."

"Are we going to have an eighth-grade dance this year? Last year Mr. Carlson said we might not."

"Well, we haven't talked about that yet. I'll let you know."

"Can you get better pizza for lunch?"

I laugh. "I'll have to try it. But I hear the food here is pretty good."

They tell me about the chocolate chip cookies that the kitchen staff bakes daily and sells—still warm—at lunch. Hearing about the cookies is enough for me to know I'd better stay away, or I'll get addicted.

During the two student lunch periods, I patrol the grounds. The kids who purchase hot lunch sit in the cafeteria; those with brown bags spread out over the outdoor picnic tables and benches. A few kick a soccer ball around the field, despite the scorching heat. The lunch area seems subdued, with quiet chatter, but experience tells me the first-day good behavior

13

won't last. A couple of kids come up to ask who I am. I haven't visited their English classes yet.

"Do you have any pets?" one asks.

"No, I'm afraid not. I'm away from home too much. But I love dogs."

The girl takes out her phone to show me pictures of her German Shepherd.

A boy asks, "What happened to Mr. Milburn?"

"He's at Henderson Elementary now—he's the new principal."

"Too bad," the boy says.

By the end of the day, I'm perspiring from walking around in the heat, but still have a spring in my step. John Carlson hasn't been in evidence. Back in the cool of the office, Gaby introduces me to a new student she is registering.

Jimmy Green's mom says hello. Jimmy is tall and lanky. He has a bad case of acne and boredom seeps from his sad eyes.

"Hi, Jimmy. You and I are both new to Hamilton. It's a pretty friendly place but let me know if I can help you."

His only response is a rude groan, the equivalent of an eye-roll.

The mom jabs her elbow at him. "Jimmy, please."

Yes, the middle school years are a challenge. I bet I'm going to be seeing Jimmy again soon.

At the end of the day, there are phone messages and emails to answer, and a few notes from teachers concerned about their class loads. I straighten my desk and leave campus close to five o'clock. I kept long hours as a teacher too, but all the walking around has taken its toll. A little dinner, a hot shower, and I begin to nod off in front of the TV. This is my life now and I'd better get used to it.

CHAPTER THREE
LUNCHTIME WITH EIGHTH-GRADERS

AS THE ADMINISTRATOR IN CHARGE OF DISCIPLINE, it's no surprise I'll be spending much of my time dealing with offenders. Mostly eighth-graders. The youngest students avoid getting in trouble and focus on whether a giant eighth-grader plans to push them around in the bathroom or break into their locker. By eighth grade, some students think they're top dogs who can defy authority and lord their seniority and size over younger kids.

Do you remember your own first days of a new school year? Most kids start on a positive note, looking forward to encountering old friends and new teachers. If they like their teachers and find the work to be engaging, they'll do OK. If not, or if they make a tiny mistake, like speaking out of turn, and the teacher immediately humiliates them, then all bets are off.

During snack break and lunch, I'm on the lookout for problems: offensive words that slip out of immature mouths, accidental bumps interpreted as aggression, or social wounds that fester and explode. Middle school hormones run notoriously rampant, so there's enough emotional drama for a daytime soap opera. Everyone can find a way to strike out at someone else. Psychology at its best!

When I met the new student, Jimmy, I predicted I'd be seeing him for misbehaving in the classroom but didn't know he'd be in a fight before the end of the first week. I come upon the scene as Jimmy and another boy are pushing each other in the middle of the outdoor lunch area.

At a distance still, I blow my whistle and they stop. Actually, it's kind of neat—everything stops. Like when you hear a siren and traffic halts. The buzz of hundreds of middle schoolers dies down and I hear only the few voices that didn't notice the whistle. Most eyes are on me.

"Jimmy, sit over there on that bench. What's your name? Ben? You sit here."

I notice Ben's cheek purpling—no doubt from a punch. I turn to the four boys sitting closest, "What happened?"

"He was butting in on our table!" offers one young man, waving his sandwich in the air.

Another points to a can on its side in a pool of cola. "Ben knocked over his drink—by accident."

A third boy says, "The kid just blew up for no reason."

The first boy continues his angry rant. "He punched Ben, man, suspend him!"

I thank the boys, noting how easy it is for kids to tell me how to do my job, and take Jimmy and Ben, now sitting sullenly, to the office to get their version of events.

Jimmy says, "He elbowed me and knocked over my drink."

Ben whines, "I didn't mean to—why'd you hit me?"

Here's my opportunity to do some teaching—while trying to break through the testosterone barrier. "Jimmy, do you think it might have been better to say something before you sat down? Like, 'Hi' or 'OK if I sit here?'"

He hangs his head. I'm on a roll.

"And Ben, Jimmy's new at Hamilton. Maybe you could have been a little...nicer."

"Yeah," says Ben, "but he hit me."

"He did indeed...and Jimmy and I are going to talk about

Chapter 3

that. Is there anything else I need to know?"

Ben shakes his head.

"Ben, go to the nurse's office and get some ice for your cheek."

Ben departs. "Jimmy, ordinarily, hitting someone is an automatic suspension and you'd miss a whole day of school. But you're new and I'm going to give you a break. You're going to stay here in the office for the rest of the day and I'll call your mom. I'm also giving you two detentions. If it happens again, I will suspend you."

Jimmy nods. I can't tell if he's annoyed over the detention or relieved it's not an official suspension. By the time I fill out the detention slips, call Jimmy's and Ben's moms, and get Jimmy some work to do while he sits outside my office, it's after 1:30 p.m. Did I have lunch? My growling stomach tells me I did not. Taking my thirty-minute lunch break after the students eat is probably a bad idea. All it takes is one scuffle and I'm tied up for an hour dealing with combatants and witnesses. I don't need to work with a grouchy attitude from low blood sugar. I vow to take my future lunch breaks early, before the kids have theirs.

AS IS TRUE FOR MOST BAY AREA suburban schools, more than half of Hamilton students are white. As am I. Janelle Owusu, whose parents came to the U.S. from Ghana before her birth, is hard to miss on the grounds, due to her towering height and dark skin. During Friday lunch in the second week of classes, she approaches me.

"Ms. Walker, the boys over there won't let my friends and me into the game. They scored ten points, but they keep playing. They told me to get lost."

With hundreds of students sharing playground space, rules are needed. If two teams are playing basketball and there's no free court, you stand to the side and wait until one of the teams

17

has scored ten points. Then the losing team must step out and you and your friends take their place. However, most students are too intimidated to force out a group of eighth-grade boys. But Janelle has no problem being assertive. She is a talented athlete whom most students hold in high esteem, but apparently not this group of boys.

I walk over to the court and step into the middle of the game. What do you know? Jimmy Green again. It appears he's made friends.

"Let's talk," I say to the group. "You know the rules. The team that lost the last round has to leave."

Janelle stands next to me bouncing on her toes, her two girlfriends behind her. The boys grumble. Jimmy is still dribbling the ball.

"Hold the ball," I order. He looks up.

I continue. "Do you understand? All of you?"

One guy says, "Each team won once. We just wanted to do a playoff."

"Doesn't matter. The last team that lost, you're out. Got it?"

Jimmy's team grumbles, but walks away, leaving the girls to play the winners. Ten minutes later, Janelle finds me again. Her team lost and yielded back to the group of boys.

"They're purposely not making baskets," she complains.

I march back to the court. "I'm going to watch for a minute, guys."

They resume play and there's indeed a lot of dribbling and passing but nobody is taking a shot at the basket. While I'm watching, Derek Simons, the handsome social studies teacher, comes by. He pauses to see what's going on.

"Hi, how are you?" I say.

"Good, good. Are these guys giving you a bad time?"

"It appears they've decided if they don't score any points, they can hang onto the court." I turn back to the boys. "OK,

Chapter 3

my friends. You're done for today. Let's have the ball."

They continue to dribble and pass the ball. Mr. Simons scowls at the kids but remains silent. I had better do something. There's no way I want a male teacher to exert authority the new female VP doesn't seem to have. I speak to them again, trying to sound calm and assertive. "Guys, the game stops now, or I'll be writing up detentions."

My heart is racing. Jimmy throws the ball in my direction. Janelle intercepts it. Good girl, as I wasn't ready to catch it. The boys stomp off.

"Your court," I say to Janelle.

"Don't worry," says Mr. Simons. "They just need to learn you mean it. It may take a little time." He rewards me with his smile and continues on his way. Whew, that was close. Would they have continued to defy me if the teacher wasn't there? I stay for a few minutes watching Janelle and her friends dribble and shoot. The boys are nowhere to be seen. Yes, this is the reason I took all those courses in educational leadership. So, I can stand in the hot August sun and solve disputes between thirteen-year-olds.

During the lunch periods, if I'm not supervising games or breaking up fights, I wander around, talking to kids and looking for anything unusual. I've heard too many stories about groups of kids playing some version of "show me yours and I'll show you mine."

One day my attention goes to a group of eighth-grade boys and girls standing in a tight circle that blocks my view. They're laughing, hooting, and slapping each other on the back. I approach with trepidation. Why are they so loud and what could be that funny?

"Hi, guys. What's up?" I ask.

One of the girls answers, still laughing, "They think I like

19

Antonio, but they're wrong!" The boy blushing in the middle of the group, barely visible behind dark bangs that almost completely cover his eyes, must be Antonio. They're engaging in harmless eighth-grade silliness.

"Well, I can see why you would," I offer, just for fun. They hoot even louder. Antonio looks at me for a moment, his sweet face tense. He has a tall, slim frame, but stands hunched over. He pushes back his hair, but it flops right back over his eyes. A tiny smile escapes the corner of his mouth.

One of the boys yells, "Hey, Antonio, Ms. Walker thinks you're hot!"

"OK, guys, I'll leave you alone. Just keep it down." My attempt at humor was probably a mistake. Knowing kids, they'll tease Antonio for months about me thinking he's cute. Live and learn.

Being an administrator requires a new set of people skills. As a teacher, you get to understand the students you see in class every day. You know who needs a firm hand and who needs soft encouragement. Administrators have to be on their toes all the time. One wrong word can create a maelstrom of trouble. And you have to deal with kids you've never talked to before, often about very serious matters.

All of this supervision and the discipline referrals that follow leave me little initiative for visiting classrooms. I'm thrilled to find a hand-written student invitation in my mailbox. From one class of the charming Mr. Simons, it reads: *Please join us on Thursday at eleven o'clock for our reports on Life in the Middle Ages.* Any opportunity to get away from the behavior referrals on my desk!

CHAPTER FOUR
TAKING CHARGE

I CAN'T WAIT TO SEE THE HANDSOME DEREK IN action. Since I'm his supervisor, it will make for a nice note in the file, enabling me to include some details for his end-of-year evaluation. "Mr. Simons actively engages students with the curriculum, using project-based learning."

Thursday at eleven I arrive and a student, on cue, brings me a special chair. That alone demonstrates Derek's thoughtfulness. He understands the challenge for a normal-size adult to get in and out of those student combo desks with the writing surface installed like a wing over the seat.

"Say good morning to Ms. Walker," he says.

"Good morning, Ms. Walker," the class responds.

The kids describe and act out roles of a Chinese scholar and tea producer, a Japanese Samurai, and an African gold trader. They're in costume and read from their reports clearly, heads held high. Derek makes ancient history interesting to kids who usually only care about what's on their phones.

Before leaving, I speak to the class. "Thanks for inviting me. You're clearly learning a lot. Good job, guys." I flash a smile at them and at their teacher before heading back to the office. The next day I find a thank you note in my box. *So glad you could join us. It means a lot to the students. D.*

I could watch this guy teach all day. His students work in small groups creating scenarios that show their understanding of the historical era. In the weeks ahead I will see them bent over their desks, talking, laughing, and writing. If one of Derek's students misbehaves, he handles it in the classroom, often calling a parent on the spot.

Derek Simons's excellent teaching, his intelligence, and his warmth make me hope he has a soft spot for me. Does he notice my long hours? Sense my deep concern for kids and teachers? I have little time for chatting with eligible men, and Derek is single and my age. On occasion, I lie awake at night imagining all the romantic things that could happen with Derek Simons. Probably not a good idea, as I increasingly stumble over my words when I see him or can't think of anything to say.

LESSON #1: DON'T FLIRT WITH THE TEACHERS!

ONE OF MY DUTIES is scheduling and conducting monthly fire drills and less-frequent earthquake drills. The first time I pick up the intercom to announce "Earthquake—duck and cover" leaves me with a heady feeling of power. Six hundred kids and their teachers stop what they're doing to listen— I hope so anyway. After the drills, I notify the fire department, check that the buildings are empty, and write a report. I laugh at myself, as one of the only embarrassing moments of my own school years involved getting caught talking during a fire drill. How times have changed.

In addition to being the school fire captain, I am called on to make decisions for sick or injured kids when we can't reach their parents. I have never had the pleasure of being up in the middle of the night with a sick child. But during lunch on an early September day, Julia, a skinny sixth-grade girl, falls off a piece of equipment on the playground. Her right arm hangs at a new angle, so Sharon and I put it in a brace. We don't think she needs an ambulance, rather a trip to the emergency room. Sharon can't reach a parent. So here I am—*in loco parentis*. The

Chapter 4

law allows me to act "in the place of a parent," and that means, with Carlson nowhere to be found, I must take Julia to the emergency room. Sharon leaves messages for both parents and promises to keep in touch with me by cell phone. I help Julia into my car for the short drive.

I reassure her as best I can. "Julia, your parents will get our message and contact us. I'll stay with you until one of them comes." She is quiet, but pale, and holds the injured arm in a tight grip.

The emergency room overflows with folks in various stages of agony. Bloody bandages on a worker's hand, a pregnant woman with a glassy stare, and elderly folks clutching the limbs that hurt. Julia remains wonderfully calm. Maybe she's in shock. After giving registration information— "No, I'm the vice principal"—we wait for a half hour before they take her in for x-rays. The doctor reports the arm is fractured and must be put in a cast.

"Of course," I say, giving my heartfelt parental approval, but worried. What if the parents don't approve of the treatment? Could they have religious ideas that don't support casts for broken arms? Sharon has still not heard from Julia's mother. I sit down to wait, leafing through a magazine, but not reading it. What terrible things might be happening at the end of the school day without me there to deal with them? Will Carlson handle misbehaving students? If he's even there.

After another half hour, Julia walks out with a big L-shaped cast on her right arm. It encases her forearm and elbow. This kid isn't going to be able to do much with that hand. She smiles, owing I'm sure to the drugs they've given her.

"You've got a lot of real estate there for your friends to sign," I quip. As I open the door for her, she turns to me at the same time that my phone rings.

"You, know, my other arm hurts too."

23

As I answer Sharon's call, Julia yells, "Mom!" Her mother rushes in and embraces Julia in an awkward hug, avoiding the cast.

"My other arm hurts," says Julia.

The mom, her face creased with worry, says, "Thanks so much, Ms. Walker."

They go back into emergency. It's four o'clock and I skip a return to school. Whatever I missed will have to wait until tomorrow. This parenting thing takes a toll.

Settled with my after-dinner glass of wine, I call Erica for sympathy. "Yeah, I had to take a kid to the hospital today. Broken arm."

"Wow," she says. "Here it's just more stacks of essays to grade. At least your job has variety." Yeah, right. I am surely behind on seeing students. I have no meetings scheduled tomorrow, so maybe I can catch up with the behavior referrals.

In the morning, I find out Julia has broken both arms. How embarrassing it must be for Julia to have her mom toilet and dress her. Not to mention how awful it must be for the mom. I'm glad my parenting duties ended at the emergency room door. And of course Carlson did nothing about the lunchtime behavior incidents. I spend the morning seeing students about cheating in a game that resulted in name calling, cussing, and a pushing match.

A few mornings later, I'm dropping off my things in the office before heading out to monitor the kids arriving, when I hear a familiar sound: "wooshshshsh." I've lived in the area long enough to recognize the noise made by a hot air balloon overhead. Because our town has a launch pad, I've been awakened at home many weekend mornings by that sound directly over my house.

I love counting colorful balloons in the air—I've seen as many as fourteen or fifteen at a time. But I have safety concerns

Chapter 4

for the riders and objects on the ground. I've seen them take out tree branches on their way down. I've seen them land in the street for lack of better control, and occasionally a passenger is injured by a rough landing. They squeeze so many people into their baskets, it's a wonder they can heat enough air to get off the ground.

I look for Carlson or the gum-chewing Sharon. She is not at her desk, but I find him standing at his office window, looking out at the crystal blue sky, presumably trying to spot the balloon.

"They're not allowed to be over school grounds, right?" I ask.

We hear the "whooooshshshsh" again.

"Oh, who cares?" says Carlson. How has this guy survived as an administrator with no respect for rules?

I step outside and sure enough, the balloon is hovering directly over the building. Joe, our day custodian, comes out and squints up. "You know they're not allow—"

"I know," I say. The balloon drifts away from the building but descends towards the ground. I can see the pilot and passengers. Apparently, the rules and the wind conditions aren't in agreement. Or perhaps it's the pilot's inaugural flight and he doesn't know what he's doing?

I shout up at him, "You can't land here!" The balloon angles towards the field. Arriving students see their day start with the VP yelling at a balloon. They run towards it, as it prepares to land.

Joe and I take off after them; my heels dig into damp grass. Where are those tennis shoes when I need them? I grab my whistle and blow several times.

"Get away from the balloon!" I'm yelling at kids. Only half of them heed my warning and stop in their tracks. Antonio, the boy with bangs over his eyes, runs towards the descending

25

balloon, with another boy, like they're trying to catch it.

"Antonio, stop!" I shout. He doesn't hear me or doesn't want to.

The balloon settles smoothly on the grass. The passengers are laughing at their predicament. Such fun. Imagine, spending time and money to take a balloon ride, only to land without welcome on a school field. A grand time indeed!

As I approach, I hear the roar of the chase vehicle driving across the blacktop, heading for the grass. They always get as close as possible. Don't want those precious passengers to walk any farther than necessary.

Ready to lambaste the pilot, I pivot my attention to the approaching van and yell, "Don't drive over the sprinklers! Or the kids!" Do I even know where the sprinklers are? Joe heads their way to direct them.

I reach the basket and turn my attention to the pilot, who stands by to help his passengers out once the crew secures the balloon with tie-downs.

"You know you're not supposed to land here?"

"Yes, I'm sorry, but the wind died, and I had no choice. We'll get out of here as soon as we can."

"OK, but I'll have to report this." That's all I can come up with. While trying to keep the kids back, I watch the passengers disembark. They walk to the recovery van.

Students are taking photos of each other standing in front of the balloon. Might as well give up on that front. There's nothing more I can do. Soon the crew will deflate the balloon, and once it's packed up, they'll be out of our hair.

Joe and I head back to the office and find Carlson and Sharon standing in front, watching the show. "Good try," he says. "But probably not worth your effort."

I linger to make sure the kids go to class before the first bell. Joe will see that the vehicles leave promptly. Here comes the balloon pilot, carrying two bottles.

"So sorry for the trouble," he says and hands one bottle to me and one to Joe. Champagne...or sparkling wine, if it comes from California. Joe offers his bottle to Carlson, who shakes his head and goes inside.

LESSON #2: REWARDS ARE FOR THOSE WHO DO THE WORK.

I smile and then call out to the pilot's back as he heads to the chase vehicle, "Thanks and hope not to see you again." One more bit of variety in the life of a school administrator.

If only I had the weekend free. You ask, "Administrators have to work on weekends?" Somebody has to supervise Saturday School, and if no teacher is up for the extra duty (and extra pay), then I'm in charge (with no extra pay).

CHAPTER FIVE
SATURDAY SCHOOL

A FEW WEEKS IN, THIS JOB FEELS LESS LIKE "vice principal" and more like "principal of vice." Most crimes are petty: talking back in class, profanity, chewing gum, or not doing homework. More severe: refusing to participate, threatening to fight, or landing a punch.

Whatever the offense, I call the kids in, check their histories, and dole out the punishments—sorry, I mean consequences. Sometimes I call a parent. For obscene offenses, I hand the phone to the student and make the culprit tell Mom or Dad what he or she did. One boy brings a photo of his parents' collection of sex toys and passes it around. You've never seen a macho thirteen-year-old break into sobs so fast, begging, "Please, I can't tell her." I insist. He tells her, in a whisper.

Consequences usually involve detention—forty-five silent minutes in a classroom after the last bell. Gone are the days of copying sentences a hundred times: "I will not pass notes in class." They're allowed to do homework, so it seems tame, but the kids hate it. They miss hanging out with friends. The kids embarrassed to serve detention do it once and then make sure they don't have to return. Most detainees are repeat offenders.

Detention becomes a big deal when they don't show up. First there's a double detention, and if the student fails to serve again, I notify the parent and the kid who thinks it will go away if he ignores it must come to school on a Saturday morning. So here I am at nine a.m.

Saturday School is much tamer than "The Breakfast Club." Today, I'll be with five students, including my friends Jimmy and Antonio, for three hours. I start with donuts (they got here, right?) with the kids seated in a circle in the school library.

"So, guys, what's so hard about serving one detention after school? How can you avoid Saturday School in the future?" I admit silently that I don't get it. Why are school expectations so damn hard for these kids?

Jimmy, who has already been sent to my office several times for disrupting class, says, "That bitch sent me to detention just for forgetting my homework. I *did* it, too!"

"Jimmy, it's Saturday, but it's still school. No swearing. Was it the first time you forgot your homework?" The others snicker.

"No, but still, I *did* it!"

"Well, that's great. But turning it in is half the task. Do you have a special place to put your school things? A backpack?" You'd think these kids would have learned better organization in elementary school. Middle school brings out their worst.

"Yeah."

"Well, try putting your homework in it as soon as it's done."

Madeline has a pink streak in her frizzy brown hair and wears tight black jeans, a ripped black tee shirt off the shoulder, and combat boots. "Why did you get detention, Madeline?"

"Talking in class." A small smile tries to erupt from her tough exterior. The group chuckles. Underneath the dark eye makeup and pierced eyebrow, Madeline is a pretty girl, but I bet she doesn't know it.

"How many times? You have several detentions from Mrs. Stein."

"A lot, I guess. She won't let me answer questions."

"Can anyone help with this?" Aren't I optimistic?

Adorable Antonio answers, "I'm in class with her. She never raises her hand. She just yells stuff out so her homeys can get a

30

Chapter 5

laugh." The others giggle.

Madeline isn't done. "Her class is sooooo boring. She asks the same questions that are in the book. And she calls on the same kids every time...the ones who always have a smarty pants answer...'Yes, Mrs. Stein, OK, Mrs. Stein'—they're such kiss-ups."

I'm aware of this teacher's lack of creativity. I sympathize if Madeline is bored in class, but that doesn't excuse bad behavior. "Any ideas for Madeline?"

"Just shut up!" says Antonio.

"Well, that would help," I respond. "I'll talk to Mrs. Stein and see what she has to say. Antonio, you're earning detentions for not turning in homework?"

He smiles and nods, his emotions hidden behind his cascading bangs.

"Look, you all need to follow the teacher's rules, including turning in homework, or you'll get more detentions." I look at the group and sigh. My voice tightens. "Why didn't you go to detention the first time and get it over with? Didn't you know what would happen if you skipped it?"

Most of them are silent. "I forgot," says Antonio. Perhaps they don't have experience with adults who are consistent with follow-up. That's going to change, if I have anything to do with it.

After the counseling chat, we spend the rest of the morning sweeping leaves off the patio, wiping down the picnic tables, and scooping trash from the grounds. I wait for them all to be picked up at noon.

Antonio leaves on foot. When I return to the office, I look up his home address. It's five miles away. Why is he walking?

My Saturday morning is shot, but I congratulate myself on getting to know a few of the students better. Jimmy needs an intervention. Madeline's description of Mrs. Stein's class is a

31

concern. And I wonder about Antonio's home life.

On my way back to the office to lock up, I'm surprised to find John Carlson's aged grey Volvo in the parking lot. Do I have to see him on a Saturday too?

As soon as I step inside, he comes to his office door.

"How'd it go?"

"Fine. I'm surprised to see you."

"I had some things to catch up on. Are you going to be here for a while?"

"I'm on my way home. Why?"

"I'd like to talk to you a bit...maybe buy you lunch?"

I can't think of a way to say no.

"Uh, OK, thanks."

We drive our separate cars to a café downtown. At a corner booth, rather than sitting opposite me, he moves closer, towards the center. Like this is a date. I focus on the menu.

Once we order, he asks, "Are you enjoying Hamilton?"

"Yes. The behavior issues are sure a challenge. There's lots to do."

"Right. Didn't you tell me you're an overachiever?" His toothy grin says he's proud he remembers my words and happy to tease me about it. Like we have some kind of intimate, inside joke. I hope my puzzled look conveys I'm not on board.

"Look, I just want to get to know you a little better. It's hard to do during the school day."

I smile, but can't say what's in my head: what on earth are *you* doing while I'm knocking myself out?

I don't know his intent, but I'd like to stick to business. "Maybe we should have a scheduled time to talk, say at the end of the day, when most people are gone."

He answers, "Sure, that's a good idea. How about Thursday afternoons at four o'clock?"

"Right. I can do that, as long as I don't have any meetings."

Chapter 5

"Good. So, tell me something about yourself. How do you spend your free time?"

"Well, John, right now I don't have a lot of free time. I read, I ride my bike with friends, I go to movies. I like to cook. Very boring stuff... why do you ask?"

"I just want to get to know you better. Are you into wine?"

"I like a good red blend. How about you?"

Over our food, we chat about our favorite beverages and cuisine. He pays the bill, but seems in no hurry to leave.

"John, I need to go. I've got chores at home and I'm seeing friends tonight."

"OK. Thanks for joining me. I enjoyed our talk. Next time, maybe we'll have some wine."

"See you Monday," is all I can squeeze out.

Is he hitting on me? I assume from family photos in his office that he's married, but not one word has been said by anyone about his wife.

The rest of the afternoon disappears into cleaning house and doing laundry. Time to focus on mindless tasks—no mental challenges. Tonight, I'm having dinner with my girlfriends. My social life has shrunk since I started at Hamilton. I long for an evening with friends—hearing about what's going on in their lives and sharing my school stories.

Erica and I have known each other since our earliest days of teaching. We've commiserated over bad principals, crazy staff members, and difficult students. We've gone hiking; we've double dated. I was her maid of honor. Too bad her marriage didn't last. Now that her divorce is final, she'll probably want to commiserate—or celebrate.

Pam and I have been friends since high school. We haven't always been close, as she has moved away from the San Francisco area more than once. But she always makes her way back. Her husband practices law and Pam sells real estate part

33

time, while raising two elementary-school-age kids. She relishes a night out with the girls.

How did I get to be thirty-five, single, and building a new career, while my girlfriends are raising kids and getting their first divorces? I've had a couple of long-term boyfriends, but the last one cheated and dumped me. I dealt with that by plunging into school administration. I may not be ready to date, but I'm definitely into catching up with my besties.

We meet in the bar at El Encanto, a Mexican place with enormous margaritas and bottomless bowls of tortilla chips and guacamole.

"So, what's it like being the boss?" asks Erica, still in awe of my administrative title.

"God, I wish I felt like the boss. The principal is pretty nasty. He does nothing to help me, but he took me out to lunch today."

"Wow," says Erica. "On a Saturday?"

"Yeah, it was kind of weird. He was there when I finished Saturday School. He's definitely a creep. Wants to 'get to know me.' Then there's the fact that he doesn't seem to do anything at school besides talking with parents. He's assigned everything to me. I'm too busy dealing with kids to boss anyone around."

"I bet you're good at it," Erica answers, raising her glass to toast me.

Pam follows suit, "To the new vice principal."

"Thanks, guys. I must say it's nice to be able to use the bathroom when I need to, rather than waiting until lunch." They both laugh.

"How are *you* doing?" I ask Erica.

"OK," she says. "Don was kind of a jerk for a long time, but now that the lawyers are out of the picture, it's better. He's leaving me alone."

"Still, it must be tough," says Pam. "There are so many

34

Chapter 5

things Roger takes care of. I don't know how I'd manage on my own."

We continue to laugh about needing to learn how to do the "guy" things—like fixing clogged plumbing.

Pam asks both of us, "So, any men worth talking about?" My married friends always want the juicy details.

"No way," says Erica. "I'm not ready to go down that road."

My turn. "Me? Too busy. But there is a very cute, single teacher at Hamilton."

I tell them about Derek—his friendliness, great teaching, sparkly green eyes.

"Sounds interesting," says Pam.

"Yeah, only I'm his supervisor and that's a problem."

Erica and I talk about our plans for December to visit Hawaii. Pam gives us all the details of her most recent listings. Although real estate talk bores me, I appreciate Pam, because she helped me buy my little house. After a plate of fajitas and coffee to combat the margaritas, I drive home, glad to have seen my friends.

Administration is a lonely world. I can't confide in Carlson. Besides being my boss, he's a large part of what I need to complain about. The teachers at Hamilton are not going to be open with a supervisor, nor I with them. And soon I'll be giving them pointers on improving their teaching—whether they're interested in what I have to say, or not.

What will it be like to give advice to teachers who are older and have more classroom experience than I do? Can I find a way to give them suggestions without offending them, without coming across as a smarty-pants junior administrator?

CHAPTER SIX
TEACHING THE TEACHERS

CAN YOU REMEMBER THE DAYS WHEN TEACHERS were free to teach what they wanted? If they wanted to spend a month of social studies time teaching kids how to weave straw baskets, they could. Or to get every student to write a poem, they could spend hours reading poetry aloud and teaching various techniques. There was no need to worry that an administrator would question their time allocation. Today, teachers must stick to the state curriculum—and the person looking over their shoulders is me. When I visit classrooms, I collect data about what is being taught and how. All to improve instruction...and test scores.

District evaluation rules require a goal-setting meeting, classroom observations, a mid-year check-in, and a final eval in the spring. Half the teachers are evaluated each year. I start by pulling the personnel files of the six teachers on my list. Settled in my office after school, I'm ready to be informed. It's a short session, as the files lack detail or follow-up, and the brief comments are too general: "Ginny continues to do a good job." Should I be surprised that Carlson has not followed guidelines for writing up observations and describing teachers' progress on concrete goals? I have to start from scratch.

John agrees to let me talk about evaluation at a staff meeting. It's important the teachers understand in advance where

I'm coming from. Some won't be evaluated this year, and some are stuck with John's laissez-faire supervision. I'd rather forewarn the teachers than surprise them later. I stand on wobbly knees and begin.

"I want to give you a heads-up on classroom observations. I'm not evaluating all of you, but when I visit your room, here's what to expect." They're making eye contact, not looking out the window or doodling on their agendas.

"I'll be looking for student engagement, instructional techniques, and evidence of the curriculum standards. If you're showing a movie, expect me to ask something like, "Which standard is this film addressing?"

A couple of people chuckle. They know teachers who use films to *avoid* teaching.

I continue. "Heck, I once took a group of kids on a field trip to San Francisco where I had to write up curriculum goals for the *bus ride*." Now they're all smiling.

"I'll be looking at the writing on your board, posted homework assignments, and the books you're using. Any questions?"

I schedule goal-setting meetings for early October and make an effort to walk through each classroom a few times in advance. The difference from one room to the next is not funny. In Bert Sheldon's science room, the kids engage in projects and experiments and rarely use a textbook. He tells the students they should be thrilled to be in his room, and most of them are. He says things like, "Someday you may have the opportunity to travel abroad and meet celebrities like I did back in the '80s. Want to hear about my lunch with Elton John?" All eyes are on the name-dropping King of Science.

George Dunning, who teaches social studies, provides a stark contrast. A skinny guy in his 50s with brown hair falling in his bland face, he appears unaware of his students. On one occasion he unwisely tells the kids to work independently from

Chapter 6

their books. Half of them are passing notes or doodling. While he lectures on the fine points of the Revolutionary War, boys in the back are throwing paper airplanes across the room. After my second visit, I find him after class. "George, do you know that a third of your students aren't paying attention? In fact, they're throwing paper airplanes."

"Uh, no," he answers.

"Look, we'll work on this in your goals, but try to notice what the kids are doing." Duh.

As I walk away, he mutters, "God help me."

Most teachers come to their initial conferences with goals in mind. I have to squeeze them out of George.

"George, have you written draft goals?"

"Uh, not really."

"OK, we need to address classroom management. Here's a basic goal:

Establish, monitor, and revise classroom procedures to facilitate learning and create positive student attitudes. What do you think?"

"I guess it sounds OK." Does he understand English? Did he train as a teacher?

His enthusiasm is underwhelming, but I go on. "I'm going to help you set up those procedures, George. You wait for the kids to pay attention before you speak and then give them positive feedback. And you need to create lessons that involve more activity and less listening."

Is that enough? We'll see if he can do this. I'll spend time in his classroom tallying student non-attention. Maybe he'll see a better way to run his room. If not, his mid-year evaluation will be a challenge.

Sam Butler does a satisfactory job teaching PE, as far as I can tell. I visit on an early morning when he has a class of sixty boys and girls. In two teams, they're running an obstacle course in the field. Sam holds two stopwatches. Janelle from

39

the basketball court beams as she runs around cones and jumps over gates. The kids are all participating, cheering each other on.

Janelle finishes her turn, sees me, and waves. I wave back.

Sam holds up his hand when the last kid on the slower team finishes. "Good job, guys," he shouts. "Gather 'round. I'm going to record your times and we'll see if you improve next week." He talks to them about the importance of supporting your team and getting exercise outside of class.

My issue with Sam is his appearance. He's quite the stud—tall and buff with blond curly hair, a mustache and blue eyes. He wears skimpy nylon running shorts and a tank top every day. It is distracting to sit in my office with Sam standing across from me, leaning on the wall, all muscular arms and legs, the substantial bulge of his private parts covered by thin nylon in my direct line of vision. Really, Sam? Are you goading me? I can only imagine the effect he must have on pubescent girls. In his goals conference, I focus on his teaching. That's easy. But none of my administrative classes covered how to talk to teachers about their clothing. I'm not ready for this conversation and can't imagine what words I'll use, but I'd better figure it out soon.

LESSON #3: HANDLE THE EASY STUFF FIRST.

UNFORTUNATELY, THE STUFF that's not easy has a way of making its way onto my plate. At the end of a long September day, I'm in my office sorting paperwork related to student behavior, evaluations, and special education, when Gloria, the PE teacher, taps on my door.

"Got a minute?"

"Of course, come in and rescue me from this pile of paper."

She sits down but shifts in the seat nervously. "There's

something I need to tell you or John...and I'd rather not talk to him about this."

"Sure."

"I overhear the girls in the locker room when they're dressing for PE. You can imagine the stuff they talk about." She chuckles, her hand going to her mouth. The worried face returns, accentuating deep lines from days in the sun. I wait.

"Today I heard seventh-grade girls talking about Derek Simons. I don't believe it's true, but I thought I'd better tell somebody."

The air-conditioned room suddenly feels too warm.

"Yes, of course. Go ahead."

"They were saying that he looks down their shirts in class. They were giggling about it."

"Oh, my."

Gloria continues. "I know. He's been here for years and there's never been a suggestion of anything improper. I'm worried if their talk spreads, it could cause trouble."

I sigh. "Can you tell me who the girls are?"

"Sure. Here." She hands me a sheet with three names. I thank her and send her out.

What a nightmare. If it's true, it's terrible—for everyone, especially the girls. On the other hand, maybe it's not true. The mere suggestion of impropriety can ruin a career. Teachers are sometimes advised to never pat a student on the back. I've been told to avoid driving a solitary student in my car for any reason. What to do? I hope the almighty John Carlson will have an answer.

I walk down to his office, but he and Sharon are both gone for the day. I leave a note: *John, I need to see you first thing.* At home, despite my glass of wine, I can't sleep. Could it be true? I'm just getting to know Derek, but he's an effective teacher and I like him. Morning can't come soon enough.

CHAPTER SEVEN
TOUCHY SUBJECTS

I STARE AT THE DARK CIRCLES UNDER MY EYES and apply concealer. Is anything going to hide the fact that I barely slept? I'm at school early and check Carlson's office frequently until he finally appears.

"John, can we talk?"

"Yeah, just give me a minute to check my messages."

I wait outside his door until he ushers me in. "What's up?"

I sink into the chair opposite him and repeat the story that Gloria told me. "I'm really concerned for Derek," I say. "How do we handle this?"

Carlson chortles and leans back in his chair. "Look, this kind of thing is not new. Whether it's Simons or Butler, the girls have wild imaginations about the handsome guys...lucky for me, I'm not in that category." He laughs again. At least he doesn't see himself as a hunk. That would be over the top, even for him.

"OK, but I think we need to follow up with the students. And don't we have an obligation to tell Derek?"

Carlson's face goes from relaxed to serious and he sits up, eyes boring into me.

"Cynthia, you can't react to every little thing that happens."

Is he kidding me? The suspicion of inappropriate teacher interaction with kids is a little thing? I scramble for words. "Would it be OK if I talk to the girls and to Derek?"

"Pffff... I guess. If that's what you want to do, it's OK with me. But don't make it into a big sexual harassment thing, all right?"

I leave his office more agitated than when I entered. There's no expert guidance to be had from him. I could call Human Resources, but that would trigger an investigation and I don't know if it's needed. Gaby is deep in conversation on her phone with a teacher standing at her desk waiting for assistance. I wait impatiently until she's free and ask her to summon the three girls.

I don't know these seventh-graders: Jeanie, Karen, and Sabrina. None of them have discipline records. Will they be honest with me? "Hi, girls, I just want to ask you about something."

They sit in the chairs that Gaby squeezes into my tiny space. All of them look nervous. Probably trying to figure out what they might have done to get in trouble.

"You're not in trouble," I say. "Ms. Burrows overheard you talking in the locker room... about Mr. Simons."

Jeanie and Karen flush bright red. Sabrina looks confused. "We were just kidding around," says Jeanie.

"Yeah," Karen adds. "We really like Mr. Simons."

Sabrina asks, "What are you talking about?"

Jeanie explains. "Karen said he looks down our shirts when he's walking around the room. Don't you remember?"

"Oh," says Sabrina. "Maybe."

Now it's my turn. I swallow and lean forward on my desk. "Look, girls. Saying a teacher is looking down your shirts is a very serious accusation. If it's true, it's important to report it."

Karen winces. "Please," she whines. "Jeanie was wearing a big scoop-necked top and he was standing over her and it just occurred to me he could probably see it all."

"Does that sound right to you?" I ask the others.

Jeanie's hand is at her throat. "I'll never wear that top again.

Chapter 7

No, I didn't notice anything. He was just looking at my paper."
Sabrina scowls. "I didn't see anything, but they were laughing about it before gym."
I give them the talk about being careful about what they say, where and when, and send them back to class. I write a note to Gloria Burrows—

Gloria, the girls were joking about what they imagined could happen, so no worries. But keep your ears open and thanks for telling me. Cynthia

I'm satisfied that nothing serious happened, but Derek needs to know. His goals conference is in a couple of days. I'll wait to bring it up. My yawn tells me there are too many hours left before bedtime.

DEREK COMES TO HIS CONFERENCE well prepared. He doesn't need guidance and has written goals about creating new student projects.

"Your class is so stimulating—I love visiting to see what you have your kids working on. And I appreciate your handling of student behavior. But don't hesitate to call on me if I can help."

"Sure," he says. "I appreciate your feedback." There's that glamorous smile.

OK, here goes. My stomach is one big knot. "Derek, there's something else I need to talk to you about."

"OK."

"It's about three girls in your third period class: Jeanie, Karen, and Sabrina. The gym teacher heard them talking in the locker room, saying you look down their shirts in class."

Smile extinguished, he sits up stiffly, eyes wide.

I continue, "I talked to them and apparently it was one girl noticing that the other girl's blouse would afford a good view to someone standing over her."

"I hope you know that I would never...my God. I've had some weird things happen before—girls writing me notes and wanting to hug me—but this is really awful."

45

"It sounds like they were just wondering what might be possible. But I thought you should know. I certainly don't want you to stop walking around the room to check student work."

"I'll keep my distance from those girls," he says, relaxing his posture a bit.

I exhale at last. "This age group is such a challenge. Thanks."

He reaches out his hand for a shake as he rises from the chair. "Thank you for telling me."

"I thought it was important."

Such a warm handshake—strong but comforting. Yes, Derek, I really want to help you, and maybe help myself to more of your company.

THE DREADED CONFERENCE OVER, I continue my evaluations. Ginny Stein teaches English to eighth-graders. She's held this position a long time, maybe too long. She doesn't collaborate with the other English teachers. The younger ones share ideas that engage the kids, like translating comics into short stories or comparing written and film versions of novels. I can't quite figure Ginny out, but she obviously does not want to be bothered. She barely acknowledges me when I walk through her room, and never smiles or greets me outside the classroom.

On a typical walk-through, Ginny sits at her desk grading papers, while her students silently read library books. A half dozen kids are doing anything but reading. My friend Jimmy has his head down on the desk. Taking a nap? Sulking? When I tap his shoulder, he sits up and opens his book. Does Ginny think silent reading is a good use of her teaching time?

Ginny arrives on time for her conference, enters quietly and sits. Her face is stone-like, without expression. Her short, curly grey hair suggests an out-of-style perm. She sports an oversized shirt with jeans. Are those paint stains on the sleeves? Not exactly professional.

Chapter 7

"Ginny, I'm happy to finally have a conversation with you." I smile. She does not. I swallow and try again. "How is it going?"

"Fine." Her voice is gravelly—too many years of smoking?

"The last time I was in your room, I noticed your students reading while you graded papers. How often does that happen?"

She frowns. "They had just submitted essays and I was giving them a break."

Yeah, right. More like she didn't want to correct papers at home. "Ginny, one of your students—fifth period, I think—told me you only call on certain kids. Do you have a method for being sure to hear from everyone?"

"I call on the ones who raise their hands." She scowls like I must be an idiot to expect anything else.

I'm not giving up. "I see. It might help if I collect some data for you. How about an observation where all I do is make notes about who answers questions? That could be interesting."

She clears her throat. "You mean you're looking for me to screw up?"

Good grief, it's like she can't hear a word. "No, Ginny, I'm trying to help. I won't write up anything from this observation. I'll only collect data for you to consider."

A chart that shows who participated during a fifteen-minute time span can be illuminating to teachers. Without me saying a word, Ginny might see which students are not being included.

I continue. "Have you ever seen how Bert Sheldon calls on kids at random, whether their hands are up or not?"

"Never been in his room."

"Well, I'm going to find a way for you to see different methods—by observing or watching a video. There are easy ways to do this, and it really makes the kids pay attention."

We manage to write goals about student engagement and collaboration with the other English teachers. When Ginny

47

leaves my office, I want to bang my head on the desk. She doesn't know me well enough to trust me, and I may need a miracle to get through to her. Too bad I don't have a stash of miracles ready to go.

Laura Gonzaga, the special education teacher, appears last on my list. Working with her comes easily, in part because of my teaching background. We get along famously, and she is a gifted teacher. She finds creative ways for her students, with all their limitations, to participate. And her individualized testing shows they're all making progress.

Spending time observing in classrooms excites me. I'm an extra set of eyes for teachers who spend many hours without feedback. The things I record can help them to feel proud about what they're doing well and discover ways to improve. However, when I'm visiting classrooms, the discipline referrals pile up. How can I find time for everything?

MY WEEKLY MEETING with Carlson arrives and I'm eager to tell him about my conferences with Derek and the others I'm evaluating. I also want to ask about the sixth-grade outdoor education program, which will take place in a few weeks. I seek him out at our usual 4:00 time, when most of the staff has gone for the day.

"Good afternoon," he booms, a greasy smile spreading as he gets up from his desk. He guides me to a seat, his hand on my back. Yuck.

"How's it going?" he continues after sitting down behind the desk. He looks like a giant inflated beach ball with a pinhead.

"Fine. First, I want to let you know I talked to the girls in Derek's class, and I talked to him. I've concluded nothing happened."

"I won't say, 'Told you so.'" But he just did.

"Could I talk to you about evaluations?"

"Sure, they're a great bunch of teachers, aren't they?"

Chapter 7

"Well, some of them are. But I'm concerned about George and Ginny."

His eyebrows raise. "Really? They're old pros."

"Have you been in either of their rooms lately?" I try not to sound sarcastic, already knowing the answer. My cheeks burn.

His smile dissolves. "What's your concern?"

I search for the kindest words I can find. "Well, George's kids are tuned out and he doesn't know it."

Carlson adjusts himself in the seat, leans his arms on the desk and folds his hands together. "I see."

"And Ginny is a cold fish. She doesn't want to listen to me, but I want to help her to engage more of her students."

"Well, that sounds like a good idea. Those two have been here a long time. They have solid reputations."

Perspiration gathers on my forehead. "I'm not so sure about that, John. There's nothing in their files that would suggest they've ever had a problem, but their teaching is just...not... good. Do you have any information—or suggestions?"

He raises both hands in a dismissive gesture. "Sounds like you're handling it. Is there anything else?" He opens the binder on his desk.

He's finished with me, but I'm not done yet. "The sixth-grade team wants an administrator to go to outdoor ed. Is that something you do?"

He rises from his chair, trying to get me to leave. "Hell, no. Overnight in the woods? I don't think so. And I need you here."

"OK, but I'd be happy to attend. I went as a teacher. It's a great way to support the staff and get to know the kids." We both walk towards the door. His hand is once again on my back. God, is he giving me a back rub? I move faster.

"OK, I'll think about it."

I stop and turn toward him. "By the way, are you scheduling a goals conference for me?"

49

"Oh, don't worry about that. We can do it after the first of the year."

That's the end of our talk. This guy is doing absolutely nothing to help me. At least he hasn't told me to leave George and Ginny alone. I may not be getting guidance, but I have the freedom to do my job. And maybe, just maybe, I know what I'm doing.

NEAR THE END OF SEPTEMBER, I'm in my office listening to an eighth-grader tell me how he didn't mean to pull up a girl's skirt— "It was an accident." The fire alarm goes off—loud blasts that can't be mistaken for anything else. Unless Carlson has mysteriously decided to do a drill, it means either some wise guy has pulled the alarm, or there's a fire.

The teachers don't know this isn't planned, so they're filing outside with their classes as I hand the boy I am with over to Gaby, who had better get off the phone fast. I jog down to the main office. Sharon and Carlson stand by Sharon's desk, eyes flitting around like they're on drugs.

"Did you pull the alarm?" I ask.

"Hell, no."

"John, we need to find..." The intercom buzzes. It's the science room.

Oh God, what has Sheldon done?

I pick up the intercom phone. "Office."

Bert Sheldon's panicky voice comes back. "There was a little fire."

"Sharon," I say, "call 9-1-1."

"It's out," he says.

I turn and yell at Sharon. "Tell them it's out." To Sheldon, "What happened?"

"We were using the Bunsen burners," he says. "Something on the table caught on fire and the next thing I know; the kid's stack of papers is going up in flames."

50

Chapter 7

Sharon yells at me, "They're coming anyway. Say they have to."

"Is everyone all right?" I ask Sheldon.

"Yeah, just a little shaken. Lucky the fire extinguisher was handy."

"I'll be right there." As I run out the door, I call to Sharon, "Tell the firefighters which classroom." John stands there watching like a child at the circus.

Breathing hard, I arrive at the science lab. The door stands open and some of the kids are outside, but others are still in the room, standing with the teacher while smoke drifts to the ceiling. He's monitoring a wastebasket, where he's put the burnt papers.

"Out, everyone," I order. Sheldon takes the remaining kids out and talks to the firemen, who have arrived in a flash, sirens blaring.

When it's over, I write up one more report. Carlson finally does something and calls the district office to explain. He makes an announcement for the student body after they're back in class, telling them, "We had a little fire in the science lab, but it was put out immediately by Mr. Sheldon, and everyone is safe, thanks to our speedy action." Yeah, like what exactly did *he* do?

51

CHAPTER EIGHT
MORE CARROTS THAN STICKS

SUDDENLY, IT'S OCTOBER. MY DESK PHONE RINGS one cloudy morning and Sharon says, "Just had a phone call from someone threatening to blow up the school. Said there was a bomb on campus." She continues cracking her gum into my ear.

"What does John say?"

"He's off campus at the moment."

"Can't you call him?"

"Well, no, he's at home dealing with some family business." Probably means he's taking a nap. What is wrong with this guy? Is he sick, screwed up, or lazy?

The caller may be a disgruntled kid playing hooky who finds it amusing to scare everyone on campus. I picture the scoundrel hearing the alarm go off and watching the kids file out of the school. But you have to take these things seriously. And act fast.

"OK, Sharon, pull the alarm and call the cops."

"Really?" she asks, rather casually.

"Yes, please."

The teachers take their classes outside and we wait for the police to check the buildings and the grounds. Fortunately, it's not raining, and the teachers keep their students occupied until the police announce the buildings are clear. Nobody needs to know the cause and our October fire drill is covered. Good job, Cynthia.

Two weeks later, I'm in Carlson's office having a meeting—a parent request for more student awards. Sharon opens the door. "Excuse me, but someone on the phone says there's a bomb on campus." She closes the door.

Ready to jump into action, I look at John. "Ah, just ignore it," he says. "It's some stupid kid."

"Yeah, but you can't ignore a bomb threat."

His look says everything: I'm too young, too green, inexperienced, too much of a rule follower. "Do whatever you want," he says. I walk out to Sharon and give her the directions, astounded that my boss would risk the lives of his students, staff...and me. We go through the usual procedures.

The policeman who gives me the all clear asks, "Do you have any idea who might be doing this?"

I shake my head but wish there were some way to find out. I ask Roxanne, the attendance clerk, "Can you print out a list of everyone who was absent on the days we've had bomb threats?"

"Sure," she says. "Give me an hour."

After lunch, I have the list. It's longer than I had hoped. One name jumps out at me: Jimmy Green. I need to figure out what to do. Jimmy keeps showing up in my office for talking back to his teachers and disrupting class. It's not a surprise, since I've seen him mouth off to his mom.

The next morning, Carlson walks by my office while Jimmy is giving me lip.

"The bitch just doesn't like me," Jimmy says, referring to one of our kindest teachers.

"Watch your language, Jimmy. We need to do something about this—you can't spend so much time in the office."

"Yeah, well talk to your f'-ing teachers then!" So much for

Chapter 8

my control over Jimmy.

I give him yet another detention and think I'd better meet with his parents and seek help to get Jimmy on the right track.

At the end of the day, I sit down with Carlson for my weekly check-in. He asks, "What's up with Jimmy? He's spending more time in the office than in class."

"Yeah." I shake my head.

"Why don't you just send him home for five days?" Carlson is referring to the maximum amount of suspension allowed by law.

"On what grounds?" I ask. Does Carlson realize there are state laws about suspending kids from school?

"Just to get him out of your hair for a while." To Carlson, this is a no-brainer.

"John, I don't believe that's a legal reason for suspension."

Sure, I could use the rules about defiance to make Jimmy spend a day at home, but that might be giving him what he wants. And maybe another opportunity to call in a bomb threat? It's a slow progression from where we are now to a five-day exclusion. Carlson thinks suspension exists to give administrators a break from unruly students. Figures.

AS A SPECIAL EDUCATION TEACHER, I used a variety of strategies to motivate students, including a drawer full of "prizes" the kids valued. Sure, we all know intrinsic reward—that wonderful feeling you get from accomplishment—is much better than extrinsic reward—the payoff, treat, money. But how do you get to intrinsic satisfaction with a student who feels stupid, unloved, and hopeless? Especially when they don't have a home life that sets boundaries and supports their sense of worth? Prizes are a way to get a little success under students' belts, so they can begin to feel they can do it on their own. *If you get 80% on the next spelling test, you get to choose a reward from the drawer.*

When I started at Hamilton, I joined the state Administrators' Association. In one of their emails, I discover a Saturday workshop on student discipline, "Using Contracts to Improve Student Behavior." Sounds interesting. A morning spent learning this method might help me with my toughest kids, the small group who take up most of my time. I sign up to trade a precious Saturday morning for new ideas.

The presenter is a rising star in the administrative ranks. My age or younger, he's already an assistant superintendent in a large district. When he speaks, I understand why. One of the most positive educators I've ever met, he talks in a charismatic way about our mission to shape young lives.

"Every one of you in this room who has power over students, whether you are teachers or administrators or parents, has a sacred trust. Building the character of a new generation. Forming the future for all of us. Scolding and punishment are ineffective tools for shaping the behavior of youngsters. There's a better way…"

He goes on to talk about a simple contract. It's not rocket science, but an agreement on paper between child and adult, signed by all parties. The formality alone has an impact. The contract reminds each person—student, teacher, parent—what they have promised to do. My new favorite person shares sample contracts and stories about positive changes in student behavior.

"This doesn't eliminate the need for good teaching, counseling, or psychotherapy when appropriate, but it can improve your relationships with your students. It builds trust and success."

I leave the workshop totally psyched and ready to try this idea at Hamilton.

Another Saturday spent on my job, but I'm looking forward to the evening, when Erica has pressured me into going

Chapter 8

barhopping with her. I haven't been to a bar to meet men for a few years, but she convinces me she is ready to test the waters after her divorce. I'm doubtful about the outcome but want to be supportive. Couldn't she just do Match.com?

We start back at El Encanto, but the bar is dead, so we go on to a place that advertises country-western dancing. Erica likes the music. Me, not so much. Too much bellyaching, heartbreak, and talk of Jesus for my taste. I do like line dancing, though, and perhaps that will help me work off the margarita I just inhaled. Do you have any idea how many calories are in a margarita?

After we find a seat and order beer, the line dancing starts. I jump up to join the line and Erica stays at the bar, getting into a conversation with the tall blond guy she is seated next to. I keep dancing until I've worked up a sweat. It feels good to let off steam, work up some endorphins and remember that I'm more than a discipline-doling bureaucrat. I need to make time in my life for fun. I make it back to my own bar stool, smiling and relaxed, just as Erica gives the guy her phone number. Way to go, Erica. One of these days it will be my turn.

ONE OF THE REASONS I WANTED to work at Hamilton is our Student Study Team (SST). The team includes teachers from each grade level and the school's psychologist, counselor, speech therapist, and our ubiquitous administrator—me. Teachers refer students who are struggling academically or emotionally. Today I report what I learned at my workshop on contracts, and everyone encourages me to give it a try. I schedule a meeting with Jimmy's mom and teachers. Jimmy will be there, as his buy-in is the most important.

I start the meeting by introducing everyone. Then I turn to Jimmy.

"Jimmy, we're all here today because we want you to be successful at Hamilton. That means getting along, not only with the other students, but with your teachers. Can you tell us about the problems you're having in class?"

Silence. I'm sure he's thinking the teachers are to blame.

Jimmy's math teacher speaks up. "Jimmy, why did I send you out of class yesterday? What were you doing?"

"Um... Janet wouldn't let me borrow her eraser."

"And?"

"I guess I poked her."

I follow up. "Right, Jimmy. Your teacher had to stop teaching because you were poking Janet. Whose job is it to have an eraser?"

"Mine?" He sounds like this is a brand-new idea. He scowls.

"Yes. Here's what we'll do. We're going to list classroom behaviors you can improve. Then we'll plan how all of us can support you. And we're going to choose a reward you can earn."

"Huh?" That got his attention.

"Is there a particular reward you'd like?"

A sly smile spreads slowly across his face and he looks directly at me. "A new bike?"

I laugh. "Well, that's a bit much for the first contract. Maybe that could be a long-range goal if Mom agrees." She's nodding. "How about something smaller? A special outing or treat?"

Mom suggests, "He always wants me to take him to the comic bookstore."

Jimmy's face lights up. "Yeah, that would be cool. And I could get a couple of comics?"

Mom nods again.

With the help of the teachers, we make a list of basic classroom behaviors: come to class with needed materials, raise your hand to speak, use appropriate language, stay in your seat, and keep your hands to yourself. Homework will come later. For a first step, we want simple cooperation in class. Jimmy agrees to the goals. His eyes sparkle with comic book dreams.

I have created a card for Jimmy to carry from class to class,

Chapter 8

with a place for each teacher to make a daily mark when he succeeds in the new behaviors. I type as we talk, including the deal that when Jimmy has 90% of the possible marks for five school days, he will get his reward. Everyone signs the agreement and I have Gaby make copies for all. Jimmy accepts his very own.

"Good work, everyone. Now, Jimmy, this is a big change in behavior. You are going to have to work at this and it may take time, but we will all do our best to help." Everyone leaving my office looks happy. It's the first time I've seen Jimmy smile.

Will Jimmy get his card marked by each teacher every day? Time will tell. Will Jimmy's mom follow through at home? It's not easy being a parent. I'm feeling more like a mother hen every day.

Every school has a Student Study Team. What makes Hamilton's special is that team members mentor the youngsters with problems. Research shows that motivation comes from any kind of attention. The teacher who advises a troubled kid, usually one not in his class, keeps tabs on the student and talks to the parents. Almost always, the student does better. The boy without a dad at home responds to a strong and caring male mentor. The girl whose mom works long hours gets to share her secrets and worries with a female mentor who listens. It's a powerful program.

I've never offered to be a mentor, given the fact that my plate is not only full, but has contents spilling onto the table and floor, and streaming out the door. But when the resource specialist hands me the file for the next student on the agenda, and I see the photo of Antonio Girardi, the boy with bangs in his eyes whom I embarrassed on the playground, my hand goes up of its own accord.

Antonio is in our program for learning disabled kids. He struggles academically. His mother, a single parent, went to jail

59

last year for a drug-related crime. He has no siblings and lives with his grandmother, an invalid. His grades are miserable. He doesn't act out, but he cuts school a lot, and the grandmother writes excuses for him. The teacher who referred him thinks he has potential, but needs a fire lit under him. More like a reason to live.

Getting to know Antonio will take creativity, given my schedule and every student's natural resistance to hanging out with the VP. I'll entice him with a late pass to class after we meet. Anything to get out of class.

The first time, I take him for a walk around the empty grounds—better than sitting in the office. He tells me about his classes. "Yeah, art is OK. And social studies."

"English?" I ask.

"No, it's boring. And math—can I get out of that class?"

We pass the picnic tables, where remnants of lunch wait to be picked up. The trees show off brilliant red leaves; the fallen ones crunch under our feet.

Looking at Antonio's downcast eyes and handsome face, barely visible below the hair, I'm concerned about his mental state. I ask him what it's like at grandma's house. He says, "It's OK."

"Do you have your own room?"

"I sleep on the couch. That's OK."

"Does Grandma cook for you?"

"She usually isn't feeling good. But I find a can of something to heat up."

How depressing. "What's with your hairdo, Antonio? Don't you want to show the world those beautiful eyes?"

He grins, but mumbles, "I haven't had a haircut in over two years."

I pause to look at his mournful face. It's not that he doesn't want a haircut. He's just a neglected kid. My arms ache to give

Chapter 8

him a hug.

"I'd like to drive you home from school tomorrow. To meet your grandma. And maybe she'll give me permission to take you for a haircut."

"OK," he says.

I call his grandmother. "He's not in trouble," I say. "I want to meet you and talk about Antonio."

The next day, he shows up at my office after school and we drive to Grandma's. The tiny house looks run down. Inside, a few small rooms overflow with magazines, junk mail, and dirty dishes. Antonio and I sit on the couch across from Grandma. Enormous, she might weigh three hundred pounds. She's ensconced in a worn, overstuffed chair in front of the TV. An oxygen tank by her side and cannulas in her nose, she probably can't walk across the room without help. She catches her breath between words.

"Mrs. Girardi, Antonio has been absent a lot and his grades are suffering."

"Yeah, he don't like to get out of bed in the morning."

Antonio squirms in his chair. "I'm too tired," he says.

"What time do you go to bed, Antonio?"

"Uh, I—"

"He stays up real late watching the tube," says Grandma.

Here I go again, giving parenting advice to people who should know better.

"You two might decide on a bedtime and stick to it. Got that, Antonio?"

His chin is on his chest, but he nods slightly.

"Mrs. Girardi, Antonio tells me he hasn't had a haircut for a long time, and I'd love to take him to my stylist. On me."

She says, "OK," and turns up the volume on the TV, signaling me to go.

I sit in the car for a few minutes, my heart in my throat.

61

What an awful situation for this young man. But what can I do? First, update the SST and get Antonio to commit to a bedtime. Baby steps. I call my hairdresser, Jeanine, and tell her the story. She'll be happy to cut a teenager's hair.

We arrive at Jeanine's salon after school on a Thursday. Antonio hesitates to get out of the car. "I don't know if I want it cut," he says.

"Sure, you do," I answer. "It doesn't have to be short. You can tell her how much to take off. I want to be able to see you under there."

Jeanine is a pro. She knows how to work with testy kids. She takes her time, shows him some pictures, explains how much she wants to cut off. He balks at getting rid of the bangs altogether, but agrees to have the hair cut just above his eyebrows. At the end, he beams as Jeanine shows him the back in the hand mirror. He is embarrassed to be in a salon and with me, but he grins at the results. Jeanine refuses payment and I leave her a fat tip. I drop Antonio off at home, assuming Grandma will be pleased.

The next day, Antonio gets teased by the other boys, but the girls are clearly giving him the eye. They can see his soulful brown ones for the first time. This first step for Antonio was a success, but there's a lot more to do. I call county social services to ask if they can intervene in the home on his behalf. Perhaps a social worker can get Grandma some help and improve Antonio's life.

LESSON #4: COMPASSION IS ALWAYS A GOOD IDEA.

CHAPTER NINE
OUTDOOR EDUCATION

THE SIXTH-GRADE TEACHERS BEG CARLSON AND he agrees to let me join them at outdoor education for one day and night. The camp, near the coast south of San Francisco, has cabins in the redwoods. Sleeping under the fragrant giants and excursions to the ocean—what could be better for a week of hands-on science learning? I help the teachers organize the paperwork—permission slips, payments, scholarships, and communications with camp staff about special student needs.

The kids and teachers go down by bus on Monday, the youngsters bouncing out of their seats with excitement or sick to their stomachs with worry. Some have never been away from their parents. They will return on Friday, filthy, sleep-deprived, and happy. In a way, it's an experiment with adulthood: being independent, getting along with others, and learning in a new environment.

The teachers will have one night when they don't need to attend dinner and evening campfire. A chance to go out for dinner and share a couple of bottles of wine. I look forward to joining them. On Wednesday morning, I drive two hours to the camp, noting the perfect weather—warm but not hot, a cloudless turquoise sky, and a cool breeze off the Pacific. I arrive in time to join one cabin group of girls and one of boys for the short bus ride out to the ocean. The kids would rather not see the vice principal, but I board the bus, chatting with Laura Gonzaga.

The camp staff plans and leads all the activities. That's a treat for the Hamilton teachers, who act as assistants. At the beach, the sixth-graders explore tide pools and listen to docents explain about the creatures they find and environmental threats to the ocean. After a short volleyball game on the beach, it's time to return to camp. As I turn to board the bus, I glimpse a boy climbing a fence post. Before I can shout a warning, he falls off onto some rocks and shrieks in pain. Not here too! A teacher gets to him first and looks at his ankle, twisted and starting to swell. The staff person calls back to camp. "We've got an injury here. Twisted ankle."

He listens and then directs us to take the boy back to camp for further evaluation. And then he asks me, "Would you contact the parent?"

Laura has all the parent information in her purse. She hands me a sheet with the boy's information. I call and leave a message for the parent. Here we go. If I don't hear from the parent and a medical evaluation is needed, I get to take over. And where might the closest emergency room be? I visualize the miles and miles of pristine beaches heading north on Highway 1, the coast road. Please, phone, ring.

Back at camp, the director has an ice bag waiting, but given how much the kid is complaining, the director says, "This requires a trip up the highway to Half Moon Bay." It's a half hour drive on a two-lane road.

After trying José's mom again—there is no other contact on his card—we gingerly help the boy into my car and I'm off, with no idea when or if I'll be able to return. If José has to go home, who is going to take him? Can his mom get here at night? That would be a tough round trip in the dark. It looks like my fun evening with the staff is off.

Three hours later, it's getting dark, and the heat of the day has been replaced by a chill ocean breeze. José is released back

Chapter 9

into my care. The doctor has determined it's just a bad sprain, but José's camp experience is over. The doctor has given him pain medication and crutches. The mom finally calls and agrees to have José spend the night with supervision at camp. She will drive down and pick him up in the morning. Hallelujah, I don't have to take him home. We settle José with the camp director, who'll be playing overnight nurse. It's late, but I call Laura Gonzaga and ask, "Where are you and is there any wine left?"

My body tells me to call it a day, but I grab my jacket and jump back in the car, determined to do what I came here to do—relax with the teachers. They're at Duarte's Tavern, an old-time establishment in the tiny town of Pescadero, a fifteen-minute drive downhill and off the coast road. The two men and three women are having dessert when I arrive, but they fill my glass and wait while I inhale a bowl of the popular artichoke soup. Then we return to the teachers' cabins for laid-back fun. While sipping wine, we tell stories about students and parents we have known, and I learn who on the staff is getting a divorce and who may retire.

One of the guys asks, "What's it like to work with Carlson?"

Perhaps I shouldn't tell the truth, but the wine gives me courage. "Well, it's no walk in the park." They all laugh.

"He has never had any interest in special education," says Laura. "We're really glad that you're involved in our IEPs."

"I'm here to support you." I raise my glass to them. "That is, when I'm not too busy with behavior referrals."

When the wine runs out, we turn in, men in one cabin, women in another. Despite the trip to the hospital, I've enjoyed my visit and the change of scenery. I know these teachers a bit better, and they have seen the lighter side of the new vice principal.

I arrive back at Hamilton the next afternoon. A stack of behavior referrals waits—Carlson has done nothing—but

65

I'm refreshed and ready to dig in. Around dismissal time, I'm sitting at my desk catching up with emails. It's the usual slew of messages inviting us to try a new photographer, fundraiser, or curriculum. Totally focused, I don't stop when a seventh-grade boy, Danny Johnson, steps through my door. This boy is unusually friendly for his age. He has brought me the occasional donut or cookie, always says hello and gives me a big grin when we pass on campus. My favorite kind of student.

I look up and acknowledge him but finish my email response. During the minute it takes me to do this, he steps behind me. I'm shocked to feel hands on my shoulders. He's giving me a shoulder massage. A good shoulder massage.

"Danny, you're a great kid and the massage is wonderful, but some people might think this a bit odd."

He doesn't stop. "Mrs. Walker, I'm just practicing. I've been learning this from my older sister—she's in massage school."

"OK, Danny, you better stop now." He walks back around the desk and directs his sunny smile at me.

"Thanks," I say. "That's going to be a hit with the girls—but please ask their permission first." He waves and goes out the door. I watch him depart and through the glass find Gaby and Derek Simons smiling at me. They have both seen the whole thing. Gaby, seated at her desk, phone still in hand, gives me a thumbs up.

Derek stands frozen for a moment, like he doesn't know whether to stay or run, then opens my office door. "I came by to ask you something. Can't keep the admiring kids away, huh?"

I feel the blush rise. The guy I talked to about looking down girls' shirts watched me get a massage from a student.

He sinks into a chair. "How was outdoor ed?"

My every move must be common knowledge. "It was great, despite a trip to the emergency room. That seems to be one of

Chapter 9

my greatest talents."

"You, or—"

"One of the kids. Twisted ankle."

"Too bad. I wanted to ask you about the Curriculum Council schedule. I'm supposed to chair this month, but I have a conflict. Can you fill in for me?"

"Sure, no problem." That was easy. But I'm surely still blushing.

"OK, thanks," he says, and rises from the chair. He turns before going out. "Have the parents talked to you about the jogathon assembly yet?"

"No. I think Jane Rogers is on my schedule next week."

"Be prepared for something fun."

He chuckles, prompting me to ask, "Now what?"

"I really don't know; they keep it a secret until the last minute, but I'm sure they have plans for you."

"Never a dull moment at Hamilton," I respond. He grins broadly and bounces down the hall.

MY SCHEDULE CALLS FOR charting student engagement in George Dunning's class. I arrive at the appointed time and sit in the back at a table. George acknowledges me with a nod. Most of the kids have their social studies books out. I quickly scrawl a seating chart and mark the desks where I see no book. George directs them to a map of the United States in the 1800s. He asks a series of questions about westward expansion.

I make tick marks on my chart when he calls on each student. After a few minutes I walk around. Some students aren't on the right page. One girl writes on a piece of paper and slips it under her book when she sees me coming. I record all of this on my chart.

After fifteen minutes, I leave. At least there were no paper airplanes. And the lesson plan was solid. I look forward to a positive conference.

67

The next day I show him my chart and ask for his impressions.

"Well, it looks like I need to be sure they've all got the book open to the right place."

"What's a good way to do that, George?"

"Walk around the room, I guess."

Yes, walk around the room. A no-brainer for most teachers, but George is not most teachers.

"Here's another thing, George. How many kids answered questions during this fifteen-minute period?"

"Let's see, one, two, three...only four of them."

"Right. Do you remember what I told you to get more students to answer?"

"Something about a seating chart?"

"Yes, you can mark on a seating chart every time you call on someone. It's easy to pay too much attention to the kids in the front. You can walk around while you're asking questions and don't hesitate to call on kids whose hands are not in the air."

That's enough for now. But this conference may be a turning point. Dunning is listening to me, asking for help. Perhaps I'm making a difference—one classroom at a time. You see, when students are properly engaged with the curriculum, it can change everything—from the all-important test scores to student attitudes about learning. That's really the goal: students who love to learn. Once motivated, who knows how far they may go in their lives? Cure cancer? Run for president? Educators change the world.

At the end of the school day, I write up my notes from my conference with Dunning and file away the day's behavior referrals. There's a new stack for tomorrow. I'm getting used to it.

Before leaving for home, I glance at the calendar. Halloween is on the horizon. But before that we have tee shirt day and the major parent club fundraiser of the year. I can't wait to find out what role they have cooked up for me.

CHAPTER TEN
DRESSING UP

I STILL HAVEN'T DEALT WITH SAM BUTLER'S WORK attire. Student dress codes are yet another nightmare. You may think it's wise to ask kids to dress in a manner that doesn't distract them from their studies. It's a good idea, but difficult to accomplish.

My last school had a dress code that defined the required length of skirts or shorts and prohibited bare midriffs, tank tops, and hats of any kind indoors. I have no desire to measure the length of shorts. And I've read enough court cases that enforce students' rights around clothing and hair that I have no desire to bring it up. Hamilton has no dress code and I like it that way. I deal on a case-by-case basis with clothing that disrupts the learning process. For example, tee shirts that advertise drugs or booze, or use offensive language.

I'm out on the grounds during the morning break when a couple of girls approach.

"Have you seen Jimmy Green's tee shirt?"

"Where is he?" I ask. They point across the yard to a group of boys kicking a soccer ball. Jimmy is wearing a black shirt emblazoned front and back with a Budweiser ad.

I call out, "Jimmy, come on over here."

He looks up, scowls, and leaves the game.

"What?" he asks with a rude voice.

"Jimmy, does Mom know you wore that shirt today?"

"Yeah, what about it?"

"Come with me."

He follows me into my office and plops down noisily in the seat across from me.

"Jimmy, you're a smart kid. You know that shirt is not OK. We don't advertise liquor or drugs at school."

"I don't see what the big deal is."

Sigh. "You have two choices. You can go into the restroom in the nurse's office, take off the shirt and put it on inside out, or we can call Mom to bring you another shirt."

He looks at me in disbelief.

"Which is it?" I ask, reaching for the phone.

"OK, OK, I'll change it around."

He comes out of the nurse's office, the shirt's logos on the inside, label flapping at his neck. "Can I go back outside now?"

"Yes, and if you wear a similar shirt again, you'll have detention to deal with."

He's out the door before I finish speaking.

At least once a year, every Student Council sponsors a fun day where kids wear school colors, put their clothes on backwards, or wear favorite tee shirts. Hamilton's tee shirt day is coming up and I put out a message to all the homeroom teachers. I want them to reinforce that tee shirts like Jimmy's are not OK.

Please remind your students that tee shirts that promote alcohol, marijuana, or other drugs, or represent nudity or obscenity may not be worn for tee shirt day. Anyone who wears an inappropriate shirt will be asked to change and will stay indoors during the lunch break.

Sigh. I'm sure there will be a few rule breakers.

To show my school spirit, I need to select my own tee shirt for the special day. I dig out the one I bought at a carnival a few years ago. It says "Shark Trainer" on the front and features a jagged cut-out side seam emblazoned with fake blood. So appropriate for this job!

Chapter 10

When the day arrives, I laugh at myself in the mirror on the way out the door. Everyone in the office wears a tee. The secretaries have dusted off their Hamilton Tigers shirts. Carlson sits behind his desk in what looks like a San Francisco 49ers shirt. He smiles and waves when he sees me. I give him points for his school spirit. I've only had a glimpse, but he must look dreadful in what must be a size XXL shirt.

During morning break, I patrol the grounds, seeing mostly sports logos emblazoned on kids' chests. Teachers send me two students with questionable shirts. One has a picture of a Dachshund and the words "My wiener does tricks." The other says "It's always 420 somewhere," and has a graphic of a marijuana plant. I make them both turn them inside out and assign the kids to sit in the office during lunch.

Kids want to take selfies with me in my shirt. One boy poses next to me, leaning over with his mouth open, like he is about to bite me. Very funny. I bet one of those will find its way into the yearbook.

JILL ROGERS, THE PRESIDENT of Hamilton Middle School's parent club, arrives at my office with Starbucks and two chocolate croissants. My kind of meeting. She's here to fill me in on the jogathon coming up before Halloween. The club raises money to pay for all the things the state can't afford, like musical instruments and supplies for shop and art classes. I should spare you my rant on those classes being non-essential. Research shows that creative pursuits enhance all kinds of learning. But the state provides little funding for anything beyond basic math and English. Sorry, I couldn't help myself. Parent club money also provides a few hundred dollars to each teacher for supplies.

Jill explains the event between sips of coffee. "The kids get pledges from their family and friends—either flat pledges or per lap. On jogathon day, they run laps for a half hour. Everybody gets a goody bag and a specially designed tee shirt. And we have prizes for the most pledges or money raised."

"Where do you get the prizes?" I ask.

"Local businesses donate them. There's usually a bike, maybe a skateboard. And we always get a trip to Disneyland!"

Wow—prizes awesome enough to motivate middle schoolers.

"How much do you usually raise?" I ask.

"Last year, $100,000."

That's more than my previous middle school ever raised from a single event.

She continues. "The assembly kicks things off, and that's where you come in."

"So, what's the theme this year?" I ask. It's always a secret until assembly day.

"Under the Sea," she says. "And we'd like you to wear a wet suit for the kickoff."

Everyone will love seeing me in costume. Or perhaps they will simply enjoy laughing at a person of authority looking foolish. I'm game for just about anything—you have to be, in a career where some administrators spend a day on the roof of their school because the kids met a reading goal.

"OK."

I've never worn a wet suit, but Jill doesn't need to know that. Scuba and surfing are not my thing. Actually, water sports are not my thing—thanks to the ease with which I get seasick. Once I became nauseous while snorkeling in Hawaii. All I could do was get back on the boat, which was anchored offshore. I hung over the side while the other tourists downed the expensive lunch I couldn't eat.

On assembly day I arrive at the gym to find papier mâché octopi and colorful fish hanging from the ceiling. A treasure chest spills fake gold coins around the podium. The floor is blanketed with faux coral and seaweed. The kids file in while

Chapter 10

I'm in the bathroom, squeezing into the wet suit. Now it's time for my grand appearance.

Here's the thing about a wet suit. The key word is "wet." It's meant to be worn in water. Out of water, it is 1) hard to get into. Maybe because it's too tight. And 2) the best sweat producer you can imagine. Covered from head to toe, I look like a human manatee. I can barely see through my goggles. I walk across the floor in fins with halting steps like the Creature from the Black Lagoon. The moms help me get down on the floor to stretch out for photos. Ouch. My body doesn't want to bend in all that rubber. The kids laugh and shout, "Ms. Walker, way to go." By the time they peel the suit off me, I've surely lost two pounds.

Jogathon day dawns overcast, with a fall chill in the air, perfect for jogging. The kids come to school in running gear and assemble in homerooms. After a few motivational announcements—"How many laps can you do for your school? Let's go, Tigers!"—everyone walks outside and takes positions around one of our two tracks. In athletic pants and a Hamilton tee shirt, I join the kids for the first twenty minutes, jogging, walking, and cheering them on. Carlson makes an appearance to glad-hand the parents, tells me he has a dental appointment, and disappears.

All of the students participate in the run. Some are really into it, running fast, totting up pledges earned. Others are out for a stroll. Many in this age group have reasons to resist: kids who are overweight, those who are too cool, and outliers who collected no sponsors and just don't care. While Janelle Owusu passes everyone by as she goes round and round the track, there is Jimmy Green slinking along. And Antonio, in jeans that are too short and a jacket too heavy for running, looking lost and alone.

At the end, even the slackers are smiling, and the sun peeks

73

out from the clouds as we send them all back inside for parent-provided treats. We've used an hour of the day and go back on the regular schedule before lunch. Now the kids just have to collect the money that their friends and family have pledged. Easy peasy! The teachers will make sure they follow up.

LESSON #5: APPRECIATE ALL GOOD IDEAS— GO WITH THE FLOW.

AT THE MIDDLE SCHOOL where I taught, students were not allowed to dress up for Halloween. Staff, however, could go all out. Some years, I wore a funny hat, but usually didn't bother with the full body costumes and makeup. Green goop on my skin for six hours? Uncomfortable, ill-fitting costumes? No thanks.

Hamilton is a different world. The parents have Carlson wrapped around their little fingers and of course *they* are at the mercy of their all-powerful twelve- and thirteen-year-olds. So, the kids get to dress up. The ground rules prohibit fake weapons and there are supposed to be limits on the amount of bare skin on the girls, all of whom would love to wear sexy French maid outfits. The costumes and parties result in a day of lost instruction and a nightmare for anyone trying to maintain a semblance of order. Yes, once again, the VP.

I've seen yearbook photos of Hamilton teachers in costume. They really get into it, so in my first year, I'd better go along with the program. What costume will be fun without completely disguising me or crushing my authority? I decide to be a pirate. Black pants and silk shirt, hat, fake hook, boots. It doesn't require applying anything to my face beyond an eye patch and a sticky mustache. Carlson tells me in advance he will be ensconced in his office with the door closed. As far as I'm concerned, his everyday costume of greasy salesman is just right.

Chapter 10

Gaby arrives dressed as a witch—green face, black hat, warts, and all. Even Sharon has dressed up, as some kind of fairy godmother—a long sparkly dress and feathered wings on her back.

The usual discipline work must still go on. I tell a couple of the less serious offenders if I see them again, they'll have to walk the plank. I think that's pretty funny, but they don't laugh. To them, I'm a dorky woman with a mustache. During morning break, I patrol the grounds, trying to walk in a swashbuckling way. Big steps and wide swinging hips. Few kids pay attention to me. They're all giggling with their friends about their own costumes.

I encounter Danny, the wannabe masseur, today a superhero. "Are you Captain Hook?" he asks.

"Not necessarily. Seen any alligators?"

Danny laughs at my mustache, which is itching already. "Weren't there girl pirates?"

"I don't think so, Danny."

The Student Council holds a costume contest at lunch. Homerooms have nominated kids who parade across the field in front of the bleachers. The officers judge the best costume based on the amount of applause from the stands, although it looks like one of those times when the kids cheer the loudest for the dumbest costumes. This age group excels at reverse compliments: "Nice shoes, Mrs. Walker," when they mean "those are the ugliest shoes I've ever seen." It's hard to nail middle schoolers for sarcasm. Since the prizes are pencils and notebooks from the student store, nobody cares who wins.

After lunch, kids in itchy costumes and makeup get restless. Or maybe it's teachers who are restless, but the office starts filling up. At one point the crowd waiting to see me includes a devil who has stolen an angel's halo. I'm sorry to see it's Jimmy, who has been doing better in the classroom. Behaving while in

75

costume simply exceeds the limits of his self-control.

"I'll take that," I say. He hands me the halo and I return it to the girl. She has a death grip on his trident, now in two pieces.

"Sorry," she whispers in an angelic way, looking at the floor. "But he took my halo first."

"Yeah, I guess I deserved it," answers Jimmy.

Without comment, I root in my desk drawer for duct tape and perform a quick repair. I spare them the plank talk and send them back to class.

A girl dressed like a baby—in a onesie and dragging a blanket—has been sent in on suspicion that she filled her baby bottle with something other than milk. One sniff confirms it's scotch. I hand her the phone. "Get your mom and tell her."

Her explanation is interrupted by yelling on the other end of the phone. The girl continues, "I...I... know where the liquor is."

Pause while Mom yells.

"It was just a joke, Mom."

More yelling from Mom.

"I didn't drink any."

Sure. Tears running down her face, she hands me the phone to finish the conversation. Soon Mom arrives to whisk her home to sleep it off.

As the school day finally draws to a close—thank God I have no meetings afterwards—I walk around campus. It's wise to be out when the final bell rings to nip any festering problems from growing into something bigger—that all too frequent promise to "meet me on the baseball field after school."

Kids walk towards the exit in various states of disrepair. Some costumes drag on the ground or threaten to fall off. Smeared makeup runs in black rivulets off sweaty faces. The kids look eager to have the school day over; I suspect they're ready to move on to an evening of candy extortion.

76

Chapter 10

Teachers begin to emerge from classrooms. There's a cute Raggedy Ann, an astronaut removing his helmet—that must have been hot—several grim reapers or ninjas, and Little Bo Peep. I'm passing Derek Simons's door as he steps out. To my amazement, he is also dressed as a pirate. Like minds?

We laugh and I announce, "Definitely looks better on you!"

Derek asks, "So did you have anybody walk the plank?"

"No, but I threatened a couple of times."

"We always go to the staff room for photos," he says. We walk there together, two swashbuckling fellows of a sort. The art teacher, who has made up her face like Frida Kahlo and carries a paintbrush and palette, takes photos. She has to have one of Derek and me together. I retrieve my prickly mustache, which has been in my pocket since lunch. Derek puts his arm around me, and I reciprocate.

We fit together snugly, his arm around my shoulder and mine around his waist. Nice feeling. Very nice. His body heat mesmerizes me, and I don't want to let go. When the photo is done, he gives me a good squeeze before releasing me. I force myself to step away and focus my attention elsewhere. An assortment of creatures worthy of the Star Wars bar scene fills the room. I survey tired, smiling faces. Even Joe, the custodian, has participated. Dressed like a cowboy, with hat, shirt, and boots, he holds a broom topped with a toy horse head.

By four o'clock, I'm ready to forget Halloween and go straight to bed, but I promised my friend Pam I'd stop by to help her kids with costumes and makeup. Her husband will walk the youngsters around the neighborhood while Pam and I answer her doorbell and have a couple of drinks.

Pam's adorable kids are blue-eyed towheads. Peter is seven and Sally is two years older. I've seen a lot of strange costumes today, but they have chosen to do something old-fashioned. Peter dresses as a girl and Sally as a boy. When I arrive, Pam is

77

applying eye makeup on a squirmy Peter.

"I don't know about this," she says. "It was their idea."

"I remember doing this switch with my brother when I was a kid," I offer.

"Hold still, dude," she says. He's wearing a long, sparkly dress and will try to walk in a pair of his mother's high heels. Those won't last one block. I help Sally tie her necktie. Small for her age, she fits into her brother's suit jacket. I've brought her my mustache, which still has enough adhesive to stick under her darling little nose. Pam has given her a small fedora, which is still too big and tries to slip down over her eyes.

Dad Roger arrives from work in time to take photos of the kids. Then they're off in search of candy and Pam pours the wine. In between dashes to the door, I tell her about my school challenges—the fire, bomb threats, outdoor ed, and Halloween.

"Remember the cute guy I told you about at school?"

"Yeah, a teacher, right?"

"Yeah. He was also a pirate today. What a kick."

"Well, you've got to do something more than dress the same if you want anything to happen."

"I know, I know, but I'm his supervisor and I'm evaluating him—it could cause a problem; at the least it could be a daily embarrassment—like if he doesn't feel the same way."

When Roger returns with the kids, they hold out their bags for inspection, their beaming faces reflecting the dazzle of what's inside.

Ever the wise mom, Pam proclaims, "Three pieces before bed. We've got to inspect all of that." And I suspect, chow down on a sweet treat before parent bedtime. That's what I'd do. I say my goodbyes before I'm tempted to dig in myself. It may be Halloween, but tomorrow is a school day.

CHAPTER ELEVEN
MORE PROBLEMS

ONE DAY IN NOVEMBER, SHARON CALLS TO TELL ME there's an urgent call from Bert Sheldon. It seems his six-foot-long python, Gertie, is missing in action. I believe Sheldon uses Gertie to intimidate his students. I once heard the students talking after he fed Gertie a live mouse. Watching the snake stalk a mouse while the tiny guy freezes in terror surely fuels nightmares.

Sharon transfers the call. My first question to Sheldon: "Could she have escaped from the room?" Her journey off the school grounds and into the creek would be a great solution.

"No," Sheldon answers. "She disappeared from the cage when both classroom doors were closed."

Since the cage has a top that closes with locks, it's hard to imagine there are no accomplices. First at the top of my list of suspects is the teacher, as I've heard this has happened before and he seems to enjoy the drama.

I ask Sharon to call for Joe, the custodian. The announcement goes out on the intercom, but he doesn't respond.

"You know," says Sharon, as she chomps on her gum, "I think I saw him leaving campus after lunch."

"Really?"

"Yeah. He may have told me earlier this week there was some meeting at the district—I don't remember."

"OK, is John around?" I can guess the answer.

"No, he's off campus too."

I could wait to see if Mr. Principal in Absentia reappears, or for Joe to return. But a headline about a python terrorizing students is not something I'm interested in seeing. I walk down to the classroom. Sheldon and I look into cupboards and heating vents, while students goof off or shiver in the corners. We find Gertie curled up under gym mats on the coat closet floor. It's hard to imagine how she got out without help. I wonder if the teacher knew where she was the entire time and just likes pushing my buttons.

I wait until school is out to confront Sheldon in his classroom. Gertie is curled up in a corner of her cage. "Look, Bert, we don't need hysterical kids or parents because a snake is on the loose."

"Ah, she's harmless," he answers.

"Do you want to explain that to any parent who hears about this and is concerned?"

"Look, it's my job to make science exciting for the kids. Why don't you let me do that? And I'll keep a closer eye on the cage."

"OK, Bert, but if anyone calls, I'll make sure they're directed to you."

This feels like a standoff. Sheldon is a good teacher, but his ego may be more than I can handle. Like what I need is another man on campus who puts himself on a pedestal and doesn't give any weight to what I think.

EVERY DAY HOLDS A SURPRISE assortment of student and parent problems. My job is anything but boring, but every minute of the day somebody wants something from me, and some days the requests come on so fast, I feel trapped in a cage myself.

Hamilton has one class for severely learning disabled or autistic students and another for emotionally disturbed (ED) kids. Each child has individual learning and behavioral goals. The program requires special teachers, who don't need my

Chapter 11

assistance. Until they do.

A few days after the snake escape, my special education skills face a test. The ED teacher is out ill, and the substitute calls for help. The class currently has two aides and six students. Paul is refusing to do anything in the classroom. I meet the tall boy and his aide outside the room.

"Hi, Paul. What's going on?"

He scowls and doesn't respond.

"Paul, look at Ms. Walker," says the aide.

He glances up. "Paul, I know it's tough when your regular teacher isn't here, but you only have two choices. You can do your work, or you can go home and miss the next class party." I repeat this, several times, giving him plenty of time to think, until the boy decides to go back to class and cooperate. That wasn't hard, but the day isn't over. It's going to be a special education afternoon.

A properly placed student with the right learning plan should be able to follow the school rules. For example, the rule that says: Thou Shalt Not Hit Thy Teacher. As a special education teacher myself, I've experienced administrators who had no idea how to handle a disturbed and irate thirteen-year-old. One time a boy punched me in the arm, after I pried a chair out of his hands, milliseconds before he would have thrown it across the room. I walked him to the office and then watched two male administrators try to force him into a chair. Before the ugly scene ended, I couldn't tell who was redder in the face, the boy or the adults. And they assigned no consequences to the student who gave me a black and blue arm. He returned to class the next day.

Now that I'm in charge, I'm determined that *nobody* will attack one of my teachers without consequences. This afternoon, a teacher's aide calls to tell me one of the autistic kids in her special class just hit the teacher. This teacher, Trudy

Young, has high energy and strong skills. Each of her students has a daily contract with points and rewards. When I get to the classroom, the boy has calmed down. Mrs. Young is fine, but the student intentionally punched her in the arm. The aide accompanies the boy to the office while I call the parent.

"Mrs. Jacobsen, it's Cynthia Walker. I'm sorry to tell you that Bryan lost his temper and punched Mrs. Young in the arm."

"Is he OK? Is she OK?"

"Yes, he's calmed down. It was about losing a point for not completing an assignment. Mrs. Young is fine, but she already has a big bruise. I want Bryan to get a clear message that hitting won't be tolerated. I'm suspending him from school. Just for one day."

"Suspension? But his anger issues are in his IEP. He's never been suspended."

"I understand, but he has broken the law and I think he can learn from this. Please come and get him."

The mom picks Bryan up, but she's fuming. Her darling boy has never been sent home from school. In reality, she probably doesn't want to supervise him for the day of suspension. She protests to Carlson before leaving with Bryan. Carlson calls me into his office late in the afternoon.

By law, a higher-up can't overturn a suspension. Dragging myself down the hall to His Highness, I'm determined to stick to my guns, no matter what he wants. He motions me to the seat opposite him.

"Cynthia, suspension for an autistic kid? Really?"

"Look, John. Do you want to have a school where it's OK for students to hit your staff? I'm scheduling a meeting to decide if the boy needs a change of placement." My words sound confident, but my heart is pounding like a drum, and I try to calm my fluttering fingers by grasping the arms of the chair.

82

Chapter 11

"You couldn't let him return to school while you do that? If it were me——"

"But it's not you." My voice is shaky, but I'm determined that he back me up. "Look, you hired me to handle special education, so let me handle it."

John's eyes widen, but he nods.

"OK, your way, but the parents will go to a higher level."

I'm still jumpy leaving his office, but confident I made the right decision. Maybe Carlson will respect my experience and decisions. The parents may go to the superintendent, and he may decide to erase the suspension from the boy's record. But the sentence will have been served. I hope Bryan and his parents will learn from this. And I've just become a hero at Hamilton. Trudy writes me a heartfelt thank you. Gaby repeats positive comments overheard in the staff room. Standing up for teachers never goes unnoticed.

The next week, I clash with a parent whose diabetic son takes insulin. From my first meeting with David and his mom, Laura, I'm convinced that this child's medical needs not only keep his mother in a state of anxiety, but that he milks it for all it's worth. Laura often talks about how well David does with his diabetic diet and how we must not give him sweets. No problem there. She has a schedule for his insulin that doesn't disrupt school. Laura schedules a meeting with me before Thanksgiving.

"Here's the thing," she says. "Halloween was tough for David. He wants to eat what the other kids are having at their parties. He's suddenly embarrassed to be different."

"What does his doctor say?"

"His endocrinologist says it's fine for David to have some sugar if he gets a small dose of insulin first."

"Well, that's your choice, if you want to give him an injection."

83

"No, I need to get out of the habit of always being around for him. We could train you here in the office and he could come in just before the Christmas party and one of you could give him a shot."

I gulp. My reaction is loud and indignant, if only in my head. I'm being asked to measure and give a dose of insulin so the kid can eat a cupcake? This is a potentially dangerous drug.

"I really don't think that's a good idea, Laura."

"You'd just have to check his blood sugar first, to verify the right dose. You could even call me on the phone, and I'll talk you through it… I need to get my own life back."

"Let me consult the district and I'll get back to you."

LESSON #6: WHEN IN DOUBT, POSTPONE.

Fortunately, this conversation takes place long before Christmas. There's time to talk with the district nurse. I skip right over Carlson—he'll probably want to administer the insulin himself, just to make the parent happy. We set up a meeting with the parents and a nurse.

I make myself clear. "I don't think staff should take on unnecessary responsibility. The goal is not worth the risk. If Laura wants David to have insulin in order to eat junk food, she is welcome to come to school and administer it herself."

We talk about the rights of kids with medical conditions to enjoy all the privileges of other students but conclude where I started the conversation. The mom will continue as her son's sugar enabler. Would they expect me to find a way for a kid with his arm in a sling to play tennis? Or for a deaf kid to sing in the choir? I feel justified, but have a recurring worry—will the parent sue me?

There's no time to dwell on this. November is rushing by.

Chapter 11

I need to plan for a Christmas trip with Erica to Hawaii. And I'm about to host my first Thanksgiving dinner in my new home.

CHAPTER TWELVE
TURKEY DAY

THE LONG-AWAITED THANKSGIVING WEEK approaches. Students will be at home all week, sleeping in, seeing friends and family, devouring turkey and pie. Parent-teacher conferences fill the hours on Monday and Tuesday, keeping both groups out of my hair. Wednesday through Friday are vacation days. I'm getting a whole week without naughty students and lunchtime supervision.

There's plenty for me to do in the short week. Monday morning, I get busy approving reports on attendance and suspensions, ordering supplies, and checking textbook inventory. Despite our best efforts to track textbooks, some disappear every semester, and we have to order more. Planning is one of my strengths, when there's time to do it.

Gaby and I are sitting at her desk preparing a purchase order. My Derek radar must be on because I spy him down the hall talking to Sharon before he comes our way.

"Hi, is there any chance you had a call from Mr. or Mrs. Stapleton, Jacob's parents?"

Gaby answers, "No, sorry. They didn't show up for their conference?"

"No, I'll have to call them. How are you ladies doing?" He graces us with that smile.

"Just ordering books," I say.

Gaby gets up. "Be right back," she says and walks down the hall.

"This must be a fun week for you," he continues, stepping closer. I catch a whiff of his piney aftershave.

"I'll say. No detention slips to write."

"What are you doing for Thanksgiving?" he asks.

Is he just making small talk, or does he really want to know?

"I'm cooking for friends. You?"

"Going to my parents' place in Gold Country."

"That's nice. Did you grow up there?"

"No, it's their retirement home, but wonderful for a visit—hiking...maybe snow."

"Snow—definitely not my thing. Brrr," I laugh.

Gaby returns and looks at him, then at me. "Is this private?" she asks with a quizzical smile. She's no doubt taking notice of my flushed face and eyes fastened to his.

I laugh, "No . . ."

"I better leave you to your ordering," says Derek. He raises his hand in a half salute and strolls towards the back door. What is it about this guy? Why did I tell him I don't like snow? Maybe he's into skiing. I sigh.

"You OK?" asks Gaby. She's grinning now.

"Fine," I say, "let's get back to it."

While placing the completed purchase order in the school mail, I meet one of the night custodians, Charles Bingham. The custodians are taking advantage of canceled classes to clean and polish floors in the gym and cafeteria. Charles is young, with blond, surfer good looks.

"Hi, Charles, how's it going?" I ask.

"Pretty good," he answers with a shy smile.

At a loss for anything else to say, I ask, "Looking forward to Thanksgiving?"

Charles looks away. "Well, not really. Nothing special going on."

"No family in the area?"

Chapter 12

"Nobody," he says.

"Me too. Look, you're welcome to join me and my friends at my house." This slips out before there's a chance to consider spending an evening with this young man about whom I know nothing.

Charles makes eye contact, a charmed look on his face. "Really? That would be great."

Before escaping back to my office, I give him my address and tell him to arrive around five o'clock. Have I just screwed up the evening? Charles with me and my two girlfriends? It could be awkward. My teacher friend Erica will be joining me, as well as Shelly, a flight attendant I've known since college. Shelly lives in San Francisco and I don't see her often.

Erica has been to my home, but it will be the first time for Shelly. I'm excited to host a holiday meal in my new digs. It's a starter home, about the same age as I, with three bedrooms and one bath. And for the first time in my adult life, I have a dining table big enough for a dinner party.

Thanksgiving morning finds me rested and ready to entertain. I assume a generous attitude about including Charles. After all, it's Thanksgiving, a time for kindness. I assemble my favorite giblet dressing from Mom's recipe, adding some walnuts and raisins to make it my own. Erica and Shelly will arrive early, to relax and catch up before dinner. I put the bird in the oven mid-afternoon and assemble my grandmother's corn pudding, while turkey aromas fill the house.

What might my school colleagues be doing today? Is Carlson having dinner with a big family group? I know so little about him. Does Gaby cook turkey or something from her Mexican heritage? Will Antonio's family gather in a traditional way? Will Jimmy behave for his parents? Does Janelle's family, from Ghana, celebrate Thanksgiving? Probably. Who doesn't love roast turkey?

89

My friends arrive and admire my new sofa and colorful pillows. We marvel over the huge amount of food we have. Erica brings sweet potatoes in addition to a salad— "Gotta have sweet potatoes," she says—and Shelly couldn't decide between pumpkin and apple pie, so has made both. An abundance of food seems to be everyone's norm for Thanksgiving.

"You know," Shelly says, "that's a lot of food for the three of us. We ought to invite someone to join us."

On cue, I say, "I invited one of the night custodians, a young guy who had no plans."

Shelly answers, "That makes four of us, but we have enough food for more! I heard the fog delayed flights at the airport this morning. There are military personnel who will miss their Thanksgiving with family."

"But how can we connect with them? And how would they get here?" Erica asks.

Shelly's excitement shows as she rattles off, "I can call someone at the United desk at the airport and have them ask in the waiting room if there is anyone who wants to come here for a meal... hey, if they want to, they can pay for a taxi—or rent a car for the night."

We three share grins all around. "Let's do it," I say.

Shelly makes her phone call, and, in a few minutes, we learn there will be two servicemen joining us for dinner.

As an afterthought, I ask, "Gee, can we be sure they know all they're getting is a turkey dinner?"

The other two laugh. "We'll make that perfectly clear," says Shelly.

We set my new table for six with a lace tablecloth and my best dishes and silver. The turkey comes out brown and beautiful. Charles arrives first. He's wearing dress pants and a long-sleeved shirt. He really is quite handsome, out of his floor-scrubbing clothes. I introduce him to Shelly and Erica

Chapter 12

and ask Erica to pour wine while I take the corn pudding out of the oven. Just as we start to wonder if they're really coming, the soldiers arrive. They've rented a car but had trouble finding my street in the dark.

We all jump up to answer the doorbell.

Charles and the girls introduce themselves, and the guys, both dressed in Army fatigues, tell us their names. Kevin, maybe five feet six inches, can't be more than twenty years old. Dartmouth is taller and a little older. He has a distinct southern accent. They both sport buzz cuts.

"Where'd you get your name?" Shelly immediately asks Dartmouth. Kind of pushy.

"My folks wanted me to go to school there—it's a family thing," answers Dartmouth. "But I joined the army instead." His smile extends from ear to ear, matching his southern accent and charm. "You can call me Dar."

As we sit down to eat, the conversation is plentiful, if a bit bizarre. Charles asks the soldiers about their tours of duty in the Middle East. "Have you killed anybody?" he wants to know.

Dar looks puzzled. "Dude, most of us don't like to talk about that. But yeah. I'll have nightmares about some of those days as long as I live."

Charles's cheeks are bright red. "Sorry. I just wonder if I could do it."

Shelly asks Charles where he grew up.

"Right here in town," he answers. "I went to Hamilton for junior high. It was just seventh and eighth grades back then. They added that whole C wing after I left."

"That must be fun, to work where you have all those memories," says Shelly.

Charles stares at her with interest, maybe more interest than is warranted. "Yeah," he says. "But it was not a good time for me. I spent a lot of time in the vice principal's office."

"Oops," says Shelly.

Despite my conviction that I have nothing in common with twenty-something fellows who have chosen careers in combat or mopping floors, we manage to talk about everything from pop music and what's playing at the movies to President Obama and the midterm elections. The soldiers appear awed to be invitees of two educators and a flight attendant. We're practically parent figures to them.

Dar reminisces about his middle school experiences. "I was too embarrassed to approach this girl I really liked. What an awkward time."

Kevin remembers smoking in the boys' bathroom. Charles acknowledges he did the same.

After consuming several bottles of wine, and before dessert, all six of us take a walk around the neighborhood. Charles walks next to Shelly, sporting a silly smile. Does he know she's at least ten years older? Has he had too much to drink? I can't tell.

Kevin, from Minnesota, says, "This warm air is wonderful. You California folks are lucky. If I'm even able to get a flight out, I'll probably be landing in a snowstorm."

We linger over the pies, naturally having to sample both. Then we hand around phones for group pictures. By nine o'clock, Dar and Kevin are on their way back to the airport, after many thanks, hugs, and promises to brag to their buddies about how lucky they were to spend the evening with us "lovely ladies."

I'd like to debrief with Shelly and Erica, but Charles hangs on. He doesn't notice that he's the only guy in the room and the women are restless.

Shelly announces, "I have a flight out tomorrow. I'd better head for home." Charles grabs his coat.

"I'll walk you out," he says, too eagerly, and follows her out

Chapter 12

the door. Poor Shelly. I know she can handle herself, but he is clearly smitten. And maybe a little drunk.

Erica and I sit down for a cup of coffee before starting on the pile of dishes. "That was great," she says.

"You don't think Charles was too weird?"

"Nah, he's just young and lonely. You made his day by inviting him."

Before going to bed, I send a text to Shelly. I know she's probably asleep already, but she can get back to me at her leisure. *Thanks for the pies. I hope Charles wasn't too much of a sad puppy.*

I collapse into bed, tired, but satisfied. Life is good. This was a perfect Thanksgiving. Shelly's response comes late the next day from London: *Tried to kiss me, but I set him straight.*

CHAPTER THIRTEEN
THREATS, REAL OR IMAGINED

WINTER BREAK WILL ARRIVE HALFWAY THROUGH December. I fool myself into thinking this short month will be easy. No such luck.

Hamilton hosts a Boy Scout troop on Tuesday evenings. I've been on campus during their sessions, so I know the supervision is less than stellar, with boys roaming the halls, out of sight of the scout leaders. On several Wednesday mornings, I have found nasty mail slipped under the office door. *Walker is a fat ass* and *Yer days our numberd* are my favorites. The scouts use the facility free of charge. They could at least be polite.

I show the notes to Gaby. "Has this ever happened before?"

"*No está bien!* Notes under the door—I don't think so. But those boys are no scouts. Joe tells me they don't clean up. He finds a mess on Wednesday mornings. The dads in charge... they're clueless." She shakes her head, a mom who knows the challenges of teaching kids to be responsible.

Too bad they don't have a scout badge for harassing the vice principal. I bring the notes to my weekly meeting with John. "These have been slipped under the door on Tuesday nights. I think it's the kids in our scout troop."

"Really? Those notes are not nice, but how can you be sure it's the scouts?" That's his response. Not, "How awful" or "I'll take care of this." Instead of supporting me, he's questioning

95

my assumptions. Once again, why am I surprised?

I respond, "I'd like to confront the scout leaders and tell them if they can't monitor their kids, they will have to meet somewhere else."

"Whoa," he answers. "They have a right to meet here. It's community property. Go ahead and talk to them. See what they say—but you can't threaten to kick them out."

Great. Carlson isn't concerned enough to get involved.

The next Tuesday evening, I corner the dad in charge. He reads the notes and shakes his head.

"Wow," he says. "I can't imagine any of our boys would do that. Plus, we're always with them."

"Paul, sorry, I don't think so. I've been here and seen boys wandering the halls while you're in the gym doing your activities."

"OK," he gives in with a tight grin, "I'll talk to them." I don't stick around to hear the talk. But on my way out, I see Jimmy in the group. Am I paranoid?

Either the dad gives a great lecture, or does a better job of policing, because my Wednesday mornings no longer begin with nasty notes.

Jimmy's contract is helping—he is coming to the office less often, but I suspect he has issues that aren't yet being addressed. I haven't done anything with the list of kids who were absent on bomb threat days, but my suspicions about this boy keep growing.

HAMILTON HAS JUST ONE counselor for the entire student body, Amy. Middle-aged, she has been at Hamilton for decades. The students and parents trust her. She knows how to get kids to talk about their problems and has great connections to community resources for troubled youth.

I share my concerns about Jimmy with Amy and set up a meeting for the two of us with Jimmy's parents. Due to work

Chapter 13

schedules, they can only meet after five o'clock, so Amy and I agree to extend our day. What does Jimmy do in the afternoons before his parents get home?

I greet the parents and Amy introduces herself. "I've only recently met Jimmy, but share Ms. Walker's concerns."

I add, "He's making progress on his classroom behavior—thanks for your help with the rewards—but he's not doing much work in class. He doesn't turn in homework. And he often seems angry."

Mrs. Green works a tissue in her hands and her face twitches. The dad speaks first. "Ms. Walker, we appreciate your interest in our son. James has always been a difficult child, who—"

"He means well," Mrs. Green interrupts. "He just doesn't know how to get along with people."

Amy asks, "He's an only child, right? Do you recall when this began?"

Mr. Green glares at his wife. She sits up straighter, still looking at her lap, and ignores her husband's gaze. "He was four when we lost—when we lost our baby." Tears spring from her eyes and she emits a quiet sob.

Mr. Green grips his knees and shakes his head.

Amy is on it. "I'm so sorry. Are you saying that's when Jimmy's behavior issues started?"

Mrs. Green blows her nose. The husband leans forward on the edge of his seat. He is red-faced and his body trembles with the effort to control his emotions. "It was long ago… crib death… nobody was to blame… but ever since, it's like, to her"—he cocks his head at his wife—"Jimmy can do no wrong."

I gulp. Thank God for counselors.

"I can see there's a lot to discuss here," Amy says, looking first at the mother, then at the father. She turns to me. "Is it OK if we postpone the academic part of this conversation while

I get to know Mr. and Mrs. Green and Jimmy a little better?"

"Of course." I direct myself to the parents. "I'm so glad you came in. I'm sorry for your loss and I know this is a challenge. But if we all work together, we can help Jimmy. I'll let his teachers know that Amy is involved."

Amy walks out with them, offering to see Jimmy for regular counseling sessions, and probably to refer the parents for some counseling of their own.

Wow. There are so many ways that kids can get screwed up. Adults too. This family needs help and I'm glad we have begun the process. It doesn't solve my immediate Jimmy problem, but insight is always helpful.

LESSON #7: COUNSELORS KNOW WHAT TO DO!

THE WEEK AFTER THE CONFERENCE with Jimmy's parents, *I'm* the one who gets in trouble. The school grounds border a tree-shaded creek, which has little water in it until winter rains fall. We're having a drought, so the creek bed is a parched ditch about four feet below the level of the field. When the bell rings at the end of lunch, I'm watching students stroll back to class, when two sixth-graders come to me on the run from near the creek.

"There's a man... there's a man down there..." The first kid is out of breath, red in the face and looks like he's seen a monster.

"He has a gun," spits out the second kid, his wide eyes glued to mine.

"You saw a gun?" I ask, not ready to panic, as kids say the darnedest things. Kids make up a bunch of crap too. At one of our assemblies, I warned the students that a hand pointed like a gun can be mistaken for the real thing.

The first kid echoes his buddy, "I saw it."

Chapter 13

"What kind of gun?" I ask, still calm, as I reach for my walkie talkie. The kids describe what might be a handgun.

While the two boys stand in front of me frozen in fear, I call the office.

"Sharon, please call the police and tell them two kids have just reported a man with a gun in the creek. Then tell Carlson I'm going to investigate."

"Okey-dokey, but he's not here," she responds. I can practically smell her spearmint gum.

"What did he look like?" I ask the boys. They describe a young man in a dark hoodie and jeans. They go to the office to await the police so they can share what they've seen. I walk toward the creek, imagining logical explanations.

A worn pathway leads down into the shaded creek bed. I look up the creek; I look down the creek. Tall oaks are covered with browning leaves. The opposite bank is visible, as well as the road on the other side. No gunman. As I'm coming back up the path, here comes uniformed Officer Strickland, badge sparkling in the sunlight, gun on his hip. We met at a district training. Then he was friendly and easy to talk to. He isn't smiling now. He frowns at me. "What were you doing down there?"

"Um, I went to see if someone was there."

"Not good, Ms. Walker. That's for law enforcement to do. You put yourself in danger."

"Look, officer, those kids could have imagined the whole thing. Maybe some rowdy high schooler pointed his finger at them."

"That may be the case, but you endangered yourself by investigating. Please go back to the office."

Cowed, I follow his orders. I'm not used to being the target of disciplinary talk at this school. I want to scream...or cry...but had better do neither. Word must travel fast. As I pass Derek

Simons's room, he leans out of the doorway.

"Everything OK?" he asks.

I swallow and put on my best face. "Fine." He's looking at me, brows knit with concern. I want to touch his arm to reassure him, to feel some comfort myself, but thirty twelve-year-olds are leaning back in their seats to see what's happening. "Just fine," I repeat, and keep walking.

The police officers do not find anything. Perhaps there was never any danger, but I spend the rest of the day in crisis control mode, dealing with Carlson, the school district, the parent club president, and the local newspaper.

A few days later, a rather excitable school neighbor claims she has seen a mountain lion in her yard. It's all over the newspaper and the local radio station. I'm in front of the school at the start of the day when a car pulls up and a guy who turns out to be a reporter leans out and shouts at me, "What are you doing to protect the kids from the lion?"

"Uh, what do you think?" I ask him. I mean, really. Does he suppose a mountain lion is going to invade the school grounds in the middle of the day? If the cat is crazed or hungry enough to look for a twelve-year-old kid to eat, what could I do?

I HAVE NOT HAD ANY CALLS from the special education teachers for a while, but I'm beginning to understand why many administrators prefer schools without special classes. I've known kids who talk to flies, cuss like sailors, chew food and spit it on doorknobs, or throw furniture. But this day begins with something new.

The special education teacher, Ms. Young, usually calm, sounds on the phone like she's going to cry. "Bobby got angry at the aide. He's...he aimed the fire extinguisher at her...we need you here now."

"Gaby," I say.

She's on a phone call, but says, "Just a minute," and looks

Chapter 13

up.

"Please call Bobby Parrish's mom and tell her we need her to pick him up." I jog down to the classroom. As I approach, I find the aide outside, covered in white powder.

"You OK?" I ask and wait for her nod before stepping into the room. There is Bobby, huddled in a corner, swinging the extinguisher and mumbling to himself. I have the teacher take everyone else out of the room.

"Bobby, it's Ms. Walker. It's going to be OK. Let's go for a walk." It takes a while before he puts down the extinguisher. I tell him his mother is on her way. By the time we leave the room, his mom has arrived. The aide has cleaned up and is laughing it off, but Ms. Young is mortified.

This was not Bobby's first angry and explosive incident. Our team will meet to decide if a public-school classroom is the right place for Bobby or if he needs a residential treatment center. My heart goes out to students who are this troubled, but when handling them in a classroom becomes impossible, I'm glad to see them go.

THE CURRICULUM COUNCIL MEETS early in December to analyze last year's test results and plan for spring. I'm relieved it's not my turn to chair the meeting. Derek, representing the social studies department, has it under control. Sitting across from him, I can study his sweet face without anyone thinking I'm doing anything besides paying attention to the facilitator.

Last year some schools cheated on the state tests. Teachers or administrators at a number of schools across the state changed students' answers to improve scores. It was a huge scandal. That's the result of high stakes testing. This year the state has new protocols for everyone to follow, to provide maximum security. That will be a headache, and guess whom Carlson has put in charge of testing? Yep, one more thing for me to do.

101

At the end of the meeting, Derek reminds us of the staff Christmas party to be held next week on the last day of school before vacation. Am I ready for a party? I'll say, not to mention the two-week vacation that follows.

CHAPTER FOURTEEN
ALL I WANT FOR CHRISTMAS

THE WEEK BEFORE THE CHRISTMAS HOLIDAYS, known in politically correct parlance as winter break, is a very stressful time. Kids are excited about their approaching Christmas haul and their vacation plans. The staff, exhausted and on edge from holiday preparations and too much eggnog, must plan lessons for tuned-out students.

On the last day before vacation, the rainy season arrives. It's coming down in sheets. Having everyone in the cafeteria for lunch adds to the noisy, chaotic feel of the day. We've changed the schedule to allow for parties in homerooms in the afternoon. Time for treats and gift exchanges. Teachers will supervise games to keep their students from climbing the walls. I've never understood the thrill of Heads Up, Seven Up, but middle schoolers still love it. It's as simple as tapping someone whose head is down and hoping they won't guess it was you—anything to keep them occupied.

If you're thinking that Hamilton is way too lax about junk food, you're right. A small group of parents have argued we should limit classroom snacks to healthy stuff, but they failed to influence the majority. Even when parents ban sweets at home and never take their kids for fast food, middle schoolers have their own money and time without Mom or Dad. If they want junk food, they'll find it. Most parents decide to save their

103

battles for bigger things, like drugs and sex.

The school vibrates with the energy of six hundred excited kids, but there are few discipline problems. The kids know that if they get in trouble, I'll send them home before their party starts. The eighth-graders don't want to miss their first dance, to be held at the end of the day.

After the indoor lunch break with the echoing noise of hundreds of kids, I return to a quiet office, delighted to have no fights to settle. Gaby ends my happy mood.

"Ms. Walker, Mrs. Scott sent Abby in. She left you a note." She hands the piece of binder paper to me.

The teacher's note includes the pertinent facts:

We're planning a gift exchange. Abby wasn't here in time to plan a gift, but I bought one for her. I went into the room during lunch and found her hiding behind the Christmas tree, with Sophie's gift ripped open. I do NOT want her back in class today!

Abby is a shy sixth-grader who moved from a rural area a week ago. From her wrinkled clothes, the approved application for free lunch, and the number of schools she has attended, it appears that this family is poor and dysfunctional. It's a tough time of year to change schools. I would have advised waiting until January, when everyone starts back fresh, but nobody asked me.

Mrs. Scott's anger is understandable, given the effort she has made to include Abby. The girl sits on a hall bench, red-eyed and gripping a sodden tissue. I bring her into my office.

"What's going on, Abby? Mrs. Scott has made sure there's a gift for everyone. Why did you open someone else's gift?"

No response. "How will Sophie feel if there is nothing for her?" I keep asking questions, but she just sits there, slumped over, flushed and sad, her strawberry blond hair matted around her face like it hasn't been combed in days.

"Look, it's hard to change schools in the middle of the year.

Chapter 14

I had to do it at your age. But stealing is stealing. I'm going to have to send you home."

Still no response. It breaks my heart to send Abby home on a party day, but delivering bad news dispassionately is getting easier. I call the home and explain what happened.

"Oh no, now why would she do that?" asks the mother.

I sigh. "I don't know. She won't talk to me. She can't go back to class now, so please come and get her."

"She was so excited about the party. We bought a big bag of chips for her to share. Will you make sure she brings that home?"

"OK. I hope she'll talk to you. And I would like her to write an apology to Mrs. Scott."

I retrieve the chips, make a note to refer Abby to the Student Study Team, and send her home. It's another sad moment, but I remind myself that every example I set with one student helps others to learn the right way to behave. Suddenly I'm tired, remembering what remains in my day.

The Student Council talked me into sponsoring the eighth-grade dance. It will be from 3:00 to 5:00, after the kids have gorged themselves on sweets. Eardrum-splitting recorded music will play. The boys will probably gather on one side of the room to avoid dancing, while the girls dance with each other on the other side.

Two eighth-grade teachers have volunteered to help me. They are making a great sacrifice, as the staff party will be going on at the same time, in the home of Bert Sheldon. Determined not to miss the party, I hope to get there before six o'clock.

Before going to the gym to spend two hours supervising hyper kids, I give Gaby her Christmas gift—a soft throw with a note that says *Enjoy your vacation and a cuddle from me. Thanks for all you do.* She opens it in front of me and puts her arms out for a hug.

"Thanks so much, Cynthia. It's my pleasure. *Mucho gusto.*"

Observing thirteen-year-olds at their first dance would make a fascinating social science study. Their anguish reminds me of my own first time. I was so scared of not being asked to dance, I sat in front of an open window in the middle of winter in order to get sick and stay home. The awkwardness of tweens makes this thirty-something feel good about being old. I walk around the gym floor encouraging them to mingle.

"C'mon guys, here's your chance to groove to the music!" They shrink from my approach. A few girls dance with me, and I drag a couple of the more adventurous boys onto the dance floor. Nobody wants to do the Twist.

"Antonio, let's shake it." He runs the other way. Finally, one of the teachers puts on a CD that plays the hokey pokey and bunny hop. Most of the kids get in a big circle and dance. They're laughing, stepping on each other, and having fun. "Put your right foot in..." You're never too old for that.

I spend part of the dance going in and out of the girls' bathroom on the lookout for smoking or alcohol or anything worse. I can't enter the boys' room, but I stand close enough to hear water splashing and toilets flushing. A male teacher checks inside a couple of times. A plumbing emergency is the last thing we need today.

We don't play any slow tunes. That will come later in the year when the kids loosen up. Then we'll have to watch out for dancing that's too close. The changes that puberty brings! These kids start the year timid with the opposite sex and end up playing tonsil hockey behind the gym.

My heart aches for the loners, uncomfortable boys and girls who would rather be anywhere else. I remember feeling like an outlier, unpopular, unwanted, like everyone is staring at you (when they're not), like you want to crawl into a hole, but your

Chapter 14

mom says you have to go to the dance: "Your first dance! You'll have a good time." You know better.

Jimmy Green stands against the wall in a dark corner, by himself. For a change, he's willing to talk to me.

"Hi, Jimmy. Having fun?"

"It's OK," he says.

I ask about his vacation plans and he talks about a family cabin at Tahoe. At least he knows someone acknowledges his existence.

By 5:45, everyone has been picked up. Even the ones who need me to call home because they forgot to tell their parent, or their parent knew but forgot to come.

One of the teachers who stayed for the dance invites me to carpool for the short drive to Bert Sheldon's home. The imposing house has an open second story, a roaring fire in the fireplace, and plentiful Christmas decorations. Inside, a decorated tree extends to the upper level and the sounds of Nat King Cole singing holiday tunes fill the space. Plates of food blanket the dining room table. The spread has been picked over, but a few bites of bread, cheese, olives and lots of Christmas cookies remain. I go straight to the kitchen for a glass of wine.

After a challenging day, it's time for a reward. The first glass goes down fast and I pour a second, trying to recall what I had for lunch—a small salad and a Diet Coke. Laura Gonzaga, the resource specialist, joins me while I'm sipping my wine.

"How was the dance?" she asks.

"Great, I think. Is John Carlson here?"

"He was here at the beginning, but I think he left. Strange guy, that one."

No kidding. She goes on. "The white elephant is going to start soon, now that everyone is here."

"OK," I say. This is the fun game where you can steal gifts. In the living room they start the long process of drawing numbers, before opening the gifts, one at a time, so everyone with higher numbers can decide if they want to steal what someone else has already opened. My contribution is a book of jokes, not very creative, but all I could come up with on a mad dash to the mall last night.

I finish my second glass of wine and load up with a few more pieces of cheese and bread. With number 22, my turn is a long way off. While I'm grazing in the dining room, Derek Simons joins me.

"Hi, Derek. How was your day?" We're alone in the dining room.

"Pretty good. Here's to vacation." He raises his glass to clink mine, gazing at me with those soft green eyes. "So, you're a wine drinker?"

"Pretty much. Especially red blends. Yours is beer?"

"Yeah, although I drink wine too. Have you seen Bert's wine cellar?"

"No, I just got here. Dance, remember?"

"Oh, yeah. Did they actually dance with each other?"

I laugh. "A little. I think they had a good time."

"Do you want to see the wine cellar? It's something you don't want to miss."

"Well, OK, what's your number for the gift exchange?"

"I didn't take one. No patience for that kind of thing. Come on." And he motions for me to follow him. I grab a bottle from the table and top off my glass, then follow him through the hallway to a staircase that goes down into the cellar. It's dimly lit and feels refreshingly cool after the warmth of the crowd upstairs. An earthy smell rises to greet me. I follow Derek, trying not to hear the voice in my head that whispers, "Remember your position. Is this a wise thing to do? Is he trying to get you alone?" The problem is another voice inside me shouts, "HE'S TRYING TO GET YOU ALONE! ALL RIGHT!"

Chapter 14

The cellar isn't finished—the floors are cement—and the walls hold old wooden racks full of dusty wine bottles. It's lit by one bare bulb overhead. Derek begins pulling out bottles and wiping off just enough dust to show me the labels. "Here's a Bordeaux that's thirty years old," he says. "I bet you'd love to try that...with Bert's permission of course." He places the bottle gently back in its rack.

"Interesting," I answer, "I wouldn't have figured Bert to be a connoisseur, but maybe the science involved in making wine interests him."

My foot catches on an edge on the floor and I stumble, sloshing wine onto Derek, who grabs my arm to keep me from falling. He now has a red stain on his blue-striped shirt. He releases my arm and for a moment looks down at me from just a few inches away. Electricity passes between us.

"I'm so sorry," I mumble, breaking the tension. "We'd better go upstairs and try to get that stain out." At that moment the door to the cellar opens and someone shouts, "Number 22, are you down there?" Derek and I climb the stairs, both of us red-faced. We emerge, greeted by wolf whistles and leers. I scan the room for Carlson, but don't see him.

"Number 22, that's me," I say and quickly pick an unopened gift off the floor. There are only a few more gifts to be chosen and then the party starts to wrap up. I can't get out of there fast enough. I grab my coat, glad my ride is ready to go, and make my escape.

I don't have time to think about whether the staff wonders if something is going on between Derek and me. I have to pack for the trip to Maui. It will be a week of sunshine, sparkling ocean and Mai Tais. A chance to get some tan on this drab white skin.

Despite my excitement for the impending trip, I lie awake thinking about that magic moment with Derek. Did he feel it too?

109

CHAPTER FIFTEEN
NO VACATION FOR THE WEARY

FROM OUR HOTEL NEAR THE HALEAKALA CRATER, Erica and I wake early, given our jet lag, to the spectacle of sunrise. The dome of sky hangs in red and gold over the dark ocean. Our modest corner room has wood paneling, ample space with queen beds, a mini-bar, and bright flowers visible through windows on two sides. Scarlet poinsettias are blooming naturally under blue skies. Nothing like the potted ones at Trader Joe's in the winter gloom at home.

I haven't finished the teacher evaluations due right after break, so have brought the last couple of files and my laptop. Over breakfast on the first morning, I mention my plan to work while soaking up sunshine on the beach.

Erica, her strawberry blond hair pulled back in a ponytail, leans in with raised eyebrows.

"You're really going to work while you're here? You've still got a week off when we get home. It'll wait."

I hesitate, but don't want to offend my friend. In my gut I know she's right. "OK, no work this week!" I mean it, but you never know what will happen.

After a relaxing first day, which includes walking on the beach and window shopping, we have dinner at a highly recommended, pricey fish restaurant. We gaze at the sunset over the water and sip wine before the food arrives.

111

"So, how's the job going?" Erica asks.

"Good, but it's exhausting. The days are long."

"Yeah, but the paycheck!" she teases. I don't bother to tell her how although administrators get paid more than teachers, on an hourly basis, there's not much advantage.

"Are you seeing anyone new?" she probes. Erica knows if I were seeing someone, she'd have heard about it, but it's still nice of her to ask. I tell her about Derek and the wine cellar.

"Sounds interesting," she says. "Does your district have rules about dating colleagues?"

I choke on my grilled Ono. "Better yet, dating people you're evaluating. I don't know. I guess I should be careful." We enjoy our dinners and listen to live jazz in the bar before heading back to the hotel.

Besides plans for lolling on the beach, wining, dining, and shopping, we've booked Maui's famous downhill bike ride. Glad our lodging is close to the meeting place, we drag ourselves out of bed to meet the group before dawn. Nighttime temperatures at the crater are quite cold, as it's at 10,000 feet. The bike ride starts at 6,500 feet. We wear shorts and tee shirts; the tour guides will give us nylon pants and jackets to wear over our clothes.

After coffee and donuts from the back of a van, we get into our outfits, don huge helmets and gloves, and get matched with the right size bikes. The crowd of twenty includes ages ten to seventy.

First, we watch the sun rise—spectacular reds and golds over the cloud-covered valley below. We'll ride twenty-seven miles in the downhill lane of the road, accompanied by cars. The guide warns us to ride single file, to neither go too fast nor rest on the brakes too hard or too long for fear of overheating them. There will be a rest stop halfway down.

"Don't think this is going to be easy," says the leader. "You'll

Chapter 15

enjoy it more if you don't expect too much of yourself. Take it slow. And don't forget to pump the brakes."

And we're off.

Erica rides in front of me, in the middle of our entourage. The cool air on my face feels delicious, even though my gloved fingers are immediately cold. Ten minutes in, my hands hurt from leaning forward. A descent this long challenges the body, which wants to tumble over the handlebars. Definitely not a good idea. We look out over the countryside revealed in the dawn's early light: palm trees and gardens, red and orange flowering trees, few houses. Beyond them lies the dark, foam-sprinkled ocean.

We arrive at the halfway point, and everyone dismounts. "This is fantastic!" is heard from more than one rider. Erica and I grin at each other, stretch our legs and drink from our water bottles.

"About one more hour," the leader says. "You're doing great."

I put my freezing hands under my parka onto my stomach to warm them up. It's going to feel great to be done with this adventure. Fifty minutes later we're finally on flat ground and I don't want to see that bike ever again. My hands and wrists are sore. Not to mention the anatomy that has been crammed onto the front of the seat. We pull off the parkas and pants, since at sea level it is already almost eighty degrees. We say farewell to the group and find a cute café for Kona coffee and brunch. We're at a table waiting for our food, listening to light rock playing on a radio behind the counter.

"Wasn't that amazing..." I start.

Erica holds up her hand, listening intently. "What... ?"

"Shhh," she says. She's listening to the radio—the music has been interrupted by a news flash from California.

"A California man is being held on charges for running over

113

another man with his car. The accused, Charles Bingham, has said the victim, Joe Hollings, paid him $500 to drive over him."

I jump out of my seat, shouting, "What?" Erica grabs my arm and gets me to sit and shut up. Charles Bingham is the Hamilton custodian who came to my house on Thanksgiving.

The broadcast goes on to other topics and we stare at each other.

"Why would he do that?" Erica asks.

I'm still in shock. "I can't believe it. You remember him from Thanksgiving? A little weird, but I can't imagine . . ."

That afternoon I send email to Carlson, asking if there is anything he needs. I get a terse reply: *Call the parent club president.* Has he forgotten where I am? On the other hand, I offered to help. Is there no escaping school?

Here I go again. Never a moment without a work issue. My call to the parent club president goes off with a minimum of excitement. We don't know if the allegations are true, the authorities will take care of it, and this custodian has little contact with kids because he works at night. She appreciates the heads up.

We enjoy water, sun, and food for a few more days and then it's back to the airport for the five-hour flight home. The trip has been restful, but my brain shifts easily to the tasks waiting for me at school. I could work on those damned evaluations, but I have a glass of wine and watch a movie.

IT'S REFRESHING TO BE HOME with another week before work. I sleep in, shop for groceries, and scan the pile of newspapers my next-door neighbor saved for me. Ten minutes in, I come across a shocking local story. A car full of teenagers had a fatal accident the night after Christmas. One of the names jumps off the page—Bernard Owusu. OMG, that must be Janelle's high-school-age brother. I put down the paper and look for my school directory.

Chapter 15

First, I call Carlson's home phone. No answer. Maybe he's out of town. I leave a message: "Did you hear about Bernard Owusu?" Who else should I call? Maybe everyone at school knows, since this newspaper is a few days old. I try Gaby's home number but get the answering machine.

Grateful for my stash of sympathy cards, I write a note to the family, adding, *please ask Janelle to see me or the counselor when school begins.* The service will take place in two days at a Catholic church. A somber formal event was not in the plan for my dwindling time off, but good administrators go to funerals that impact the school community.

The afternoon of the Owusu service arrives. I head to the church, determined to be strong. The community will surely be out in force. The church vestibule holds a couple hundred people. I don't notice any Hamilton students; most of the youth seem to be Bernard's age. I pick out Sam, our PE teacher; George Dunning; and Derek standing together in the crowd. They all taught Bernard when he was at Hamilton, and Derek had Janelle in his class last year. I join them and we walk inside together.

"Awful stuff," Derek says and sits next to me. He looks good in his suit. The navy blue brings out those green eyes.

OK, Cynthia, you're here for a funeral, not to flirt with Derek.

The service begins, with family members and coaches speaking about Bernard and his dreams, permanently interrupted. Janelle and her parents sit up front with a few other Black adults. The attendees, mostly White, remind me what a homogeneous community this is.

I can't help tearing up when the speakers talk about the potential that Bernard had. Losing kids is devastating, even when you don't know them personally. My tissues must be in the bottom of my purse, but before I can find one, Derek whips

115

out a pristine handkerchief. I blot my eyes and whisper thanks. When the service ends, we approach the family to say our condolences. They greet us warmly and thank us for coming—a presence from the school means something to Janelle and her parents. They introduce the uncles and aunts that are with them. I give Janelle a hug and she hugs me back, tears in her eyes.

"We'll see you at school," Derek says to her. "Come and talk to me any time before or after class."

After the service, Derek and I stroll to the adjacent hall for refreshments. The other teachers have disappeared. We try the coffee and cookies and make small talk with a few church members and work acquaintances of the Owusus. Derek says hello to one or two high school teachers and former students I don't know.

Derek walks me to my car. He says, "Tough day, huh?"

"Yeah, I'm glad you were here." I smile weakly. I mean it in the most proper way. The service and socializing would have been much harder, had I been by myself.

"Me too. I mean I'm glad to see you… well not in these circumstances. You know what I mean." And there's that smile that I can't help but return.

"See you at school." I get into my car. He turns and walks away. Should I have suggested we go somewhere for more coffee?

IT'S THE FRIDAY AFTERNOON before school begins again in January. The temperature is in the 40s when I arrive at Hamilton to get organized. When I see Carlson's car in the lot, I almost turn back. But Monday morning is coming fast, so I continue. Walking past his office, I call out "Hi, John."

"Hey, wait a minute," he says.

I stick my tongue out at nobody, turn around and step inside. "Yeah?"

Chapter 15

"Happy New Year," he says, a gloppy grin glued to his face.

"You too."

"How long are you going to be here today?"

"An hour or so. Why?"

"I'd like to talk to you a bit... buy you a drink at the Watering Hole." That's the name of the closest bar to the school. Not that I've been inside. It looks like a hangout for types I don't hang out with.

"Uh, I don't know, John."

"Come on, be a good sport. Just one drink with the boss."

"OK, give me an hour." I sigh on my way to my office.

An hour and fifteen minutes later, we're seated at the bar. It's three o'clock in the afternoon. The place isn't exactly jumping. One guy at the end of the bar nurses what looks like a whiskey. The bartender scurries around polishing tables, setting out napkins, and cutting up lemons, perhaps getting ready for a big Friday night.

"What would you like?" John asks.

"I'll have a glass of Pinot Noir."

"OK, and a Bud for me," he says to the bartender.

"How was Hawaii?" So, he does remember I was away.

"Nice. Great weather. We did a killer bike ride down Haleakala. John, what did you want to talk about?"

"Can't a colleague buy a colleague a drink?"

"I guess, but I can't stay long. I have things to do at home." My fingers tap nervously on the bar.

He puts his hand on the bar next to mine. "Look, we just don't have much time to talk at school and I want us to be friends." I'm speechless.

"Don't you like me even a little bit?" he asks.

I take a sip of wine. "Why would you even ask that?"

"Because I like you and...we're a team."

"I...I don't know what to say." Rare, but true.

"OK, let's talk about crazy Charles Bingham. Have you heard anything more?"

We talk about the custodian who was dumb enough to take money to drive over his friend. Charles is on administrative leave while the police sort it out.

I tell him about the Owusu service.

"Thanks for going," he says. "I couldn't make it." What else would I expect?

Next, he fills me in on the strike the teachers' union has threatened for the second week in January. Happy New Year, indeed.

CHAPTER SIXTEEN
THREE STRIKES...

KNOWING THE TEACHERS PLAN TO STRIKE tomorrow, I moisturize my Hawaiian tan and steel myself for a tough day. Teachers' strikes usually have deep roots in disagreements about money. Yes, teachers are underpaid, administrators too. You've already heard part of my treatise about the responsibilities of school employees—the lives in our hands, the future we influence—compared to those of much higher-paid employees in private business. We're all underpaid. But, like wily sellers in a Middle Eastern bazaar, unions often negotiate for something beyond reason.

Early in my teaching career, I participated in a strike, because the teachers' union told me to. I stood across the street from my middle school, watching kids leak out. One would slip out a classroom door and take off on the run. Then another. And another. The local newspaper caught a photo of me and a colleague crying—it was that painful to abandon our responsibilities. A school strike divides the teachers, pits them against administrators, and confuses and hurts students.

Carlson calls me at home the night before to strategize. Or rather, to dump the bulk of the duties on me.

"I think all the teachers will be on the picket line," he says.

"Will we have substitutes?"

"Yes, they're sending us ten. A lot of the kids will stay home. So, we'll plan on ten rooms, with the kids assigned by grade and last name." That's ten rooms out of the usual twenty in operation.

"OK." I hope we don't have to squeeze fifty kids into a room.

"I want you to be out front to greet the subs and send them to the office. Sharon will hand out assignments. When you're done with that, help the students find the right rooms. They won't change classes but will stay in one place."

I wonder what he'll be doing while I'm running around. Probably drinking coffee and watching from the window.

What will happen in the classrooms remains a mystery. Will the subs arrive with their own plans? Each classroom's sub folder might have emergency plans for a fifty-minute instructional period. Even if those can be found, they won't last all day.

This plan needs help. The substitute teachers—and the students—will benefit from specific lesson plans. I go through my boxes of teaching materials and pick out a handful of simple activities, like graphing points on a grid to create a picture, word puzzles, and writing prompts. I'll go in extra early and make copies for people who need them. The subs should have a break in their day too, so perhaps I can take each class for a half hour of PE. That will keep me busy all day. If there are any major behavioral incidents… I suppose, Carlson could handle them. Yeah, that's about as likely as the whole strike being called off. The behavior problems will have to wait for the next day. Little do I know that my biggest headache of the strike will not be the kids or the subs.

I arrive at 7:30 and copy my lessons. The picket line slowly gathers. Teachers are decked out in hats and gloves, prepared to spend hours in the frosty morning air. The school has one main drive-in entrance, used by school buses and parents. The staff park in a side lot. The teachers are forming their line about twenty feet inside the grounds, a barrier the subs will have to cross. They're strung out like a human necklace, facing the parking area. I smile at the teachers, some of whom smile back.

Chapter 16

Others look at me like I'm the enemy. What do they expect me to do? Join them on the line?

The first sub arrives. As she tries to walk through the line of teachers, I can see them talking to her, nasty looks on their faces. I move closer to the line.

"Scab, we'll never ask for you again!" shouts one of my own.

At first, they link arms to keep her from crossing, then let her through. Face drawn and shoulders shaking, she looks terrified. I put my arm around her and usher her to the office.

"Thanks for coming. We'll make sure you have a good day."

I hurry back out, as a few more subs arrive. One of the teachers is passing out signs on sticks that say, "Teachers Deserve Better Pay" and "Support Teachers". The picketers become more daring, yelling in a chorus, "Go home, scabs," and raising their arms over their heads, threatening like they're trying to scare off an angry bear. Or perhaps they are the ones feeling like angry bears. It's like the subs must cross a roiling river and I'm there on the other side to pull them out to safety.

Soon a bus full of students approaches and tries to pull into the lot, aiming for the drop-off point at the bright yellow curb. The picket line immediately moves to block the bus. Kids stare from the windows—curious, amused, scared. The bus driver brakes, so as not to run over any teachers. As I approach, the driver makes eye contact and shrugs. Grateful for my walkie-talkie, I call the office and ask Sharon to summon the police. If they're not too busy at some other school site.

I scan the teachers with whom I have worked so hard to form relationships: George Dunning, who has earnestly listened to my suggestions for improving his lessons; those who have shared their most personal stories of divorce and illness; Derek, whose devotion to the kids makes this painful—he must be feeling the way I did when I was on strike years before. He gives me a narrow smile.

"Come on, folks," I call out. "You can't block the school bus. The police have been called. I know you don't want to hurt the kids. Come on."

Some are wavering; others are too angry to hear my words. Next thing I know a KQRS-TV truck pulls over on the street and someone shoves a microphone in my face.

"Are you the principal?" the cute young reporter asks. Maybe five feet tall, with auburn hair down to her waist, she looks like a recent high school graduate. A tall guy with a video camera stands directly behind her, aiming it at me.

"Vice principal," I answer. I can't keep myself from adding, "You're really not helping." The reporter turns her attention to the picketers. Bert Sheldon, the site rep for the union, steps up to the reporter.

"You know, teachers in this district have been patiently negotiating for months, but the district is not working to resolve this. They let us down time and time again. We're just trying to do what's best for students."

Suddenly, Carlson appears by my side. "I'm the principal," he says. "Do you want to talk to me?"

A patrol car creeps along, coming our way.

"John, the cops are here." He's busy trying to get the attention of the reporter. I turn once again to the teachers in front of the bus.

"The police are here, folks. It's time to let the bus in." Laura Gonzaga, the special education teacher, moves aside slowly; others follow. The bus driver gives me a salute and slowly moves the bus forward, pulling into the curb. The reporter, camera crew, John, and Bert are all swept aside like debris on the beach pushed by an incoming tide. The bus parks, doors open, and the kids are released.

Now I have the job of convincing students, some of whom are trembling, that this is just another day at Hamilton Middle School.

Chapter 16

"Ms. Walker, what's going on?" they ask.

I put on my best fake smile, pat as many shoulders as I can, and announce over and over, "It's a strike. The teachers are exercising their rights."

A few kids approach the picket line, wanting to chat, but I shoo them away. Jimmy Green has walked to school and looks confused.

"Jimmy, come with me and I'll help you find the right room."

"We're going to rooms 10 through 20 in A-wing. Look for your grade and the letters of your last name on the door."

Are the subs all in place? I've lost count of how many have arrived.

I usher the first busload to the classrooms and check in with the office. Gaby is here—bless her heart for not honoring the picket line—and she comes out to help me. Another bus pulls in, this time without a problem. We direct the kids in the second load and then return to greet those who are arriving on foot or by car. The police have parked out front and the picketers are letting kids through without comment. I make eye contact with parent drivers as they stop at the curb. Many faces are set with worry, but when they see me smiling and waving, they smile back and let their kids out.

"We've got teachers," I say more than once. "He'll be fine... she'll be fine." I hope I'm right.

Finally, it looks like everyone has arrived. It's 8:15 and I'm exhausted. I poke my head into the office.

"How many subs?" I interrupt Sharon from sipping her Starbucks coffee, with a half-eaten Danish in front of her.

"We got all ten," she answers.

"Good. Tell John I'm going to take each group for PE to give the subs a break."

"Really?" she says, looking at me like I've announced a plan to slit my wrists for public view.

123

The rest of the day goes as well as could be expected. Some subs have arrived with lesson ideas in several subjects. Others use my worksheets. One guy has his seventh-graders read parts from Shakespeare, except the words are rewritten in street slang: "Yo, Romeo, Romeo! Where you at?" They're having a blast.

I go room by room, taking the kids into the gym for a game of dodgeball, about the only game I know. Just divide them into two teams. No skills required. Acting like I've played this game since elementary school, I do a quick sweep of what they're wearing and get an idea.

"OK, kids, everyone wearing a hat or a tee shirt, you're on Team A; everyone else is Team B. We make a few changes to even them up and go over the rules.

"Ms. Walker, were you a PE teacher?"

"In your dreams," I answer. They must be feeling sorry for me or just happy for the break because they don't throw the ball too hard or aim too high.

Watching kids I know interact in a game with their peers is eye-opening. Some of them are naturally aggressive towards the opposing side and angry when they're out. Others participate minimally, just trying to stay away from the ball. I don't see Antonio—he probably used the strike as an excuse to stay home—but Jimmy does a surprisingly good job aiming the ball. He even passes it to other kids on his team. Maybe there's an athlete hiding under his negative attitude. I give him a high five at the end of class.

"Good job, buddy."

He grins.

At lunch, I take a minute to look in on the temporary teachers in the staff room. Several of them thank me for my support at the picket line or for the worksheets. They're having an OK day.

I'm gratified to know, as the clock approaches three, that

Chapter 16

this is a one-day strike. Rather than having their people out day after day, losing wages, the union has threatened one-day walk-outs, with little notice. When the last bell rings, the picket line has disappeared. Students and substitutes file out unimpeded. Everyone is glad this day is over.

The local evening news covers the strike and shows a video of my back as I'm talking to the teachers on the picket line, with the bus waiting behind them. Next, they switch to Carlson saying, "We have a great school here. We'll get through this." Right.

My friends call to say they saw me on TV. "You're famous," says Shelly. I'm surprised it made the San Francisco news. Pam sends me a text: *Looks like you're in charge. Take care, girl.*

Erica is more concerned. "Are you OK?" she asks.

"I'm fine. I just wish I could sleep in tomorrow. But I have to do a presentation for the teachers."

The next day is a scheduled planning day, meaning the kids will be at home and staff will be on campus for professional activities. Anticipating a normal day—silly me—I'm slated to lead the opening session on a new approach to reading.

After dinner and wine, I sleep like a rock. I can rest because I organized the reading presentation weeks ago. But no amount of preparation is enough for the crises that happen every day at school.

I arrive at my usual time, spread out my materials in the library, and am ready to begin, colored markers in hand, fresh easel paper on the chart stand. I'm primed to get teachers psyched about a new way to make reading enjoyable in all classes.

The teachers file in looking beat and sit around the table. Their usual laughter and kidding are missing. The bell rings, I stand and greet them all, starting in on my spiel.

"It's great to see you, everyone. Today we're going to learn

125

about a new—"

"Wait a minute," says Bert Sheldon. "You're not going to talk about what happened yesterday?" Some teachers mumble in response.

"Um, I was going to talk about the reading program."

Ginny adds, "You need to know you hurt us yesterday."

"Hurt *you*?" I ask. My mouth is suddenly dry and heat rises to my face.

"Yeah," echoes Bert, gesturing wildly with his hands. "How could you treat those scabs that way?"

"What way?"

"You know," adds someone else. "Putting your arm around them and all."

"Yeah, you comforted them when they were working against us!"

I'm speechless. Perspiration beads on my forehead. I take off my jacket and throw it on the back of the chair, then sit down. They go on about what a terrible day it was for them and how their demands should be met or there will be another strike and how administration doesn't support them. I let them talk. Well, frankly, I have no idea what to say. Where's Carlson?

Laura Gonzaga gazes at me with concern. "Look," she says to her peers, "this situation with the district is not Cynthia's fault. She's just doing her job."

Bless you, Laura. Derek sits in the back, staring at the floor. He looks uncomfortable, but will he speak? This day is shot. Their minds are not ready to focus on reading. Whether or not I can salvage any of my presentation, damage has been done and I have to do something to appease them. When they finally seem to have talked themselves out, I gather my wits. I'm beginning to understand why Carlson stayed in the office yesterday.

"Look, I know where you're coming from. I've been on

Chapter 16

strike and it was one of the worst days of my teaching career. What some of you don't get is that yesterday those subs were my teachers and I treated them the same way I would treat you if you had to move through an angry crowd to get to your classrooms. I cared about them the same way I care about you. We can talk about this more later, but right now I'd like to tell you about an amazing reading program."

Derek finally speaks. "I think we should hear the presentation. Those who want to talk more can see Cynthia later."

Thank you, Derek. I talk about reading and perhaps some of them are listening. It's not my finest moment, but with a little help from my friends, I muddle through.

LESSON #8: PLAN AHEAD, BE PREPARED TO CHANGE COURSE.

IN THE FOLLOWING WEEK, the district and union make progress in their negotiations, so it looks like this strike may have been a one-off. Will this day color my relationship with the teachers for the rest of the year? There's no way to know. If I had it to do over, I'd put the training off until the afternoon and give them time in the morning to chill out. Maybe go from room to room listening to their individual concerns.

I hope I haven't lost the teachers' good will, because soon I'll be knee-deep in mid-year evaluations. That means one-on-one meetings with those I'm evaluating. I still need to observe Ginny Stein for a class period. Despite numerous notes in her mailbox, asking her to choose a day and time, she hasn't gifted me with a response. It's time to be less considerate. I leave her a note: *I'll be there Thursday fourth period, conference to follow Friday morning during your prep.*

Near the start of the instructional period, I find a place to sit in the back of the room. Ginny glances at me with pursed lips, dark circles under her eyes. The required novel, *The Giver*, by Lois Lowry, is open on most students' desks. With a soft voice, she asks them to talk about the difference in meaning between *distracted* and *distraught* in the first chapter.

"How did the teacher in the story know that Asher meant to say distracted? What does that word mean?"

A few students raise their hands, and she calls on them until someone correctly defines both words.

"OK, now I'd like you to read aloud, from page five."

Oh my. How am I going to observe her teaching if she's just going to have the kids read? Is she doing this to defy me? She picks students randomly to read aloud. That's good, at least the random part. They all seem to be following along. What will she have them do at the end of the reading? They read pretty well, with few stumbles, and come to the end of the chapter.

"Now, students, open your notebooks. Please write a paragraph about what you found interesting in that chapter. We'll discuss this tomorrow."

I can't believe it. She thinks that's a lesson? I walk around the room to see what the kids are writing. A few do nothing, unable or unwilling to begin. Most are writing something. Wouldn't it be better to have a discussion? On my way out of the room, passing the desk where the teacher sits, I catch a whiff of something. Alcohol? The students are bent over their desks and Ginny gives me a weak smile as I open the door to leave.

After school, when I know she has left campus, I return to Ginny's room. Not sure if the smell is still there. Is it OK to open her desk drawers? No, that would be wrong. I sniff around some more, find nothing, and go back to the office.

The next day I go to her classroom at the start of her prep, first period, with my notes from the observation. She's writing on the board.

Chapter 16

"Hi, Ginny. Can we talk here?"

"OK." She sits down at her desk. I pull up a chair. There's that smell again. As I talk about what I observed, which isn't much, her face has no expression. I lean in. Sure enough. The alcohol smell is coming from her. That scent you have when you've drunk too much and it's coming out of your pores.

"Ginny, is everything OK? You may not be aware...but...you smell of alcohol."

Her eyes flash wide and her mouth opens, then closes again. She looks down at the desk, folds and unfolds her hands and finally says, "It must be from last night."

"OK, but your students will smell alcohol on you. Do you feel OK?"

"I'm fine," she says with an angry tone. "I went to a party. It won't happen again." She's still avoiding my eyes.

I wrap up the conference and tell myself I'd better talk to John about how to handle this. This vice principal has no idea.

It seems like the week will never end. The Student Study Team meets at lunch and discusses Abby, the girl who stole the Christmas gift. The teacher who referred Abby has talked to the mother and shares the sad story of a drug addict dad who is often missing. The family has been moving from one relative to the next. They don't have the resources to have their own apartment. The teacher contacted social services, who have promised to meet with the mother. One of the men offers to be Abby's mentor. A caring man to encourage her sounds like a good idea.

"If there's anything the girl needs for school that the family can't afford, please let me know so we can use our parent club emergency fund." That's my two cents. The discussion continues about how to get Abby connected with other kids. She's always alone at lunch and break and doesn't speak up in class. The meeting wraps up and I return to the office preparing to seek out Carlson. As I reach the office door, Antonio Girardi intercepts me, on the run. He bumps into me, nearly knocking me over.

"It's Mr. Sheldon...he...he fell down...he's on the floor...help …"

I grab a walkie-talkie from the office and jog across campus to Bert Sheldon's room. The kids huddle on one side. Sheldon lies on his back on the floor next to his desk. Kneeling, I feel for a pulse on his neck. His face is grey, but he's alive. "Bert," I say as I shake his arm. No response. I speak into the walkie-talkie: "Call 9-1-1. Sheldon has collapsed. He has a pulse but seems to be unconscious."

Now for the kids. "All of you go out and stay close to the room. He's going to be OK." I hope.

They slowly move outside. Soon we hear the sirens. Sharon has remembered to tell the firemen how to pull up close to the classroom. She calls me on the walkie-talkie. "They're here."

"Sharon, is Carlson on campus?"

"I don't think so." What else is new?

"OK, please see if you can reach him, but first make an all-call announcement that we're handling a medical emergency, and everyone should stay in their classrooms and ignore the bell. Also, see if you can reach Bert's wife."

The paramedics take over and I go outside to calm Sheldon's students. Some are flushed and teary. Others have blank faces as the paramedics wheel him out on a gurney a few minutes later. He already has an IV hooked up to his arm and his face has some color. That must be a good sign. They tell me which hospital they're going to and I relay that to Sharon for the wife. I bring the kids back in and spend the rest of the afternoon in the classroom.

The students are full of concern, but all I can say is, "He's in good hands" and "thanks, Antonio, for your quick thinking."

Chapter 16

When the last period class comes in, I ask, "What have you been studying?" Eighth grade science is definitely not my lane. They start talking about matter, energy, gravity. Physics? Definitely not anything in my teaching repertoire. But I did go to Pisa a few years ago, so I tell them the story of how Galileo dropped balls of two different sizes and weights off the Leaning Tower to prove weight has no effect on gravity. They want to know more about Pisa.

"Ms. Walker, did you walk up the tower?" they ask. "Was it hard to do?"

"I did and I leaned on the wall. It was not easy to balance."

There's a quiz at the end of the appropriate chapter in their text. I divide them into two teams for a little competition to see who can get the most answers correct. It's kind of fun—as long as the teacher's manual provides the answers.

What a day. I still have to talk to Carlson. A soon as the campus clears out for the day, he's back. He's chatting with Sharon, so I figure he knows about Sheldon. Then he goes into his office and shuts the door.

I knock. "John, I need to talk to you."

"OK. Come in."

"Any word on Bert Sheldon?"

"Only that he's at the ER. His wife is with him."

"Thanks."

He says nothing about my heroic efforts, so I continue. "I want to talk to you about Ginny Stein." He nods as I take a chair across from him.

"She smelled like booze this morning and admitted to a party last night. The same smell was in her classroom yesterday."

"What did you tell her?" He leans back in his chair, his arms crossed on that big belly.

"Nothing. I'm not sure what to do. That's why I'm here."

"Well, the truth is, she's probably an alcoholic. I've heard

131

rumors in the past that she has a bottle in her desk." He does not sound particularly concerned.

"Yikes. Should I check?" My voice rises, along with my frustration.

"I don't know where the law is on that." Well, can you find out? Instead, I ask, "What has been done in the past? Isn't it wrong to ignore it?" I'm on my high horse now. I can't help it. This is a big deal. "We have an obligation not only to the kids but to her."

He sits up straight, hands on the desk. "Look, young lady, you've got to understand a school has a culture. You can't just come in here and turn things upside down."

That's bad enough, but then he adds, "Milburn never made such demands."

Now I'm furious. He's comparing me to the previous vice principal, who survived this job to go on to be a principal.

I lower my voice, but I'm leaning forward in my chair, eyes staring into his. "With all due respect, John. If a teacher has a problem with alcohol, that's not the school culture. And if you ignore it, you're condoning it. This is not good for kids and if your precious parents were to find out, they'd have a fit."

"Are you done?" He's red in the face, just inches from mine, and spitting his words out. "Let me think about what we should do. I'll get back to you." He falls back in his chair.

With that, I'm dismissed. I walk to the door but turn back to say, "Please let me know what you hear about Bert."

"OK," he answers.

Walking down the hall to my office, I say to nobody, "And thank you, Ms. Walker, for handling the situation so well." I hope Bert Sheldon is OK. I can't imagine how we would handle the death of a teacher.

CHAPTER SEVENTEEN
STAYING CALM

THE NEXT DAY, SHELDON'S WIFE CALLS TO report he spent the night in the hospital and is now resting at home. It was a mild heart attack. The guy who loves to talk about all things scientific can now lecture about his stent. January is off to a bang-up start.

Once in a while, my trajectory on the administrative learning curve hits me smack upside the head. Today it's kids and prescribed medications. I taught students who took drugs for ADD. If they needed to take their meds during the school day, they simply went to the office and the nurse or clerk dispensed them. Now I'm one of the people who does the dispensing. We keep ADD meds, antibiotics, and epi pens in a locked cupboard in the nurse's office. Whenever we administer a pill, we record the name, date, and time.

I handle the medicine cupboard without incident until the day Tim Hastings, or someone who looks a lot like Tim, comes to the office for his ADD medication. He comes in at the same time every day and it's an easy routine. I'm the only one in the office, so I ask, "Here for your pill?"

"Yeah," he responds.

We go into the nurse's office, I unlock the cabinet, get out a pill, hand it over with a small cup of water, and watch him take it. He then goes dutifully out to lunch and I record the time. When Sharon comes back in, I tell her Tim has taken his pill.

"Tim Hastings?" she says. "But he's absent today."

My heart sinks. "Oh, no, could that have been Nathan, you know, Nathan Hartley—the two of them look alike, don't you think?"

Sharon stares at me with the contempt she reserves for newbie administrators who don't know what they are doing, while she, who is paid so much less, knows it all.

"Better get Nathan back in here," I moan.

The rest of the day disappears in the follow-up. I contact a nurse to ask about possible effects of this medication on someone for whom it is not prescribed. Fortunately, she says, "He may be jittery or have trouble sleeping, but will be fine tomorrow." Then I call Nathan's mother and do my best groveling while I apologize profusely for the mistake and assure her Nathan will be OK, but perhaps she should take him home early.

What I really want to do is scream at Nathan, "Why the hell would you take a pill when you don't ever take medication at school?" But I'm stopped by the spaciness of this age group and the desire of kids to do what the authority figure asks. I keep my frustration to myself and instead apologize to Nathan and suggest he tell me his name each and every time he sees me.

Will the parent sue me or have me fired for this mistake? What if it was a drug that could do great harm to the unintended recipient? I don't want to think about that. No more medicine cabinet for me. "You need your pill? Have a seat. Sharon will be back in a minute."

Near the end of this horrible, no good, very bad day, I stop in Carlson's office. I must be a glutton for punishment.

"Did you hear about my little mistake?"

"Which one?" He gives me a devilish grin.

"Giving the ADD meds to the wrong kid?"

"Oh, yeah. Not good, but don't torture yourself. You took care of the kid and the parents."

"I did what I could. Do you think they'll sue?"

Chapter 17

He gets up from his chair and approaches me. He puts both hands on my shoulders. His arms are short, so his face is just a few inches from mine. Stray whiskers and bad breath. "Hey, not to worry. I'll call the mom and make sure everything is OK."

"Thanks," I mumble and back out of his grip.

I hope to spend the rest of the afternoon in my office with some boring paperwork, feeling sorry for myself. But as I approach Gaby's desk, I see her wiping tears from her eyes.

"Everything OK?" I ask, knowing it's a stupid question.

"Can I talk to you?" she asks. We sit down in my office, door closed.

"It's my Sal," she says.

I wait.

"He was coming home late last night from a work event. The cops pulled him over. He got a DUI. I'm so embarrassed."

"I'm sorry, Gaby."

"He wasn't really drunk, you know, but he's not a big guy—he's my height—and if he drinks at all...well, you know. Anyway, it's the first time, but he'll have to go to court and his name will be in the paper...and his boss will find out."

"How awful."

"*Estoy preocupada*...I'm so worried he'll get fired."

"Maybe he should tell the boss up front," I say.

"Maybe. We have to talk tonight."

Gaby is too upset to get much done, so I send her home before four o'clock. I leave a little early myself. A big glass of wine and some loud pop music will give my brain a rest from thinking about who might sue me for poisoning kids and whether Gaby's husband will soon be unemployed.

In the morning, Gaby isn't at her desk at the usual time, which is strange, because she's always early. She arrives while I'm on the phone and I watch as Carlson stomps down the hall to her desk. I have to focus on my conversation, so don't get what he's saying. Once I hang up the phone, I step out to see what's going on.

Carlson has left. Gaby's crying again. "It's John," she says. "I'm sorry I'm late, but Sal and I were up half the night. I called and told Sharon I'd be a little late. You know me, I'm always here early! But John, he walked down here and scolded me. Told me I better not be late again...'or else,' whatever that means."

"Don't worry about it, Gaby." I rub her shoulders and add, "Why don't you get us some coffee. I'll be right back."

I walk down the hall to Carlson's office. He's alone, sitting behind the desk. "John?" I drag his attention from the computer screen.

"Yeah?"

"John, I thought I was Gaby's supervisor."

"You are, but I won't tolerate people who are late for work." This from the guy who is always off campus with no explanation.

"John, you might have talked to me first. She is *always* early. She has some personal stuff going on at home right now."

"What stuff?"

"I don't have her permission to share."

"That mouth of hers doesn't get on your nerves?"

"I know she talks too much, but she's a great employee. The next time you have a concern about Gaby, please let me handle it. She's truly a gem and I don't want to lose her."

He looks at me with a blank stare. I turn and walk out. Maybe this wasn't the best way to work on my relationship with John, but who else will stand up for Gaby? Besides, pushing back feels good.

The next day, Gaby takes me aside to fill me in on her husband's DUI problem.

Chapter 17

"He told his boss and they're giving him a break this time."

"That's great, Gaby."

"Yeah, he better make sure it never happens again. Or he'll have me to answer to."

I imagine what Gaby might be like when righteously angry. She may be petite, but she is a powerhouse. And on my team, thank heavens.

SOME PARENTS ARE CLUELESS. I, who have no children of my own, get to talk to kids like a parent. And to parents about appropriate consequences at home. I tell the mother whose kid sent profane texts to others, "Don't ground him for a year. How about taking away the phone for a couple of weeks?"

Then there are the parents who want to be on my speed dial. Jane Forman writes a check for every fundraiser, volunteers in her kids' classrooms—even when not invited—and shows up with weird requests of teachers and administrators. It's like she thinks her generosity guarantees country club privileges.

Jane and I have a friendly rapport, until her sixth-grade son, Marv, gets in trouble at lunch. He's horsing around with some boys, one of them loses his temper, and Marv gets caught up in the fight that follows. It's their first time and results in no blood or bruises, so I give them all detention. Marv doesn't show up and earns a double detention. Jane storms into my office, unannounced.

"Mrs. Walker, what is this double detention slip you gave to Marv?" Red-faced, her volume rises a couple of notches above normal. I use a calculated calm tone.

"Um, he was in a fight. He didn't tell you?"

"Why didn't you call me immediately so I would know what was happening?" Her volume continues in an upward spiral.

Does she have any idea how many kids I see in a day? And what it would take for me to call every parent every time? Well, no, she only wants me to call *her* every time.

With my softest voice, I answer, "It was a minor scuffle, Jane. Marv is a good kid. I gave the boys a warning, along with detention. But Marv didn't go, and then it was doubled. Why don't you sit down?" I point to a chair.

"If you told me, I would have made him go!" she shouts and remains standing. "I don't want this on his record."

I have surely earned an award for stubborn patience. I keep my voice as syrupy as possible. "Look, Jane, nothing will be on his record. This is not a big deal. You have to let Marv start handling his own problems. He needs to serve two detentions, and then it will be over."

She sprays saliva through partly clenched teeth. "Would you stop being so damned calm?"

Reaching the end of my politeness, I stand. "Jane, Marv knows what he has to do. Have him serve the two detentions."

"I'm going to talk to John about this!" and she storms out. Great, what I need is another confrontation with John.

CHAPTER EIGHTEEN
WHO'S A RACIST?

AT THE FINAL BELL AFTER A LONG, TIRING DAY, I'm anticipating some time to think about anything other than misbehaving students. No such luck. Janelle Owusu walks in with another girl.

"Tell her," says the friend.

"What is it, Janelle?" I ask.

"It's not that big a deal. It's happened before…"

"What's happened before?"

"It's the eighth grade boys. They're calling me names."

"Tell her!" the friend repeats, louder.

"OK, they called me a monkey from Africa."

"What?" I gasp. Oh, the blessings of working with middle schoolers. "Janelle, please tell me who said that."

She doesn't want to tell, but I get it out of her. It's two of the boys who gave her a bad time on the basketball court in the fall—my friend Jimmy and his buddy, Kevin.

"Janelle, it's never OK to ignore racial slurs. Do you understand? If it ever happens again, you need to tell me immediately." I look at the friend. "You, too. Got it? And thanks for bringing Janelle to see me."

Tomorrow morning is now planned for me. I'm glad there is nothing on my calendar to keep me from jumping all over the two boys. Too bad it's no longer appropriate to apply soap to the source of the words.

In the morning, I send for the boys.

"Do you know why you're here?" I ask.

"Nope," says Jimmy.

"Someone overheard you calling racist names."

"Huh?" says Jimmy.

"Damn," Kevin mutters. He knows exactly what I'm talking about.

"Kevin, can you fill Jimmy in?"

He turns to his friend. "You don't remember?"

Jimmy looks desperately dumb.

"Janelle," says Kevin.

"I'd like to hear the words you said, Kevin."

"Do I have to?"

"Yes."

"We called her...we called her a... monkey."

"That's not racial," says Jimmy.

"Interesting that you're puzzled, Jimmy, when Kevin was too ashamed to say the words to me. It's definitely racist. Can you imagine being one of the few Black kids in this school? How would that feel? And to have someone call you a monkey?"

Jimmy shakes his head. "We didn't mean anything by it." Kevin hangs his head.

"So, here's the deal, guys. I'm going to call your parents so they can help you understand how terrible this is."

Kevin groans. I continue. "You're going to spend your lunch break here with me...and I want you both to think about how you will apologize to Janelle. I want you here tomorrow at the beginning of morning break to give me your plan. You'll have no free time until that has been handled. Oh, and one more thing. Did you know Janelle's parents came here from Ghana? You have a special homework assignment from me. I want you to do some research tonight and write me one page about Ghana, something interesting. Bring it with you tomorrow."

The boys sit and listen while I inform their mothers, both

Chapter 18

women understandably shocked and disappointed. I'm pretty certain the boys will have an interesting evening at home.

I have one more call to make, to Janelle's parents. I want them to know their daughter was the victim of racial slurs and hesitated to report it, so they too can talk at home. Mrs. Owusu answers the phone. I tell the story.

I hear a deep sigh on the other end of the call. "Thanks Ms. Walker. We've had to teach Janelle to be tough. Perhaps that's why she didn't want to report the boys. It's something we have to deal with and just get on with our lives."

"I understand. I just wanted you to know we aren't going to tolerate that kind of language at school. The boys' parents are deeply concerned. I think they'll make sure their sons understand how serious this is."

Kevin and Jimmy show up the next morning with their essays. They have learned about the slave trade from Ghana in our country's early history, as well as details of Ghana's rich cultural heritage. I look over their notes to Janelle, noting that Jimmy's still says, "I didn't mean anything by it."

YOU MIGHT THINK THAT'S enough racial drama for the week, but the next day, Sam Butler, the PE teacher in skimpy shorts, sends me Junior Buddle with a note, "Needs to talk to you—something going on at home."

"Have a seat, Junior." Small and wiry, he sashays to the chair and plops himself down with a thud.

Here's what I know about Junior: He's from a large Black family. Mom, a big, blustery woman, rules her brood with a firm hand. Junior has learning problems and occasionally gets pushed around by other kids on the playground.

"What's up, Junior? Mr. Butler says we need to talk."

"Nothing."

I wait.

"My mom's mad at me because I lost my PE clothes and Mr.

141

Butler keeps marking me down for not changing."

"Have you looked through the lost and found?"

He nods. Staring at the floor, he wipes tears off his face with his hands.

"What is it, Junior?"

"My mom... she... she's really mad at me. She says she's not going to get me new PE stuff, and if I don't find them, she's going to beat me and lock me in my room."

I move to sit in the chair next to him. "OK, Junior. We can give you new PE clothes. But I want to know more about the beating so I can help you. Does it happen often?

He pauses, glances at me, then looks away. "Yeah, whenever... when I mess up."

My hand rests gently on his back. "It's OK. Can you tell me what she hits you with?"

He whispers, "A paddle." He sniffs and hiccups, wipes his nose with the back of his hand.

He's doing great, but I need more. I keep my voice low and warm. "Junior, where on your body does she hit you?"

"On...on my butt." Tears continue to trickle down his face. I grab the box of tissues from my desk and hand it to him.

"Does it hurt afterwards?"

He stops to blow his nose. I hold out the wastebasket for the deposit. "Yeah, sometimes I'm sore after." He's perking up, no doubt relieved to share his burden.

"And how long does she make you stay in your room?"

"All day on Saturday. I get hungry."

"She doesn't feed you all day?"

He bursts into tears again, sobs, then takes a breath and answers, "No."

"How can we expect kids like Junior to grow up to be sane and responsible, after being mistreated by their parents? Junior's tears have dampened his shirt front. I give him a sideways hug

142

Chapter 18

and he leans into me. "I'm so sorry, Junior. I'm going to have someone talk to your mom."

"Please don't tell her...she'll be really mad," he begs, and takes another tissue.

Gaby gets Junior new PE clothes. I give him time to get himself together and send him back to class.

As a teacher, I phoned Children's Protective Services numerous times. The state law requires a report for mere suspicion of abuse. No proof is required. Using a paddle and food deprivation are both reasons to report Mrs. Buddle. She will surely be upset if they contact her, but I have no choice. I make the call. They listen to the story and direct me to send in the paperwork. Sigh. More work for me.

Two days pass and I find a note from John Carlson on my desk after lunch: "See me today."

I walk down to his office. Sharon is away from her post. Through the open door I see John behind his desk talking on the phone. He summons me with a wave of his majestic hand. I sit down on the chair opposite him.

"Yeah, Julie, it was a great party. I'm so glad you invited me. Thanks." He hangs up and grins. "That was the mayor. I was at her home last weekend."

"Great. You wanted to see me? Is it about Jane Forman?"

"No," and his smile disappears. "Mrs. Buddle came in very angry. She thinks you're a racist."

"What?" I mutter. "What did she tell you?"

"Something about Children's Protective Services and you not respecting her as a parent."

I relate the story about the PE clothes and what Junior told me about the beatings and being locked up all day.

"Well, I know you needed to report it, but she's threatening to go to the school board."

"What?" I can't believe it. What did he say to her—did he

143

stand up for me?

He continues, "I told her we'd set up a meeting for the three of us. So, she can tell you how she feels."

"But I was following the law, John—the law!" My face feels ablaze and I'm hanging on to the armrests like I'm overboard and they're a life preserver.

"Yes, but she has a right to have her say. Maybe if we meet, she won't go to the school board." He gets up out of his seat and comes over to me. I'm stunned, frozen in place. He stands behind me and puts his meaty little hands on my shoulders. Their clammy perspiration seeps through my blouse. That wakes me from my angry reverie.

"Yeah, OK." And I ease out of the seat and away from his hands.

Gaby stops me as I return to my office. "*Qué pasa?* You OK?"

Not only am I red-faced, but steam might be coming out of my ears. "Carlson," I say. "I'll be fine." I brood the rest of the day. How could the woman call me a racist? What will she say to the school board? They won't know about the incident with Junior, because it's confidential.

I understand that Black parents in a mostly White community may suspect the school too easily disciplines their kids. But I'm more likely to be biased in the other direction—giving the Black kids a pass when I shouldn't. And this isn't about Junior; it's about Mrs. Buddle and the laws on child abuse. And what about Carlson? Between his not supporting me and his need to touch me, it's hopeless.

As Gaby is getting ready to leave for the day, I approach her desk.

"Gaby, can I ask you something?"

"Sure, anything."

"What do you know about Carlson's marriage? He is married, right?"

Chapter 18

"Yeah, I met the wife once, a few years ago at a party. She's very quiet. No kids that I'm aware of."

Nobody else is in our part of the office, but I whisper, just in case, "Is he touchy-feely with all the women here, or just me?"

She furrows her brow. "Hmmm, he's never been that way with me. Maybe because he doesn't like me." She laughs. "Maybe I'm lucky. I've heard rumors, but nothing specific. He's just a strange guy."

"Thanks, Gaby."

A few days later, the Buddle meeting takes place after school in Carlson's office. Mrs. Buddle ignores my extended hand. She has brought two of her youngest kids with her. They're not likely to stay in a chair. I go out for paper and markers and sit the kids down on the floor. Mrs. Buddle nods at me without smiling. John asks us to sit at the small round table in his office.

Maybe he'll say something in my defense. Silly me. He begins. "Mrs. Buddle, I understand you have some concerns about Ms. Walker. My purpose is to clear the air and let you know we only want what is best for Junior. Would you tell us what you're concerned about?"

Mrs. Buddle turns to look me in the eye and says, "You reported me to Protective Services, when I was within my rights as a mother. You clearly do not understand the African-American community. I'm a good mother. How dare you question that?"

"Ms. Walker?" says John, with a smile. Is he enjoying this?

"Here's the thing, Mrs. Buddle. It's not my job to judge your parenting, but the law requires me to make a report if there is even a suggestion of abuse. No evidence or proof is required. Junior told me things that required a report. Protective Services decides if the report requires follow up, not me."

"Well, they called me," she says. "Do you have children?"

I shake my head. Only six hundred I'm responsible for during school hours Monday to Friday!

145

"Then you don't know how hard it is, being a parent. And Black kids come into harm's way easily. I just want to make sure that my children do what they're supposed to and stay out of trouble. That's my job."

"So maybe you can understand that I was doing my job?"

She pauses. "Humph, I have a mind to go to the school board meeting and tell them how racist this school is. Marking my kid down because he lost his PE clothes. Sending him to the office. Calling Protective Services." She shakes her head. "You wouldn't do that to a rich white kid."

I look at John; a pleasant smile is still plastered on his face. Does he have anything to say? Evidently not. I continue. "We would do exactly that for any kid, Mrs. Buddle. And we took care of getting Junior new clothes for PE."

John finally opens his mouth. "We appreciate your coming in to talk. I hope you're feeling better about everything. You can call me any time on my private line." And he hands her his card.

The meeting is over, but has John said anything in my defense? Nope. Has he explained how the law on child abuse works? Assured her that I handled her case just as I would any other? That he would have done the same? Not at all. Does he even ask me to remain behind so we can talk about what just happened? No. He says his goodbyes to both of us and closes his door. What a poor excuse for a supervisor.

I want to kick something, but instead slow-walk back down the hall. Perhaps I look as distraught as I feel, because Gaby puts down the phone and follows me into my office. "Is Mr. Carlson giving you a bad time?" she asks. Just like Gaby to be concerned about me.

"You could say that." I motion to a chair and close the door. I sink into my chair.

"*Dios mío*, he's not a good man, Ms. Walker. He…"

146

Chapter 18

"Cynthia—Gaby, call me Cynthia."

Her small hands wave and gesture as she talks. "He puts people down. The clerks, the teachers. Nobody likes him—*nadie*. One time I was on the phone, and he stormed down here and glared at me. I was trying to tell the person I was talking to that I had to get off the phone and he just pushed the button and disconnected the call. I try to stay away from him."

Leaning back in the chair, I take a deep breath and let it all settle. "Well, I don't have that option. How did Bruce Milburn handle it?" Bruce is my predecessor, whom I met at the administrative retreat in August. He worked at Hamilton for years until they promoted him.

"Let me see..." She frowns. "Bruce didn't tell me much, but I could hear him and John arguing from time to time."

"Thanks, Gaby. I may give Bruce a call. I really appreciate your support." We get up and hug before Gaby goes back to her desk.

Late that afternoon I dial Bruce's number, hoping for some advice.

"Hi, Bruce. I finally had to reach out. It's been quite a week." I tell him about the meeting with Mrs. Buddle, without revealing any names.

"Yeah, that's John," he says. "He'll never stand up for you to a parent. He doesn't want to risk losing their love and support."

"He's off campus all the time, Bruce. Was it like that with you?"

"Yeah. You just have to learn to handle it all yourself. Believe me, the folks at the district office are watching. They know what's going on. This could work to your benefit in the long run."

Call over, I write a note about Junior to Amy, the school counselor. Perhaps she can include him in a group or at least check in on him from time to time to see how he's doing.

147

I drive home deep in thought about what Bruce said. What was he referring to about the district office watching? Do they have spies in the school? How could this awful situation benefit me? I'm supposed to be learning from John; instead, I'm having to handle it all with no help. Sink or swim. And right now, I'm exhausted from treading water, ready to go under.

I attend the school board meeting, prepared for anything. If Mrs. Buddle accuses me of racism in a public place, I'll have to do something. But she doesn't show up. Junior has new PE clothes. Neither he nor his mother bothers to say thanks.

It feels like a millennium has passed since school started in August. The job does not get easier—every day presents new challenges. I'm staying at work until six o'clock or later and my exercise program has disappeared, along with any expectations of a good night's sleep. There's too much to worry about.

CHAPTER NINETEEN
SUPER-VISION

AFTER OBSERVING GINNY STEIN TEACHING, I arrange a meeting to discuss my notes.

"Ginny, why don't you call on students in the back of the room, even if their hands aren't raised? That will get everyone to pay more attention, thinking they might be next."

"OK," she answers.

"How is Jimmy Green doing?" I ask. It's time to renew his contract. His behavior in class has improved, but I'm concerned about his work.

"He has a solid D minus."

"Yikes. Have you talked to the parents?"

"No, not yet."

"Please call them while there's time for him to improve." I make a mental note to check in with all of his teachers and revise his contract to focus more on work production.

On my next pass through Ginny's classroom, she once again only calls on students who raise their hands. Has she heard anything I've said? She's supposed to be collaborating with the other English teachers to get ideas for more engaging lessons. I doubt it has happened; her class continues to be a snooze fest. Then there is the possible alcohol problem. Carlson said he would advise me on this, but he hasn't said a word.

In contrast to Ginny, George Dunning has made a good effort to improve his students' attention. He observed Derek once to get ideas for classroom management. I'd like Derek to take George under his wing. I've been putting off talking to Sam, the PE teacher, about his attire.

I place a copy of each teacher's goals in their mailboxes, with a request to write a self-evaluation before we meet. Gaby sets it all up for the last week of January. Now I have to find time to sit down with my notes and fill out the evaluation forms.

How long will that take? Probably close to an hour per teacher, combining notes from two or three classroom visits and one or more conferences. Plus, I want to add comments on their adherence to curriculum standards. It's like writing a term paper with a pile of notes from different sources. Except my evaluations will remain in their Human Resources files forever. For those who aren't doing great, I'm documenting problems that could be used in the future to push them out of the classroom.

Writing has never been a challenge, but time is another matter. I can't work on evaluations during the school day and don't have the energy after hours. This task calls for a dedicated time and place to do nothing else for five hours or more. A place with no phones or doorbells or social engagements or need to prepare meals. A weekend in the woods!

Occidental is a charming town in the redwoods with a reasonably-priced B&B. There's great Italian food in the two-block downtown. I'll get there on Friday night, have a quiet Saturday to work, and come home on Sunday.

I've barely seen Derek since the Owusu funeral. In truth, I may be avoiding him, to squelch any rumors about something going on between us. His participation in the strike seemed less than enthusiastic. He appeared quiet, even somber, on the picket line. I appreciated that, but maybe his colleagues did not. After school on the Monday before my evaluation weekend, he pokes his head into my office. My heart skips a beat. His sky-blue shirt contrasts with his dark hair. He looks fresh

150

Chapter 19

and relaxed, despite the time of day. Is my hair a mess?

"Can I talk to you?" he says.

"You're here late—sure."

He closes the door behind him and sits in the chair where the culprits usually squirm.

"I want to apologize for the way the staff embarrassed you at the Christmas party."

Heat rises to my face. "Don't worry about it. It's not your fault."

"They're like a bunch of frat boys when I'm around a single woman." He smiles. Poor Derek. It's tough being the good-looking single guy on the staff.

"I can take it," I say, and grin back at him, my eyes glued to his.

"Well, in that case, would you like to go wine tasting with me this weekend? One of my favorite wineries is having a special event."

All concerns about professional distance and embarrassment evaporate. "Uh, I'd love to, but I'm going to be away, working." I tell him my plans for Occidental.

"That's a great area," he says. "How about a hike there on Sunday when you're all finished with your work?"

"I'd love it. And I want to talk to you about George Dunning, so we can consider it a work outing." Silly me, still trying to sound professional, when my heart is racing at the thought of a date with Derek.

Could I think of a better reward for a day of writing evaluations? No, Sir. We agree he will meet me at my B&B at ten a.m. on Sunday.

I arrive in Occidental early Friday evening and scarf down spaghetti and meatballs before checking in at the B&B. Once my laptop and printer are set up on the desk in my charming Victorian room, I collapse into bed. In the morning, full of

151

motivation, I start on the evaluations. Without distractions, it's rather enjoyable. I have the challenge of praising Dunning for his cooperation in learning new methods, while rating him as *Needs Improvement*. My recommendations include observation and counsel with a colleague to learn new techniques. If he keeps working at it, I'm hopeful he'll become a good teacher. And I'm counting on convincing Derek to mentor him.

By the end of the day, the evals are finished and I start thinking about my hiking date on Sunday. Am I making a mistake to have any kind of date with Derek? Especially since I'm evaluating him, too. I've given him a positive report, perhaps even downplaying what a great teacher he is. The professional implications give me a headache, but there's no way I'm going to deprive myself of a possible life-changing relationship.

Sunday dawns cool and fresh with a bright, cloudless sky. I dress in my most flattering jeans and a shirt in my best color— turquoise. I usually wouldn't put on makeup for a hike, but this is different. It's a first date.

Derek shows up right on time, cheeks pink and eyes sparkling. He carries a backpack and wears hiking boots and an old army jacket.

"Hey there," I say, grabbing my fanny pack and climbing into his SUV. We make a stop for deli sandwiches. My stomach butterflies disappear, because it's so easy to be with him. He drives us past Westminster Woods, where I once attended an outdoor education program, to the Willow Creek Road trailhead. He knows the area well.

"This one will take us several miles up. Is that, OK?" he asks.

"Sure, as long as lunch is at the top."

"Lunch with a view," he answers.

We hike up through the cool shade of towering redwoods to open sunshine. I breathe in the plant-scented air and carefully

Chapter 19

step over roots in the trail. Please, Cynthia, no tripping or falling on this outing. We chat about random things, none of them school related. This is strictly getting-to-know-you conversation.

"I grew up in Redwood City," he says. "I went to UCLA and decided I wanted to teach public school, rather than slog through a Ph.D. to become a history professor."

"I wish I'd had a good history teacher," I say. "History classes were always so boring." Will this confession make him like me less? Will he think I'm a philistine? Maybe I am.

"The problem is teachers who focus on names and dates and don't explore the reasons behind events. You know the saying—we have to learn from the past. So we won't repeat it." He smiles. I hope he doesn't think I'm a complete idiot.

"I'm ready, Mr. Simons," I quip.

He laughs. "Anyway, I started teaching in L.A., but when I had the opportunity, I came back to the Bay Area to be near my parents and sister. I didn't want my whole life to be so far away from them. I've been at Hamilton for five years."

"Derek, you are such a good teacher. Have you ever thought about going into administration?"

"Maybe someday. For now, I'm just enjoying the subject matter and the kids."

We stop at the top at a bench strategically placed to afford a view of the shaded canyon and woodlands below, as well as the rugged coast and ocean not far away. I wipe my sweaty face and sip my Diet Coke. It's lovely to sit quietly with this fellow by my side. It's been a long time since I've felt so at ease with a man. My turkey sandwich tastes delicious after the climb. We share potato chips and a big chocolate chip cookie Derek insisted on buying for me.

He asks, "Have you been married?"

"No, but I had one long-term relationship that ended badly.

153

After seven years, he started seeing someone else behind my back, then dumped me."

"Ouch." He scrunches his face in a sympathetic way.

I go on. "So, I went back to school to get my administrative credential."

The sun glistens on Derek's dark curls while he gazes at the view.

"I have a similar story," he says. "I was engaged two years ago. Then she went on a business trip and met someone she liked better."

"Double ouch. So sorry. Sometimes I look at couples who have been together a long time and wonder how they do it."

"Well, maybe they study their own histories and figure it out?" He smiles and turns towards me. "I think you just have to find the right person." He brushes a stray hair off my face.

"Thanks." I feel a blush rise and look away from those dazzling green eyes to the horizon, where the coast meets the Pacific under puffy clouds. Could Derek be the right person for me? And I for him?

On the way down the trail I ask, "Would you consider mentoring George Dunning?"

"What would that entail?"

"You'd observe each other teaching. Then you could give him suggestions. He would learn so much from you."

"You think so? Can people really learn this stuff? Or do some of us simply have the ability to motivate kids and keep them on task?"

"I don't know, but I'd sure like you to try with George."

"OK," he says. "I'm willing to give it a go."

Derek returns me to the B&B and time stops while we stand by my car talking. I've learned about his family and background. Sharing our relationship disasters has forged a connection.

154

Chapter 19

"Well," says Derek, reaching out and taking my left hand in both of his, "we had better be getting back." We easily melt into a hug.

"This was great," I say.

"We'll do it again," he answers. We're both smiling like fools. My pulse quickens when he gives me a peck on the cheek. Then he's gone. I get into my car and check out my lingering grin in the mirror.

MOST OF MY EVALUATION MEETINGS go well. Dunning receives my comments and the *Needs Improvement* without getting visibly upset. He tells me he and Derek have already set up a regular time to meet. I'll cover Dunning's class, so he can observe in Derek's room. Then I'll cover for Derek so he can observe Dunning. I'm excited about the possibilities for both of them. Am I becoming the change agent I have always wanted to be?

Next, I have to meet with Sam. I have pondered different approaches to talking about his clothing, but I need to just get it over with. He arrives at my office at the appointed time and settles his nylon-clad bottom on a chair.

"Sam, has no supervisor ever commented on how you dress for school?"

"Uh, what about it?" he asks defensively, but with a sly grin. He knows exactly what I'm talking about.

"Look, Sam. I get your need to wear athletic shoes and sporty attire to do PE. I don't expect you to wear a suit and tie. But your skimpy shorts and tops have got to be distracting for the kids—the adults too!" I wait for a reply. The grin is still on his face.

"And you?"

I take a breath. "I'm going to pretend you didn't say that, Sam. Can you make an effort to at least wear long pants?"

Silence.

155

"This is important enough to include in your final evaluation if you don't agree to make a change. I've checked with other schools and *nobody* has men walking the halls all day in running shorts!"

"OK," he says. "But I'm going to talk to the union."

"That's fine with me." I'm sure the union will not make a case out of this. How many of their members care what Sam wears?

Ginny is still an enigma. She hasn't met with her colleagues—I checked. Still unsure how to handle the alcohol issue, I have not mentioned it in my evaluation. I wrote that she's not collaborating with her team or increasing student engagement. This is definitely a *Needs Improvement*.

When I share what I've written, her face sinks deeper into a sullen grimace.

"Ginny, I'm willing to work with you, but I can't help if you won't let me."

"OK," she says, and signs the form. At least she doesn't smell like a wino.

Focused on meeting with teachers and students, I have not seen Derek since our date. On Thursday, I receive a typed invitation from his last period class: *Ms. Walker, if you can join us tomorrow at 2:15, we're having a debate about water rights.* Derek has written at the bottom: *Applying history to problems of today! D,* followed by a smiley face.

Oh, my. I should never have told him of my dislike for history. Now he needs to educate me. Or am I overreacting? Actually, it's kind of sweet. I show up at his room on time, nod to Derek, and take the guest-of-honor-seat. The kids present opposing sides of two different cases, one from ancient Mesopotamia and another from arid parts of current-day California. Who has rights to use the water? To dig canals and siphon river water? Or in modern times, to build developments that drain the

Chapter 19

water table?

The students have done their research. The rich and powerful have controlled water for millennia. Derek has pushed his students to filter their learning of ancient history through what they know today about the environment. They conclude that water belongs to everyone and must be conserved.

When they're done, I stand and applaud, longer than necessary, but I'm blown away by the maturity and power of this lesson. And by the kids' ability to make the connection between ancient times and current problems.

The final bell rings, but I have no desire to make an exit. The students pass through the open door, smiling and thanking me.

"Very impressive, Mr. Simons," I say. He comes over to the doorway, where I linger. "Really, Derek, you're doing so much more than teaching history. You're motivating these kids to change the world." I'm misting up. OK, Cynthia, cut that out.

He comes close and puts his hand on the door frame. "You see, history can be very exciting." I'll say. My heart rate is up and I'm tingling all over.

We're standing transfixed when I sense movement behind me. I turn my head and see Carlson.

"Everything OK?" he asks.

Derek steps back. "Absolutely."

Carlson looks at me. He shakes his head in a disapproving manner and walks off. I put my hand up to my forehead. "Damn," is all I can say.

"No worries," says Derek. "We were just chatting. How about if I call you later?"

"I've got to go," I say and make my escape.

I want to kick myself. What does Carlson think he witnessed? If he's concerned, will he bring it up with me? Or report to someone at the district office? And why did I walk away from

157

Derek, whose teaching moved me to tears? And whom I really, really like?

It's still January and I need to focus on the challenges that lie ahead, including a requirement that I play in a basketball game—with Derek.

CHAPTER TWENTY
WILL JANUARY EVER END?

EVERYONE ON STAFF IS INVITED TO PLAY IN THE annual student-teacher basketball game. At five foot, eight inches, I'm tall, but that doesn't make me a basketball player. I won't be much good to my team; I just hope I don't embarrass myself in front of the whole school. The six-foot guys have an advantage over the students, but the kids are faster, so it should be an interesting competition.

A week before the game, the staff coach, Sam Butler, schedules an after-school practice. I've sent for Antonio just before the final bell, to discuss his attendance, which is slipping again. He strolls in smiling.

"Hi, Antonio. I want to talk to you about your attendance. You've missed five days in the last two weeks. What's going on?"

His smile disappears and he hangs his head as he settles into a chair. "It's my mom."

"Your mom?"

"Yeah, she's back at home and it's great to see her and all... but it's a little crazy."

"I see." His mom was in jail for a drug-related crime. "How's it crazy?"

"She fights with my grandma all the time...and she's drinking."

"Are you still sleeping on the couch?"

"Yeah. Grandma goes to bed early and my mom sleeps in the room with her, but not until really late."

"You have to stay up until your mom goes to bed?"

"Most nights, I go out for a walk, just to get out of there."

"Antonio, I'm so sorry. Does the social worker still visit you?"

"Not since Mom got out."

"Would you like me to talk to Mom?"

"I don't know. She'll be mad I told you."

"OK, let's phone the social worker. Maybe she can help."

"OK."

It's late in the day, but I call and leave a message.

Antonio listens, then adds, "Sometimes I stay at my cousin Brian's house."

"Where does he live?"

Antonio gives me the details and we call the uncle. He says he'll make arrangements with Antonio's mother to have him move in for a while. When we're done, the boy's smile is back.

"You can get to school from your uncle's house?" I ask.

"They'll drop me off," he says.

"Great." I pat his arm. He waves on his way out.

I'm finally ready for basketball practice. I do a quick change into my running pants and jog over to the gym. Sam is giving orders and he's wearing long pants. Hooray! He has divided the players into two teams for practice drills. It's clear I'm the slowest in the group, although I could argue the rest are warmed up. It's more a laugh fest than a true practice, as half of us miss shots, trip and fall, or gasp for air after one jog down the court. Carlson is of course missing. He would probably go into cardiac arrest if he had to hobble down the court once. I can run but have no sense of my body in space, so I constantly bump into people.

"Hey!" one of the guys shouts when I step on his foot.

Chapter 20

"Sorry...sorry..." I repeat. It would help if I could get the ball in the hoop, but there's no such luck. Derek, the other young guys, and the two female PE teachers move fast and make baskets. The older folks and the rest of the women don't contribute much.

"OK, you guys. We'll do our best," Sam mutters with a scowl, and dismisses us. The others head somewhere for a beer, but I'm not finished in the office.

Sitting at my desk in my sweaty tee shirt and running pants, I review my notes about Stefan Kostic. Small for his age, he wears thick glasses, and his lips are often blue. At his recent IEP meeting, his teacher explained that Stefan was born with a heart deformity. It prevents his body from getting enough oxygen. He's lucky to be alive.

I need to make this call but haven't been able to get myself to pick up the phone. After our IEP meeting, which addressed his educational needs, I consulted with a nurse and called Carolyn, a friend of the parents, who don't speak much English.

"Can't something be done for his heart?"

Carolyn answered, "He could have had heart surgery as an infant. I don't know about now." The parents, who long ago emigrated from the countryside in Yugoslavia, believed that Stefan's deformity was God's will.

I protest, "Times have changed, and they're not in the old country anymore."

Here's the question: is denying surgery to a sick child a form of abuse? Someone with more knowledge of the law needs to provide the answer. Carlson has pushed everything back at me, so why bother talking to him? At long last, I pick up the phone and call Children's Protective Services, explain the whole situation, give the names of the knowledgeable parties, and hang up. My stomach is in knots. This could get ugly. But I've done what I think my student needs to be well. That's my job, right?

161

ANTONIO IS STAYING WITH HIS UNCLE and has made it to school three days in a row, but I don't know how long the relatives will keep him. The social worker gets back to me, listens to the story and promises to look into it. Maybe she can work out something long term with the uncle or help sort out the situation at Antonio's house. I breathe a sigh of relief that someone else is on the case.

The night of the basketball game arrives, and the gym fills with cheering students and parents. The parent club, never missing an opportunity to earn a few bucks, sells fresh popcorn and sodas. The gym smells like a carnival. We're playing short quarters, not that I know what a normal quarter is. I'm glad to be on the bench at the start. I know a few of the students who are playing, including Janelle.

The adults tire quickly and before long Sam points at me. "Walker, you're in."

With my height advantage, guarding one of the girls goes well, but when the ball sails to the other end of the court, I'm the last one to make it down there. The big men control the ball and tease the kids by passing it back and forth at a height the students can't reach.

"Think you're fast, huh?"

"Reach for it, dude!"

Derek passes the ball...to me. Are you kidding? I fumble it immediately; Janelle picks it up and races to the other end for a basket. Great.

The crowd laughs and shouts, "Go, Tigers." I hear, "You can beat those teachers!" I'm too out of breath to know if I'm having fun. Sam sends me to the bench again. Perfect. I look around and see Janelle's parents in the crowd. I spot Stefan and his family in the bleachers—both parents and two teens, who must be his older sisters. Should I talk to them? Maybe one of the older kids can translate.

Chapter 20

The game continues and once again I run down the court and try to get the ball. It comes to me once and I succeed in tossing it to one of the other women without an interception. Thank goodness that Sam, acting as referee, doesn't call out us old folks for moving without dribbling or other errors. Then it's half time. After visiting the water fountain, I make my way over to Stefan's family.

"Hello, Mr. and Mrs. Kostic. I'm glad to see you here."

Stefan touches his mother's arm and says, "Miss Walker."

The mother nods at me and then whispers to one of her daughters. The daughter says, "OK," and addresses me.

"My mom wants to know why you called Protective Services. Do you think she's a bad parent?"

"No, please tell her I'm concerned about Stefan's health."

The daughter translates for her mother. The mother nods her head and gives me a little bit of a smile.

"I only want what is best for Stefan." He steps carefully over the benches and comes to stand next to me. He says, "I'm going to see the doctor at UCSF next week."

"Great. I hope that goes well, Stefan." He gives me a smile and a hug and walks back to his family.

On my way back to the teachers' bench, I notice Mr. and Mrs. Green in the bleachers.

"Hi, where's Jimmy?" I ask.

"Oh, probably running around with his friends," answers the mom.

"How's the new contract working?" I ask. We've added a homework requirement and there's a new bike on the line if he brings up his grades before the end of the year.

"Oh, fine," she says, with a smile. Structure and consistency don't come easily. Has she figured out how to reinforce her son's improved behavior? And get him to do homework?

Walking back towards the bench, I hear a familiar voice.

163

"Cynthia!" Carlson shouts from the bleachers and waves me over. Really? I climb over people to get to where he sits, surrounded by smiling parents.

"Yeah?" What could he want from me here and now?

"I just wanted to say you're looking good out there." His grin says so much more than his words. Will the parents who are listening get the sleaze factor? Or think he's being nice?

Sam blows his whistle to end the break. I shrug and make my way back to the gathering of teachers, where Sam starts his pep talk.

"You're doing OK, guys." His fake smile shows what he really thinks. "We're slightly ahead. Just try to keep them from scoring."

Despite the break, we're all still sweaty and red in the face. Please, let's not have any medical emergencies tonight. We do that team spirit hand slap, roar "Teachers," and go back to it.

I get two more outings on the gym floor and am starting to feel less like a detriment, even stealing the ball once. Close enough to the basket, I shoot, but miss. *C'est la vie.* It's finally over and the teachers laugh with relief. The kids squeaked by us by two points, but my guess is the men let that happen. The students cheer and hug the kids who played and then the gym slowly clears out. The staff group invades a downtown pizza place for mugs of beer.

Derek comes over to me as I stand at the bar waiting for a drink.

"Not too bad," he says and holds up his hand for a high-five. I give him a good slap and join in the idiotic grin we can't seem to avoid when we're together.

"Yeah, only falling and breaking a leg would have been worse. You, on the other hand, are a good basketball player."

He explains. "I played some in high school, but that was a long time ago."

164

Chapter 20

"Some people are just athletic. I can jog for a half hour, but I'm no basketball player."

"Maybe, but you have other stellar qualities." He holds up his glass in a toast.

"Hmmm, go on... "

"Well," he says, and leans closer, "you're a good vice principal. You work hard and you care about kids... and teachers... and you have a warm and lovely smile."

"Gee, thanks, I don't get positive feedback often."

My glass of beer arrives, and we move away from the bar, but maintain our distance from the crowd of teachers, now seated at tables they have pushed together. Perhaps they're too engaged in their own talk to notice Derek and me. Perhaps not—maybe we should be more careful.

He didn't call me after that awkward ending to my classroom visit. But my heart is racing, and it's no longer from running around the gym. Derek likes me! Or maybe he's just a flirt.

Derek points to the door and I turn to see Carlson coming in. We separate and join the others for pizza and more beer. After Carlson leaves, when the party breaks up, Derek walks me out. It's dark and we talk until our two cars are the only ones left in the lot. "So how about dinner and a movie next weekend?" he asks.

Whatever hesitation I've had to continue getting to know Derek has disappeared. I respond, "Sounds great."

"All right if I call you at home?" he asks and puts his arms around me for a hug.

I hug him back. "Yes, I'd like that." And we kiss, just a short kiss, but soft, on the lips...delicious. He holds the car door while I get in and closes it gently, waving as I pull out.

The following week Stefan's family friend, Carolyn, calls to tell me the result of the UCSF cardiology visit. A call from Protective Services prompted the parent to make the

165

appointment. Stefan is too old and his heart problem too advanced for him to have surgery now, but a younger child in the extended family—a cousin—has the same issue, and the family may take her for surgery. Stefan's life will likely end within a few years, but my anguished child abuse call may save another life. I thank Carolyn, my voice trembling with a mixture of sadness and gratitude.

LESSON #9: YOUR DECISIONS TRAVEL FAR AND AFFECT MANY.

Speaking of hearts, soon it will be February and that means love is going to be in the air for a few weeks. Maybe longer if my date with Derek goes well.

CHAPTER TWENTY-ONE
GUILTY AS CHARGED

MY ENTHUSIASM FOR MY DATE WITH DEREK IS tempered by worry. Before the lights dim for the movie, I scan the theater for Hamilton staff or parents. Or students—they would spread rumors faster than anyone.

Derek takes me to Rosetti's, the town's classy Italian restaurant. As we walk to our table, I feel his eyes on me as I scan the occupied booths.

"Are you looking for someone? An old boyfriend?"

He's grinning, but over salad, I confess my fears. "Derek, I don't know if this district has a policy about colleagues dating. What will happen if someone—maybe Carlson—says something to the district?"

He knits his brow and answers, "We've had couples on the staff in the past, but they didn't include an administrator. Do you think the district cares?"

"I don't know. Worrying, however, is one of my best skills."

"OK, next time we'll go somewhere out of town."

"Sounds good." Good that he's already thinking there will be a next time. On the other hand, a fair number of staff live out of town.

The evening ends with a lovely kiss at my doorstep, but I don't invite him in and he doesn't ask. Maybe he shares my concerns about a relationship mixed with work. If we get serious and then have an ugly breakup, it would be a disaster to see each other every day at school.

167

SHARON CALLS ME ON THE PHONE one afternoon while I'm in my office with a student. "I've got John on the line for you," she says. That's weird. Usually, he just summons me to his office.

He launches into a request about bringing him papers from a file.

"John, aren't you in your office?"

"No, I'm working at home, but I need that file on the new security system."

"And Sharon—"

"I want *you* to bring it to me."

What? I'm getting a creepy vibe, but I answer, "OK, if you insist. Let me just send this student back to class. What's your address?"

I find the file and tell Sharon where I'm going. She nods. Nothing unusual to her? The school day may be almost over, but there won't be an administrator on campus once I leave.

John's small house sits on a narrow street that dead ends at a forested park. Nice location. But why is he always here and why does he want me here? I vow to give him the file and get out as quickly as I can.

He answers the door with a big grin. He's wearing a track suit, too much like pajamas, and I doubt he can run a block.

I hold out the file, ready to dash back to my car.

He steps back while intoning, "Come in, come in."

I pause, step over the threshold.

"Come on, have a seat. I want to talk to you." He's walking towards the living room couch.

The house is very quiet, so it appears nobody else is here. If I'd had any expectations of John's home, they would have included piles of unfinished paperwork and overflowing ashtrays. But the furnishings are modern and minimalist. A few framed paintings, no clutter. Who is in charge here? I sit down at one

Chapter 21

end of the long couch. He pulls up a chair opposite me.

"What's this all about, John? I'm uncomfortable being here. And there's no administrator at Hamilton right now."

"They'll be fine," he says. "I want to talk to you about your Mr. Simons...and I thought it should be off campus."

"What about him?"

"I know what's going on between you two."

Oh my God. What does he think is going on? Do *I* even know what's going on?

"There's nothing 'going on.' We're friends. What does that even mean?"

"It means I may have to report you to the superintendent for inappropriate behavior with someone you are evaluating. You've heard of sexual harassment, right?"

I don't know whether to laugh, scream or burst into tears. The latter are gathering in my eyes. "There's no harassment. We've gone out a couple of times, that's all. He's a great teacher. He has nothing to gain by associating with me."

"That's for someone else to determine, if I report you."

"What do you mean?"

"Well, only that I'm thinking about it. Maybe we could discuss this and your future in the district at greater length. Over dinner somewhere?"

Now I'm on full alert. He's threatening to get me in trouble with the district if I won't have dinner with him?

Beginning to tremble, I bite my lip to get control. "John, I...I... just don't understand. You want me to have dinner with you so you won't report me?"

"Something like that."

"That wouldn't...I don't know...I have to think about it."

I grab my purse and bolt for the door. I start to drive down the street but have to pull over. Tears overtake me. What have I gotten myself into? I need to talk to someone, but it can't be Derek. Counselor Amy isn't at Hamilton today. I dial her cell and leave a message. "I need to talk to you Amy, today if possible. It's...personal."

I can't go back to school. At home I blow my nose and wash my face. The call from Amy can't come soon enough. She agrees to come to my home in a half hour. By the time she arrives, I've written a bunch of options on a yellow pad: *Go to dinner, ask HR abt policy, stop seeing Derek, report the bastard.* None of them feel right.

Amy arrives and I pour us each a cup of tea. No wine for me in this fragile state.

"You look like you've had a really bad day," she says.

"You won't believe it." I give her the details and show her my notes. "What do you think?"

"Well, *you* haven't done anything wrong. John is the one who is in the wrong, but you can't control his behavior—only your own. What do *you* think is the right thing to do?"

"I guess I find it hard to believe he would seriously report me when his behavior towards me has been so...inappropriate. But would they believe me?" I don't tell Amy about all the times he's put his hands on me—it always looks innocent, but it doesn't feel that way. *She* might be the one making a report if I told her.

"You don't need to be in a hurry. Take some time to get yourself together. Maybe nothing will come of this. But if John repeats his demand, keep a written record."

Amy has slowed down the windmill of my mind. When Carlson doesn't seek me out over the next couple of days, I decide to wait and see. Maybe he's all talk. Maybe he's watching me twist and turn from afar. I avoid being alone with him and skip our usual weekly meeting. Maybe he's realized *he* could be the one in trouble with the district.

Chapter 21

I CAN'T SPEND ALL MY TIME worrying about Carlson, since student misbehavior never takes a break. My biggest discipline challenge so far involves a girl. Yep, girls are often the toughest nuts to crack. Madeline, whom I met at my first Saturday School, uses the power of her personality to push other kids around. She has been in my office several times, but I've never been able to nail her on anything. It's petty stuff like calling kids names and making threats, but these things are upsetting, even frightening, to eleven- and twelve-year-olds. And they're always too afraid to tell on her.

Today's report, however, goes beyond calling names or tripping someone. A group of seven girls were going home on the school bus. The district recently reupholstered the seats, at great expense. When the bus returned to the barn after dropping off the students, several seats had permanent red marker scrawled all over the new grey fabric. I notice Madeline's name on the list of passengers and know this is going to be tough. She most certainly played a part.

How to get to the bottom of this? Some vice principals punish students based on hearsay, without proof. I'd rather let a guilty kid go free than risk punishing someone who is innocent. If I confront Madeline first, I'll get nowhere. If she's the responsible one, she's not likely to own up to it. Do I dare set the kids up against her? The rest of the names aren't familiar, but I start with a sixth-grader who I hope will tell the truth. Gaby squeezes chairs into my office. Girl #1 enters, and although she won't make eye contact and grips the seat for dear life, she coughs up pretty quickly that Madeline took the marker out of her backpack and drew on the seats. I have her remain seated and we call in witness #2.

"Jodie has already told me what happened to the seats. Now it's your turn." This continues with each witness, all of them repeating the same details, until six of them are crammed into my office. Then Gaby sends for Madeline.

She saunters in, looking totally unconcerned, even puzzled about why this group is gathered. The other girls look away from her, like they want to escape. I say, "Everyone here has told me what you did to the seats on the bus, but I need you to tell me too." The distress to the other girls is the reason I hesitated to do this. They squirm in their seats and stare at their hands or the floor, surely all imagining how and when they're going to get beat up for telling on Madeline.

She blurts out, "I didn't do anything." She crosses her legs and smooths her purple-streaked hair, nose to the ceiling.

I read aloud from my notes the exact words of the assembled girls, then say, "We'll wait." Doesn't matter if it's kids or adults who have something to confess—waiting is a good strategy. Let them squirm.

"It's important, Madeline, for you to take responsibility for your actions. Somebody is going to pay for the damage to those seats and it should be the person who did it."

Madeline glares at me, then adjusts her top and looks at her shoes. We wait in silence for a few minutes, the witnesses restless as birds in a cage. Madeline maintains a defiant scowl. Finally, she speaks, so quietly I can barely hear her. "I don't want to be here all day. You want me to say I did it, OK, I'll say I did it."

Success! Not exactly a soulful confession, but good enough for me. The other girls have earned their release. Carlson walks by my office as they're filing out and waiting for Gaby to write them passes back to class.

I suspend Madeline, call her mother, report to the district, and write a referral for Madeline to see Amy. Maybe the counselor can get to this girl. At least the parent is apologetic; Madeline's mom knows her kid is a troublemaker.

Chapter 21

LESSON #10: PERSIST UNTIL YOU NAIL THE PERPS.

When I hang up the phone, Gaby tells me Carlson wants to see me. I find him back in his office, stretched out on the couch. We haven't had a private conversation since a week ago at his home.

"Close the door," he orders. And here I thought he was going to let it all go. I comply, but stand in front of him, refusing to sit down.

"What was that about with all those girls?"

I tell him what Madeline did and that I've suspended her.

"Good, good. What is it with kids, anyway?"

"I don't know, John. Attention seeking? Some of them definitely have problems."

"Don't we all." He pauses, eyebrows raised. "Have you decided to have dinner with me?"

"I've been too busy to think about it," I lie.

"Well, let me know soon. At the very least, stay away from Simons—for your own good."

Another threat? "Is that all?"

He nods and I escape.

CHAPTER TWENTY-TWO
VALENTINE'S DAY

CROCUSES AND DAFFODILS BURST THROUGH THE greening landscape, signaling the arrival of California spring. February may be Black History Month, but this age group is focused on Valentine's Day. Student organizations often sell flowers or candy for delivery to students during the school day. It's a great money maker, but I always feel bad for the kids who don't get anything.

Carlson started the year advising the Student Council, but he hasn't shown up for their last two meetings. The officers track me down to request a hearts-and-flowers type of event on the fourteenth. I gather them together in my office one day at lunch.

"What are you thinking you'd like to do?" I ask.

"My mom can get us a deal on See's suckers," one girl offers.

"Cool! We could tie red ribbons and message cards on them," suggests a boy.

Someone else says, "We could sell them for a dollar."

I respond, "OK. It would be nice if this sale benefited a charity or community group. What do you think?"

They decide to donate half of what they make to the local Heart Association. They'll design the message tags, get the word out to the student body, and fill me in on their progress next week. It's a great plan, but I can't stop thinking about the students who will feel unloved on Valentine's Day.

Carlson's threat is with me every day, but I still want to cook

175

dinner for Derek, out of the public eye. I send him an email and we set a date for the Friday night before Valentine's Day. Since we both like Italian, I'll cook my favorite lasagna. While I make a mess in my kitchen, I'm still puzzling over the plan for Valentine's Day. The house smells of tomato sauce, onions, and garlic. French bread warms in the oven and a green salad is ready to be dressed. I've had no time for baking but picked up cream puffs for dessert. The Cabernet Sauvignon is open and breathing when he arrives. I open the door to that lovely grin and when he steps inside, his hand emerges from behind his back to reveal a bouquet of red tulips.

"For the cook."

"Aw...how sweet. Tulips are my favorite—how did you know?"

Instead of answering, he gives me a one-armed hug, steps back, says, "two lips" and kisses me squarely on mine. A nice long kiss that stirs me to the core and sends my mind off into a tizzy of questions. Is this going to get intimate tonight? Does he think the dinner invite implies something? Do I want it to? Am I wearing sexy underwear? We sip our wine and sit down to eat. Soft folksy music—a local band with moderate success—plays from my phone.

"Delicious," he says after his first bite. "Hey, is that the Rangers?"

"Yeah, I heard them at a festival last year." I pass him the French bread.

"Would you believe I'm related to one of them?"

"Really?" I set my glass down.

"Yeah, the lead singer, Chuck, is my cousin."

"Cool," I answer. I want to know so much more about this man.

Soon I bring up the Valentine's Day plan, and that I'm looking for some way to make the day special for everyone. He puts

176

Chapter 22

down his fork.

"That's so sweet of you." He touches my arm. "What if I could get the band to do a mini concert at school that day?"

"Wow! That would be awesome."

"I've never asked them before and they may not be available, but even a half hour at lunch would be a treat."

Derek helps me clear the dishes and put them in the washer. We move to the sofa with our coffee and cream puffs. His does not get eaten, but nerves make me inhale mine. As things get cozier, I have to speak.

As he puts his arm around me to pull me closer, I say, "Derek, I think we need to talk about this...and our jobs. Are we ready for the next step?"

He straightens up and sits back. "Did you think..."

"Well, the flowers, the kiss. What were you planning tonight?"

He takes both my hands in his. "This is the most comfortable I've been with anyone for a long time. I want to get closer to you. But I don't want to push you—especially if you're worried about the district."

His words give me chills. It's possible I've found a guy who can talk about his feelings and is concerned about mine. A diamond in the coal mine of dating. On the other hand, Carlson's threat hangs over me.

"I really like you. I'm worried about Carlson using this against me. He's threatened...well...let's not go there. In any case, it's not just the district. I worry about what would happen if we had a bad breakup and still had to work together."

His face colors and he squeezes my hands. "Carlson has threatened you?"

"I don't know. It's a long story, but maybe won't amount to anything."

His gaze is soft but intense. "I think we just need to promise that no matter what happens, we'll remain friends and

177

teammates. And you know you can talk to me about anything, right?"

"It's a deal. But let's take it slow. It's such a crazy time of year. I'm overwhelmed planning for state testing, then spring break...but I don't want to disappoint you."

Those dazzling green eyes are still with me. "You're not disappointing me. In fact, I'm rather impressed by your wisdom." He releases my hands and moves a few inches away, leaning back on the sofa. "Speaking of spring break, do you have plans?"

Is he going to suggest we do something together? Too bad I booked my flights long ago.

"I'm going to alligator land to visit my folks...not very exciting. You?"

"I'll be in New York with college buddies."

"Could be a lot of talk about sports and cars."

"Well, maybe. But they're an interesting bunch. Maybe you'll meet them someday."

Any someday that includes Derek in my life sounds like a grand idea to me.

DEREK WASTES NO TIME contacting his cousin and the next thing I know we have a commitment for the band to play in the gym during the last period on Valentine's Day. The Student Council will deliver suckers with messages to students in their homerooms and then everyone will make their way to the gym for the concert. I write an article for the school newsletter about the donation to the Heart Association and a parent who is a doctor donates a hundred bucks to encourage the kids in their efforts. The parent club buys more suckers, and the Student Council encourages everyone to send one. No romance required. See's practically gives the suckers away when they hear we are donating half the proceeds. I invite the parents, someone from the Heart Association, and the See's

Chapter 22

manager to join us for the concert.

Valentine's Day arrives and the school buzzes with excitement: the usual anxiety of kids wondering who likes them enough to send them a treat, as well as anticipation of a special concert. The sales have gone better than expected—even the teachers are buying—and with the donations we've received, it looks like we'll be giving at least $300 to the Heart Association. Hamilton has never done this kind of fundraiser before, and everyone is psyched. Despite the kids' high energy level, there are no discipline problems. The council reps pass out the suckers.

The mood in the gym is upbeat as the band warms up. I don't see Carlson—he's probably sulking because he's not the center of attention—so I introduce the special guests and turn it over to Derek. He and the band leader, Chuck, have their turn.

"Thanks so much for coming," says Derek. "Students, let's show Chuck and the band that we appreciate them joining us today." The kids cheer.

Chuck takes the mic. "We didn't want to miss an opportunity to thank you for your generosity to the Heart Association. Happy Valentine's Day! Let's hear some music."

They play for most of an hour, with kids swaying in the bleachers, singing along to old familiar ballads. I look for Derek in the crowd and finally find him, but he's watching his homeroom kids closely and doesn't look my way.

The kids stomp their feet and cheer after the last tune. They file out to waiting buses and cars. When the campus has cleared, I make my way back to my office, light on my feet. What a great day.

On my desk I find three suckers, handwritten notes attached. The first one is from Carlson: *Dinner soon? John.* The second reads: *Thanks, Mrs. Walker. Have a nice day. Antonio.* That brings a tear to my eye, before I pick up the third. In Derek's immaculate script is written: *Wishing for many more Valentines with you.*

179

CHAPTER TWENTY-THREE
PICTURE DAY

SCHOOLS HAVE MANY REASONS FOR PROMOTING picture day. You think those beautiful annual shots of your kids are for documenting their growth and filling yearbook pages? Actually, schools get a kickback from picture sales. They negotiate the price of photo packages offered to parents; if the school picks a higher percent of return, package prices go up.

We've scheduled picture day for early March during the kids' PE classes. Instead of changing into their stinky gym clothes and running off some energy, they sit on bleachers in the gym fixing their hair and makeup. The PE teachers keep things under control while the kids wait their turn.

Teachers are supposed to go to the gym for their photos during their free periods. But not everyone is eager to smile for the camera. Gaby helps me track down the shirkers and we escort them to the gym.

"Do you want last year's awful picture in the yearbook again? No? Then you'd better come with me."

I sit for the photographer early in the day before sweat from running around campus smears my makeup.

I pass Derek in the hall, on his way to get the deed done. "Good morning," he beams. Nobody else is around.

"Looking good," I reply.

"Suppose they'd do a couples shot of us?" He laughs.

"Yeah, right. Centerfold in the yearbook."

We giggle and continue on our separate ways.

I check in at the office, thrilled nobody has been sent out of class.

Mrs. Owusu, Janelle's mother, waits at the front desk, where Sharon usually sits.

"Hi, can I help with something?"

She holds up a red, flowery blouse. "I brought this for Janelle. She left this morning wearing a tee shirt, but I want her to look nice for her picture."

"We'll make sure she gets it." I take the shirt and ask Gaby to send for Janelle.

When the girl comes in and sees me holding her blouse, she frowns. She is indeed wearing a plain grey tee shirt with her sleek running pants.

"This is pretty," I say.

"My mom was here?" she grumbles, not pleased.

"Yes, she wants you to dress up for your picture."

Janelle smacks her palm with her fist. "She's always telling me what to do. I don't care about my picture."

This is the first time I've seen Janelle angry. "Let's talk," I urge, and usher her into my office.

Once we're seated and the door is closed, I continue. "OK, so you don't care, but your mom wants a nice picture of you. Does she give them out to relatives...hang them on the wall?"

"All of that...but since my brother...she doesn't let up on me."

She slumps in the chair and a solitary tear slips down her cheek.

"I'm sorry, Janelle. This has been a tough year for you and your parents. Have you talked to a counselor about any of this?"

It's another referral to the wonderful Amy, who will listen to Janelle's complaints about her mom and probably talk to the parent about giving Janelle some space. I persuade the girl to come in for the shirt when her PE class is called for pictures. Then she can change out of it as soon as her picture is taken.

Chapter 23

Everybody wins.

By lunch, I'm exhausted from chasing down staff members and going back and forth from the office to the gym, a distance of nearly a city block. The kids, animated after getting gussied up and having their moment under the lights, need supervision. There's a ruckus across the yard and I go to see what's up.

Darlene Glass has come to school in a party dress, which should make a nice photo. She sits at a picnic table with a couple of girls, surrounded by a group of standing boys.

One boy laughs hard and then teases. "Wooo, Darlene, you look so gorgeous...like a five-year-old."

Another chimes in, "Yeah, you should be in kindergarten where you can play with dolls."

Darlene brushes something off her skirt—the boys are spitting sunflower seed shells at her. Her face is blanched and tight.

A girl at the table yells at the boys, "Back off, douchebags."

"All right, guys," I say, "unless you're looking to spend time in detention, go somewhere else. And ladies, watch the language."

Darlene looks up at me, tears in her eyes. "Mom will kill me if my dress is dirty." Something about the way she says the words suggests they're not a euphemism. Her eyes have a pleading quality.

"Darlene, why don't you go wait for me at my office so we can talk, OK?" She nods, gathers her lunch things, and moves slowly in that direction.

When lunch ends, I'm ready to question Darlene. "What's going on at home?" I ask, settling into the chair next to her. Her tears flow again and I put my arm around her.

"My mom...she gets...so angry. At every little thing."

"Like what?"

"Well, if I don't wash the dishes right after dinner, she threatens to whup me."

183

"And does she...whup you?"

"Sometimes."

"And how does she do that?"

"With an old belt that Dad left."

"And where on your body does she hit you with the belt?"

Darlene sobs. I give her a sideways hug.

"It's OK, Darlene. I just want to help."

"Will you tell Mom I told you?"

"I won't tell her, but I have to call Children's Protective Services. They'll probably contact your mom. But they know how to do that so she won't hit you again."

The crying continues quietly. "She whups me on my back."

"OK, sweetie. I'm so sorry. If I looked at your back, would there be marks there?"

"Yeah, probably."

Darlene is too upset to go back to class, so I let her sit with a book in the outer office while I call CPS. Here I go again. Soon they'll know me by my first name. They're too short-staffed to send someone today, but make it clear I should not let the child go home until the situation is checked out. At their direction, I call the police. The switchboard tells me they'll send a youth officer before the end of the day.

In the meantime, I have one more picture day nightmare to get through—the eighth-grade photo. The teachers have cooked up the idea of having a middle fold spread in the yearbook of all one hundred eighty-nine eighth-graders. We can sell prints to make extra money. It will be a unique remembrance for the kids. The photographer has set up risers on the field so that we can have three or four rows of kids standing in the picture. At two o'clock, I make the announcement: "All eighth-grade classes, please come out onto the baseball field."

The teachers try to keep their groups together, but the noise level is off the charts. Kids stand in clusters, moving around, as

Chapter 23

this age group always does—no quiet waiting in line for them. Using my trusty megaphone, I ask each homeroom group to come forward as soon as the photographer is ready to place them on the risers.

"Mr. Sheldon's homeroom, you're next," I shout. They move like turtles. The boys elbow each other; the girls smooth their hair.

The photographer calmly separates each group by height and tells them where to stand or sit. "Tall boys, over here. You guys, come up front."

The din of eighth-graders who think they're ready for high school is alarming.

"Yo, Joey, nice shirt!"

"Don't push me!"

"Get out of my way!"

We finally have all the kids on the risers, but they're facing different directions, talking and laughing. "Hey, eighth grade," I yell through the megaphone. No change. "Eighth-graders, we need you to stop talking and look at the camera!" The short kids in the front row are now looking at me; the ones in the back are still punching each other and talking. I'm waiting for someone to fall off a riser. I've had it. What a day.

I scream into the megaphone, "SHUT UP!"

Silence happens, but I'd better take advantage of it quickly. "Thank you. Now please listen to the photographer and remember, if you make any funny finger gestures, you'll be erased from the picture!" As if on cue, Carlson strides over from the office, positioning himself at the end of the first row. He never misses a chance to pretend he's involved.

The photographer knows how to handle kids. He takes many shots, including a couple where he says, "Let's see your grumpy look" and "How will you look on the last day of school?" At last the teachers lead them back to class and I return to the office.

185

Darlene sits holding her book. Gaby has the phone to her ear, but motions for me to wait. She hangs up.

"Officer Keaton is on her way," she says, "a woman."

There are only twenty minutes left until the end of the school day. "How do you get home, Darlene?" I ask.

She straightens up in the chair, but looks at me with brows knit, eyes searching. "My mom picks me up."

"OK. Someone is coming to talk to you. Come into my office."

The officer arrives and the two of us sit down with Darlene. The uniformed policewoman, in her forties, has a soft, encouraging voice and dark hair pulled back in a ponytail.

Darlene repeats what she told me about her mother hitting her with a belt.

"When was the last time this happened?" asks Officer Keaton.

"A couple of days ago, I think." Darlene speaks clearly, without emotion, but she keeps glancing at the clock on the wall and then at me.

Officer Keaton continues. "Darlene, would you unzip the back of your dress? Just the top, so I can see if there are marks? Ms. Walker will stay here. And don't worry about your mother. I'll talk to her when she gets here."

I pull down the rarely used shades on my windows and door. I've examined kids' arms for marks in the past, but I would never do this kind of inspection on my own. I'm shocked to see Darlene's back covered with horizontal lines. Most of them are old brown scars in her skin, but others are still red and in a couple of places where the skin has been broken, there are scabs.

"OK, Darlene," the officer continues, zipping up Darlene's dress. "I'm so glad you told Ms. Walker about this. I'm going to make sure it doesn't happen again. You're not going to go home

Chapter 23

with Mom today, but you'll come with me to a safe place."

Darlene slumps in the chair, hugging herself. The next thing I know there is a noisy commotion outside my door. Darlene puts her hands over her ears and makes herself small. Lifting the edge of the shade, I see a woman who I presume is Darlene's mother, arguing with Gaby. She's young—late twenties—with dark, angry eyes. She towers over petite Gaby, but what my wonderful clerk lacks in height, she makes up for in attitude.

"You can't go in there."

"Don't you tell me what I can do."

"That's exactly what I'm doing!"

Thank God for the police. The officer goes out to talk to the mother. They must go into another room, because it gets very quiet. I pull up a chair next to Darlene, who has removed her hands from her ears, but is still slumped over.

"The officer will take good care of you, Darlene. It's going to be OK."

Officer Keaton comes back in. Darlene sits up and looks expectantly at the policewoman.

"Your mom is going home. We'll talk to her in a little while to help her understand that she can't hit you with the belt anymore. You and I will go down to the police station and then you'll have a nice family to stay with tonight while we sort this out."

I expect Darlene will stay in a foster home until the authorities determine they can safely send her home. My heart breaks for her, but it's the best the system can do.

After Darlene and the officer depart, I'm at my desk writing up the report for CPS. Carlson bursts in, bounces over to me and slams his fist down on the desk. "My office, now!" He turns and storms out.

My mouth hangs open. I can't imagine what has upset him. Nor can I believe he's treating me this way in front of the office staff, who are preparing to leave for the day. Totally unnerved, I follow him to his office. Gaby and Sharon sit wide-eyed at their desks, watching.

As soon as I close the door to his office, he yells, "You called the police without telling me?" His red, sweaty face appears apoplectic. We face off, standing about three feet apart.

For the first time, I raise my voice to match his. "CPS told me to."

Still angry, he shouts, "I don't want cops on my campus without knowing what's going on. I have parents calling me, asking what's happening."

"Well, this is a confidential matter, isn't it, when they take someone into protective custody?" I haven't attempted to mask my sarcasm.

"I don't care about confidentiality. You have to tell me what's happening."

He has gone too far. How can he say such a thing when he never does anything but sit in his office, entertain parents, and go home for naps? I'm shaken by what I have witnessed with Darlene and exhausted from a long, trying day.

"Look, John, I'm handling all of the discipline, all of the student problems. When am I supposed to fill you in?" Once again, this man has me on the verge of tears, struggling to hold it together.

"Before you leave here every day, I want to know what has happened."

My hands clench and I shout, "Well, great, if I can find you!"

There's a long pause while he glares at me. I'm shaking. He walks to his desk, sits down and looks up at me. Suddenly his tone is soft. "You realize I am your supervisor, right?"

I get the message and mirror his tone. "Yes, but it's been a very long day. Can we talk about this tomorrow?"

He wipes his moist brow and smiles. Relishing his power

188

Chapter 23

and my discomfort? If only I cared more about what he thinks of me or felt the deference he craves. God save me.

As I walk back down the hall, it appears everyone has left. They surely heard us yelling at each other. After this day, I need a drink and a friend. Before I leave for home, I call Derek. An hour later, he rings my doorbell, carrying pizza and a bottle of wine.

"My favorite person," I say and inhale deeply. "Something smells delicious."

Once inside, Derek puts down what he's carrying and hugs me. "At your service, Madam."

"Mmmm, I needed that an hour ago."

We settle at the dining table.

"So, what's going on?" he asks.

I tell Darlene's story without mentioning her name and fill him in on the fight with Carlson.

"Poor you," Derek says. "The guy sounds unhinged."

"We'll see what happens tomorrow."

I feel a bit better after dinner but am painfully aware I could lose my job. Or this fight might spur Carlson to talk to the district about Derek and me. Derek hangs out until my yawns are back-to-back.

In the morning, Gaby greets me with a serious look, her eyebrows raised. "Is everything OK?" she asks. I nod and smile, but shrug, as if to say, "Who knows?"

I walk down to Carlson's office. Door open, he's having coffee with a parent, but pauses. With a tone that is brisk but not angry, he calls out, "Please come back in thirty minutes."

When I return, the parent has gone. Carlson remains in the armchair at the back of his office and points me to the sofa.

"Feeling better today?" he asks and offers a plate of pastries.

"Yes—no thanks—but there are several things I'd like to talk about besides yesterday."

189

"OK, but first, at the end of every day, I want you to jot me an email with any happenings that involve the cops, or someone likely to be angry or make a scene."

I sigh. "I can do that. We haven't been doing our weekly conferences."

"You're right. Let's do that again." He helps himself to a pastry and spills powdered sugar down his shirt and tie.

I'm not done. "So, have you thought at all about Ginny and whether we should check for booze in her classroom?"

"Oh, yeah. No, that's a tough one." He's trying to brush the sugar off, but it smears.

"Just so you know, her mid-year evaluation wasn't good. She won't—or can't—do the things I'm suggesting."

"OK, I'll talk to her." He grabs a yellow pad and pen from the coffee table and jots something down. I have no confidence he'll follow up.

"What about that dinner?" he asks. "I'm being patient with you... for now. Still seeing Simons?"

"My personal life is none of your business, John. You're going to talk to the district when I could just as easily tell them you're pressuring me for a date?"

"You think they'd believe you?"

"I've got to go." I go back to work, relieved he hasn't fired me on the spot. I'm proud I stood up to him again. But am I going to make it to the end of the school year?

No matter what happens, Derek has become my new best friend, someone I count on for support when there's trouble. Being Carlson's VP is lonely. I can vent with Gaby, but worry she'll repeat things she hears from me. Derek is the only one at school I can confide in. I trust him to keep the things I share to himself. But I'm worried about what isn't happening between us. We're becoming such good friends, is he looking for romance elsewhere? I certainly have no reason to expect anything else. I could just ask him, but perhaps I'd rather not hear the answer.

CHAPTER TWENTY-FOUR
SURPRISE, SURPRISE!

I HAVEN'T SPENT AN AFTERNOON OR EVENING with my friends Pam and Erica for ages. But we set aside a Saturday afternoon in March for a movie matinee and early dinner. Pam will still get home to put the kids to bed. We argue over which movie to see—a popular chick flick or the indie foreign film with rave reviews. We let the show times make the decision—indie foreign—as a three o'clock film gets us out in time for dinner without having to fight crowds or make reservations. We like the Thai place close to the movie theater. The film turns out to be a tear-jerker about twin sisters separated at birth.

We're leaving the theater when I almost choke. Coming out the door, with his arm around a lovely woman, is Derek. He's looking at her and talking, so doesn't see me. I take off, jogging towards the restaurant, and only stop to wait for my friends when I can see that Derek and his date are not coming our way.

"What's with you?" asks Erica.

"Oh, my God, it's Derek...with a date." I groan. "A cute date."

We get to the restaurant and settle in, but my day has been ruined.

"It's no big deal," says Pam.

Erica adds, "You don't know she's his date."

They try to engage me in analyzing the film, but I'm totally bummed. Derek is seeing someone else and I'm history.

I haven't stopped thinking about it on Monday. From the moment I arrive at school, I avoid Derek at all costs. I am no good at hiding my feelings. He'll know something is wrong and I won't be able to explain. I steer clear of his room all day and avoid the teachers' room during his lunch and preparation periods. That's good, but there's more stress coming, thanks to Carlson.

Now accustomed to dealing with difficult parents, I have no qualms when Carlson asks me to be around for a late afternoon parent conference. Silly me.

"What's it about?" I ask.

"It's an ugly custody battle and I've asked both parents to be here to talk with me. The mom wants to move the boy to another school and the dad and I are trying to persuade her to leave him here."

"Who's the boy?"

"Ignatius...I think his first name is David."

I don't know him. I agree it's not a good time of year to change schools. Spring break is coming up, followed by state testing. Then only two months remain until summer vacation. That would be a better time for a change, but maybe the mother has a good reason to move him now.

The conference is at 4:30, when the office and grounds are empty. I walk towards John's office and hear shouting. On the front lawn, a man and a woman are screaming at each other.

"John, is this them?" He comes out of his office.

"Damn, let's try to settle them down."

As we open the door, the woman, about five feet tall, starts pushing the guy, who is a lot taller.

"You can't tell me what to do with my son," she shouts.

He moves closer to her and grabs one of her wrists.

"Guys," Carlson says, "guys, let's go inside."

The man lets go of the woman's wrist and turns to John.

Chapter 24

"She won't listen."

Carlson manages to get his bulk between them.

"Cynthia, why don't you take Mrs. Ignatius inside and Dad and I will chat out here."

I am thinking this is all a very bad idea and maybe I should call the cops. But I take her arm gently and lead her towards the building.

"That son of a bitch isn't getting my boy if I have a breath left in me to fight," she mutters, hands on hips. I ask her to sit down in John's office, but she won't sit.

"Look," I say. "Can you tell me why you want to move David?"

She takes a deep breath and lowers her arms. "Because it's hard for me to get him here and get to work on time. If he were at Washington, it would make it so much easier on the days he's with me."

"I see. And I guess Hamilton works better for his dad?"

"Yes, that bastard..."

"Look, Mrs. Ignatius, we'll do whatever you and his dad agree on. It might be easier on David to stay here until June, but I understand your problem."

She keeps talking about how difficult this divorce has been and how she wants what's best for her son, but she can't be late for work every day, yada, yada, yada. I got the point a long time ago. She finally sits down.

"Just a minute," I say and go to check on the other half of the problem. It looks like the dad has also calmed down. I crack the door and poke my head out.

"You want to come in now?" I ask. Carlson looks at the dad, who nods. They step inside and approach Carlson's office. Before I can say one word, the mom is on her feet again and shouting at her ex.

"I'm going to call my lawyer and file for sole custody. You

can't do this to me." She lunges and takes a swing at the dad, just missing his chin. Carlson once again gets between them.

This is enough. I go to the phone and dial 9-1-1. "We have an altercation between two adults in the Hamilton Middle School office. We need help."

Despite their shouting, all parties seem to have heard this. They are now silent. The dad heads for the door, repeating "Sorry, sorry," I presume to John and me. The mom goes right after him still shouting obscenities.

They're outside now yelling at each other. We watch as the police car arrives. Two officers emerge, a man and a woman. Mr. and Mrs. Ignatius stop their rants long enough to listen. Soon they get in their cars and drive away. The male officer comes to the door. I go out to greet him. John is already back in his office on the phone.

"They would benefit from some counseling," the officer says and smiles.

"Really," I respond. "That was a bit scary."

"Probably not a good idea to try to handle this at school."

I look towards John's office. He's still on the phone.

"I'll pass that along," I say.

"Do you have any other concerns?" he asks. I shake my head.

"Don't hesitate to call us when you need us," the officer says, and departs.

LESSON #11: YOU CAN'T SOLVE EVERY PROBLEM.

I walk back down the hall to my office, a headache starting. That was scary and a waste of time. Carlson should never have thought he could manage this kind of encounter. I'm gathering up my laptop and purse when he appears at my door. What now?

Chapter 24

"Cynthia..."
"Yeah?"
"That was awful. I need to unwind. Can we go somewhere and talk?"

I look at my watch. Unwinding sounds like a good idea, even if it's with the guy responsible for the stress. I must be forgetting his previous attempts to get me alone and the looming demand for dinner, because I hear myself say, "OK, but not the Watering Hole."

"How about Rosetti's? We can have a drink in their lounge. Very respectable."

I consent and follow him in my car, thinking up an excuse for leaving after one drink. Would he believe I have choir practice?

Their bar is a comfy area adjacent to the dining room. Soft music, sofas, and chairs around tiny tables, carpeted floor. Very soothing. I slide onto a sofa and sink in. To my dismay, Carlson slides in beside me. Will this guy never give up? I should have chosen a chair. I drag myself farther away. He orders beer for him and wine for me.

"So, John, I made a mental note to never deal with warring parents again. I'm going to tell Gaby, if a parent becomes violent, don't wait for me to tell you, just dial 9-1-1."

"Yeah, I thought I could persuade the mom to leave the kid here," says John.

"That's a discussion for the lawyers."

"I guess. So, no other police reports?"

"Not this week," I smile and lift my glass of wine.

He asks another question. "You're enjoying yourself?" Is he asking about the job or life in general? What is it he wants? Is he hoping I'll talk about Derek?

"It's mostly good. Exhausting, but good."

He may have an agenda, but I have no clue what it might be. "I'm glad you're enjoying it. Cynthia...I wish we had more

195

time to talk. I think you're pretty special."

"John, don't..."

"Don't worry. I just don't have anyone to talk to."

"About what?" He wants to confide in me?

"About anything."

"Don't you have a wife?"

"Hah, that's a good one. Things aren't good at home. My in-laws are always stirring things up."

I ask, "What about all the parents and politicians you hang out with?"

"They're not really friends...I need...a friend." He looks at me with puppy-dog eyes. Is he kidding?

"Have you tried a therapist? You know, a person you pay to listen to your problems who isn't part of them. I can't do that for you, John...I mean...you're my boss."

He whines a bit more and I suggest he ask Amy to refer him to a marriage and family therapist. He'll probably try to unload on Amy. Ugh. I tell him I have a book group to get to. That's sort of the truth—I have a book group, but it's tomorrow, not tonight. Maybe I should finish reading the book.

He frowns when I put a ten-dollar bill on the table, preparing to make my escape. This was a business meeting, not a date. Everyone has a burden of some kind, but I'm not taking on Carlson's. I'm still crushed that Derek is seeing someone else. I had such high hopes. He was so perfect for me. And I risked my job security for a relationship that now seems to be over.

MY BIRTHDAY FALLS IN MARCH, although I have no desire to share that information. One of the teachers keeps track of staff birthdays and delivers a cupcake to each person on their special day. That's enough. If the students or parents know it's my birthday, there will be some combination of gifts and pranks. Derek did once ask for my birthdate, but he

196

Chapter 24

probably has forgotten—or no longer cares. I haven't talked to him since seeing him at the movies.

On my birthday I wake up thinking there won't be any special attention—beyond a cupcake—coming my way. Before leaving for school, I study myself in the mirror. You know, that now-I'm-a-year-older examination. My brown hair has new grey strands and I'm sure I see the beginnings of crow's feet, but the changes are minor. The job is challenging, and Carlson is obnoxious and incompetent, but I'm learning to work around him. My social life could be better, but you can't have everything.

There's a strange smile on Sharon's face when I walk into the office, and I hear Gaby tittering as I walk down the hall. She and the attendance clerk, Roxanne, are standing by their desks with big grins and I can't figure out what's going on until I turn to my office. Through the glass windows and door, I see that the entire space is filled with balloons. Black balloons from ceiling to floor. When she catches her breath from laughing, Gaby says, "*Feliz cumpleaños.* Happy birthday. I don't know who did it. It wasn't me."

Is this funny or annoying? I'm not sure which. When I open the door, a couple of balloons float out. The helium-filled escapees float to the ceiling directly above Gaby. I push more of them towards the doorway but can't get to my desk. Roxanne is taking video with her phone.

"Oh, well." I finally laugh and smile for the camera. Soon teachers come by to join the party. Derek is in the group and gives me a sideways hug.

"Did you have anything to do with this?" I ask.

"Me? I'm sworn to secrecy. But when you find your desk, there's something from me."

Soon it's time for them all to go to class and I move enough balloons out to get to my desk, where I find a vase of ruby-red

197

tulips. The card from Derek reads *Wishing you the best birthday ever! Dinner out Saturday?* I slip the card into my purse and sit down with that dark cloud of balloons over my head, confused. He still likes me. But who was that other woman?

Gaby comes in with a tray of something that smells sweet and delicious.

"I made you my pineapple tamales—only for special occasions. Happy birthday!"

I get up and give her a hug. "Thanks, Gaby. *You* are what's special."

I peel back the corn husk and take a bite. Sweet, but not too sweet. The combination of corn *masa* and *piña* is wonderful. Soon Sharon and Carlson join us for a little party. Maybe public birthday celebrations aren't so bad after all.

As they're on their way out, carrying extra tamales to munch on later, Carlson turns back and asks, "How about a birthday drink later?"

"John, I just can't..."

"OK, OK," he mutters and stomps down the hall.

Later in the day, when I open my mail, I have to catch my breath. In January, I learned that the Rotary Club was seeking a Grand Marshal for the Founder's Day parade in May. With the wild idea that we could select a Hamilton student for the honor, I filled out an application. And promptly forgot about it. Now I've got great news. What a lovely birthday I'm having!

It's after lunch and Gaby is away from her desk. I float down the hall to Carlson's office. His door is closed. Sharon sees me bouncing up and down, letter in hand, probably looking like a kid who has found a huge stash of candy.

"He's in there, but he's with Mrs. Rogers," she says. "Do you..."

"I'll come back," I answer and run off.

I walk around the grounds, considering the best way to pick

Chapter 24

one student to lead the parade. The theme is "Proud of My Town, Proud of My Country." I like the idea of a written competition. The essay should demonstrate strong emotions, showing the topic is truly special to the student. I make my way back to the office and find Carlson free.

"John, this is really good news." I slap the open letter down on the desk in front of him.

He looks it over and then up at me. I'm bouncing from foot to foot.

"Founder's Day, huh? Sounds good. We could have one of our super athletes do it. Someone like the Rogers boy, what's his name?"

"Joel." The son of the parent who just left his office. Joel happens to be a great basketball player.

"No, John, there's no reason for it be an athlete. And it has to be a fair process. I'm thinking of an essay contest."

"Well, OK. Keep me informed. And be sure to tell the newspaper."

It's still my birthday, and as many surprises as I've already had, it's not over yet. I haven't had a moment to analyze the tulips and card from Derek. I stop by his room after school to thank him, but he's not there. Was he just being nice? Buttering up the VP? But the dinner invitation says it's more than that. We haven't been on a date for several weeks, and now that I've seen him out with someone else, it doesn't make sense. Who was she? If he doesn't tell me, I'll have to ask. That question will be sure to keep me awake tonight.

The phone rings as soon as I get home. Birthday greetings from my parents, then Shelly. My Facebook page overflows with birthday wishes. There are people who love me, after all. Tonight, Erica is cooking a birthday dinner for me and a few teachers from my former school, a reunion of sorts. I bring a nice bottle of wine and look forward to getting Erica's take on Derek.

The former colleagues talk about their students and principals, like the old days. I share a few of my own stories. There are gifts and cake and lots of laughter. It's a lovely evening, but I can't wait for everyone to leave so I can talk to Erica.

"He gave me red roses and a card and asked for a dinner date Saturday. What does it mean?"

"You doofus, it means he really likes you, Cynthia."

"But that other woman…"

"Look, he hasn't promised to date you exclusively. Or maybe she was just a friend."

"Or maybe I'm a friend, dinner included."

"Well, you're going to find out Saturday. Take a breath, girl."

Granted, it's Wednesday and I'll know soon enough. But it's a long time until Saturday when your heart is in a vise.

Derek calls to firm up the time and place. After I thank him for the flowers, I ask, "Is this dress-up, Derek?" It's a fancy restaurant and maybe our usual casual style isn't enough. "I guess I'm asking, are you wearing a sport coat?"

"Yeah," he says. "I thought we'd make it special…for your birthday."

I picture my embarrassment if Derek were to arrive and find me wearing jeans and a sweater. This new wrinkle requires a Friday evening trip to my favorite boutique. I find a dress that's simple but flattering, in a dark green that accentuates my hazel eyes. "God, Cynthia, you have really lost it," I mutter, as I pay the bill.

He picks me up on time and starts with a hug. I'm a little stiff, but he seems not to notice. At the restaurant, we sit at a corner table in candlelight and listen to soft music. The wine relaxes me as we chat about school, his mentoring of Dunning, and a bit about Crazy Carlson. As I'm working on my entrée, a perfectly cooked piece of salmon on a bed of delicious veggies

200

Chapter 24

that I can't name, I finally have to get it over with.

"Derek, I saw you a couple of weeks ago at the movie theater."

"Really? Why didn't you say hello?"

"Um, I was with my friends and we had to get to dinner... who were you with?"

"The French film? Wasn't it wonderful? Let's see, that was Becky." I must be giving him a strange look because he keeps going. "Becky, my sister Becky."

"Oh." I'm sure I'm as red as a beet.

"Did you think...?"

"I didn't know what to think. I'm the one who has put you off. Silly me, so worried about my job. You can certainly be seeing other people...for whatever reasons..." I'm staring at my salmon now, both hands on the table.

Derek puts down his fork and places one hand over mine. "Hey, birthday girl. Let me be clear. I'm not interested in seeing anybody else. It's you I want...and I'll wait."

I look up at him, wide-eyed and melting like the wax candle between us.

I can only smile the smile of maidens rescued from the railroad tracks seconds before the train arrives.

"Tell me about your sister," I say.

Derek tells me about his younger sister Becky, who likes skiing and computer programming. And he invites me to Easter dinner with his family. The rest of the evening speeds by and our goodnight kiss feels like the beginning of a new chapter.

201

CHAPTER TWENTY-FIVE
IT MIGHT AS WELL BE SPRING

EASTER FALLS IN THE FIRST WEEK OF APRIL. Anticipating "dinner with the parents" keeps me awake at night, as I wonder what Derek has told them about me. But his commitment to our relationship, no matter how slow I want it to go, has a positive effect. I'm newly confident in him—in us as a couple—and I look forward to meeting the folks who hatched this lovely man.

I fuss over choosing an outfit and a hostess gift. I don't want to overdo it but need to make a good impression. I choose a skirt and blouse and purchase artisan chocolates. Derek is bringing flowers for his mom.

We drive an hour and a half to Gold Country. It's where gold was discovered, starting an onslaught of migrants to California in the 1840s. I once panned for gold at a place where they added gold flakes to the trough, so if you worked at it, you'd have a worthless sample to take home.

Derek is behind the wheel. He talks about school events coming up before spring break. We've both volunteered—in my case it was more like having my arm twisted—for the dunk tank at the school carnival. He tells me how much fun it is to be soaked by students. I have my doubts.

I'm still excited about the Founder's Day essay contest. The teachers have recruited the English department to help.

They'll announce it in their classes, collect submissions, and select finalists. I'll pick the winner. The teachers have promised to get the finalists' essays to me right after spring break. I ask Derek what he thinks.

"I've heard the kids talking about it," he says. "Sounds like they all want to do it."

"Great. I hope they won't be too disappointed when we pick one winner. Maybe there's a way to share the essays with the community."

"You could approach the newspaper and see if they'd be willing to run some of the best ones," he suggests.

"Excellent idea. I'll do that."

I need to talk about Ginny Stein and Carlson's apathy. "I don't want to give you all the details, but I have some major concerns about Ginny."

"You mean her drinking?"

"OK, so it's not a secret. But that's not all of it. Why is Carlson so hesitant to take action when a teacher is clearly in trouble?"

"Well, I once heard that John and Ginny had an affair way back when. Just a rumor."

"That would explain a lot. He *is* still married, right?" Carlson's mention of his wife over drinks didn't provide much information. Not that I wanted to hear it. And that sterile home environment provided no clues.

Derek answers, "He never talks about his wife or family."

"Don't you think that's weird?"

I'll have to ponder Carlson's marriage another time. Derek pulls off the road and up a driveway in the woods. His parents have retired to a home fashioned out of logs. The air, cooled by the forest canopy, holds scents of pine needles and wood smoke. Becky comes out to greet us, reminding me of my shock when I saw her with Derek at the movie theater.

Chapter 25

"So nice to finally meet you," she says. "I've heard lots."

"All good, I hope. You too—I understand you're quite the skier."

Inside, Derek introduces me to Helen and Ray Simons. They're younger than my parents. She's petite and makeup-free, very wholesome. He's the source of Derek's green eyes, with greying hair, still a good-looking man. They greet me with warm smiles and Derek hugs them both, giving his mom a big smack on the cheek. Ray shakes my hand and promptly offers a mimosa before dinner. You've got to love a man who has a good relationship with his parents. We eat ham, asparagus, and potatoes. They ask about school and we both share amusing anecdotes.

"Where did you grow up?" I ask Helen.

"Los Angeles, but then I met Ray and he persuaded me to move north. I was a high school teacher."

That may explain Derek's natural skills and dedication to teaching.

Over homemade lemon meringue pie and coffee, Ray, who owned his own automotive business, asks me, "So what's it like being Derek's boss?"

"He's such a wonderful teacher, it's easy." Well, yeah, except for the specter of a sexual harassment accusation by Carlson.

We stroll around the property after dinner. Helen shows me the vegetable garden she is preparing for planting. The piney air reminds me of a childhood park that I loved. Soon it's time for us to depart. Hugs all around. Becky promises to be in touch.

Back in the car, I tell Derek how much I like his family. "They don't hug just anyone," he says. Derek puts the radio on a classical station and we're quiet for most of the ride home. He takes my hand and I lean back and close my eyes. I've always thought being comfortable enough with someone to be happy without talking is a blessing. I've been smitten for a long time, but am I actually falling in love? What a perfect spring this could turn out to be.

BERT SHELDON IS AN ACE at keeping it interesting in his classroom. Hence his annual egg drop. The teacher challenges each eighth-grader to create a container that will keep a raw egg from breaking when Sheldon drops it from the school roof, a fall of some thirty feet. I think the project is a good one, scientifically and educationally. What bugs me as I watch it in real time is that the other teachers feel free to bring their classes out to watch. All day long. Does he encourage this so sixth- and seventh-graders will work up enthusiasm for being in his class? Am I being uptight about something that's good for kids? Perhaps the vice principal is just cranky today. And has anyone ever questioned the advisability of Sheldon—the fire and heart attack guy—climbing up a ladder to stand on the roof?

For the third time today, I abandon the more important tasks I should be doing—returning parent calls, observing teachers, seeing students. Time to supervise another egg drop. It rained overnight, and close to midday the pavement is still wet. The target Sheldon painted on the surface has not completely bled out and features smeared raw eggs from an earlier period. A crowd gathers as Sheldon waits on the roof, for dramatic effect. He wears a baseball cap—to protect his balding head? With his jeans and tee shirt, he looks a lot like a student. Wait. Two students are also on the wet roof. Has the man completely lost his mind? The two boys are lining up student-created egg packages, high above me.

I get as close as possible, directly below where the teacher stands. "Bert," I call up to him. He doesn't hear me. The crowd is too noisy. Or maybe he doesn't want to hear me.

"Bert," louder this time. Where's that megaphone when I need it? I give up on the teacher and focus on the kids.

206

Chapter 25

I ask one of the eighth-graders, "Who are those two boys on the roof?" I get their names and move as close as I can to where they're standing above me.

I belt out, "John, Davey, get down from there right now!" One throws up his arms in disgust and my lip-reading skills tell me there's some cussing going on, but both boys move towards the top of the ladder.

Now Sheldon sees me. He shrugs. I grab the bottom of the ladder to steady it while each boy climbs down, yelling "Wait," when Davey starts to get on the ladder before John is all the way off. "You guys," I say, full of relief but pissed at the same time, "you do not belong on the roof, *ever*, got that?"

"Yes, Miss Walker," they both grumble and join their classmates as the event begins.

The crowd quiets and Sheldon says something self-important about all he has taught the kids about gravity and the strength of an eggshell. He tosses the first package, a Styrofoam cube with inflated balloons tied around it. It bounces a couple of times and stops. The student engineer removes the balloons and tape holding the Styrofoam together. *Voila.* The egg is intact. The audience cheers. The next egg package is a cardboard box. When it hits the ground, it opens and spills pieces of foam, packing peanuts, and a broken egg.

"Aww," moans the crowd. The third egg comes out of its packaging and goes splat on the pavement. The next student up is Antonio. His egg contraption uses Styrofoam and plastic air pillows. Looks good, but the egg breaks. By the time they're done, six or seven broken eggs and assorted packaging material cover the target. Creators of the few surviving egg transports will be lauded back in the classroom. What a mess. Poor Joe, the custodian. I'll remember to thank him; will Sheldon do the same?

I make a mental note to talk to Carlson about why teachers

207

feel free to abandon their work and transform their students into Sheldon's fan base. Perhaps before next year's event there might be guidelines limiting the invitees.

NEXT UP IS THE SPRING CARNIVAL, hosted by the Hamilton parent club. With longer, warmer days, students' families are invited to play games, eat junk food, and raise money for the school. The Student Council runs a face-painting booth, a hit with elementary-school siblings, and art and shop teachers sell student projects prepared especially for the carnival. What parent can say no to purchasing their darling's framed art?

As I'm strolling by the tables and canopies, enjoying colorful displays of food and games, a mom approaches, eager to report a problem.

"They're harassing the kids helping in the booths, trying to get free food, and just being a pain," she says. "There…" she adds, as Jimmy Green and Kevin race by, carrying cotton candy.

I thank her and follow them to the other side of campus, where I find them bent over laughing, holding their cones of cotton candy high.

"That was so bad," shouts Jimmy, in between convulsions of laughter.

"Hi, guys," I say. "And did you purchase your cotton candy?"

"The girls gave it to us," says Kevin.

"Shall I go check with them? Are they going to say they offered it to you?"

"Whatever," says Jimmy and starts eating his. Perhaps he plans to wolf it down before I take it away.

After a quick check to confirm that the boys are here without their parents, and they bullied the girls into giving them samples, I take the culprits into my office.

"You're done here," I say.

Chapter 25

I call both parents. Mrs. Green sounds weary on the other end of the call. "OK, I'll come and get him."

I wait for the boys to be whisked away before returning to the carnival. Several parents approach me to ask about the Founder's Day essays.

"Ms. Walker, Jacob is so excited about Founder's Day. Any hints about what you're looking for in the essays?"

Is this mother going to write it herself? "We're looking for someone whose thoughts on pride really mean a lot. The most compelling reason for leading the parade will win."

A small group of parents has gathered. One man comments, "No matter who wins, it's a tribute to the school."

"Wonderful," I say as I move on. It's time for me to make an official appearance.

Two parts of the carnival I'm not looking forward to are the dunk tank and the sponge throw. Of course, I have been asked to donate my body to the cause. First, I will sit on a platform in my bathing suit above a tank of water, waiting to see if those who have bought tickets hit the right button with a heavy beanbag. If they succeed, I'll drop into the water below. I've never done this before and do not look forward to my virgin voyage. The one upside is that Derek is doing it too. So maybe we'll have to go home together all wet and need to strip down to dry off and... sorry, back to the carnival.

The second event I've been talked into requires me to stand in a refrigerator box with an opening for my head. At a distance of about ten feet, ticket holders will throw wet sponges at my mug. I'm not sure about this one. I figure it's a bit like pie in the face, but with nothing delicious to lick up. Administrator abuse seems to be a popular pastime today. But these events raise much-needed funds for the school, so I'm a willing victim.

I'm doing the sponge throw first. That way any water dripping from me will prepare me nicely for the dunk tank. The

209

huge industrial sponge, the kind you might use to wash your car, sits in a bucket of water. I imagine it holds a pint or more. The parent in charge apologizes as she places a hairdresser's cape over my clothes.

"So sorry, Ms. Walker. Thanks for doing this."

I can only smile as she ushers me into the box, painted to look like a puppet theater. On the front in bold red letters it sports: *Face Off—show them what you think!* Oy, as my grandmother would say. The first few people who step up are sixth-graders. They're laughing but you can tell they're shy about throwing something at the woman who's in charge of discipline.

"It's OK, guys. Let's find out how this works." The first two throws fall short of the box. I get an idea of how much water the sponge holds. A lot. The kids giggle. Now there is surely dirt mixed with the water.

"Sorry," I call out. "Try again, guys!"

A woman I don't know approaches. She escorts a group of teens who are all busy looking at their phones.

"Let's try this one," she says and exchanges her ticket for the sponge. "Here goes." She tosses the sponge underhand. It bounces off my chin and back out to the ground. Not bad.

"Come on, Mom, let us try," says one of her youngsters.

"One more," she says, and throws the second one with more force, but still underhand. This time it hits my forehead and spills its contents down my nose and chin. I'm blinking like crazy.

I ask the mom in charge, "Is it cheating if I duck?"

She laughs. The teens step up, grinning.

"Did you go to school here?" I ask.

"Yeah, we graduated last year. How come Carlson isn't in there?"

"I don't know, but I'm the nice vice principal."

I'm still grinning when the first sponge comes straight as an

Chapter 25

arrow—if an arrow could be filled with water—and hits me smack on the nose, exploding the sandy solution all over me. And it hurts.

The kid's friends are laughing and shouting, "Way to go, Bruce! My turn!"

"How much longer do I have?" I whine, while the mom reloads the sponge.

"A little longer."

After ten minutes of this, I feel I have been assaulted. This is no fun. I get out, dry off, and decide on a bite to eat before I hit the dunk tank. Hot dog and soda in hand, I walk to the tank to observe. I find Derek sitting on the platform. He's positioned a couple of feet above a tank holding about four feet of water. He looks very cute in his long swimming trunks and tee shirt. The students have lined up to wait their turns and he taunts them.

"Come on, guys, you couldn't hit that if you tried ten times!" He says this just before one of the big eighth-graders hits the button solidly with the heavy beanbag and Derek drops, with a huge splash, into the chest-high water. He is now drenched from his head on down. I decide to keep my tennis shoes on, to cushion the impact. I wave at Derek, who has climbed back up on the platform and still grins and teases the kids. He's a natural for this. Me, not so much. Can I yield my time to Derek the Brave? Not likely. Dunking the VP is a coup for any student.

I go inside to change and decide to wear my Tigers tee shirt over my swimsuit. It's bad enough to be the target for such inane activities. The last thing I need is for someone to make fun of my suit or my body.

Derek climbs out of the tank and gives me a bear hug in front of everyone. They hoot with laughter, thinking he's doing it to get me wet, but I know better. The hug is delicious and encouraging, but the water he transfers to me is quite cold. I climb up on the bench. I look at the familiar faces in the crowd.

Stefan and his family. Danny, the massage artist. Nobody that hates me, as far as I know. The crowd watches and waits.

"OK, guys, let's spend some money for Hamilton! If you dunk me, you can take a picture to share with the world!"

The crowd laughs and a few students step up.

"Sorry, Ms. Walker," says one seventh-grade girl, before she slams the button with her beanbag. I fall into the water, hitting hard, like I just jumped into a pool feet first.

"Nooo...prob...lem..." I answer, after coughing and pushing wet hair off my face. I smile for the photo op and manage to get my dripping arm around the girl, who giggles.

Fifteen minutes later, I'm drenched and cold, but laughing. I've done enough for my school today. This is better than spending a whole day on the roof, which many administrators have done. But I have another physical test coming.

IN THE SPRING, EACH sixth grade class spends a morning at the county ropes course. It's the same location I visited with administrators in August. Seems like a lifetime ago.

One of the teachers invites me to join her class and, without asking Carlson, I say, "Love to." I leave him a note telling him I have some sixth-grade business that morning. If he can be off campus all the time, I can do it once in a while! I pray there will be no bomb threats or major injuries while I'm away. Gaby knows how to reach me.

Rather than riding on the bus with the kids, I drive myself, making it easy to leave if necessary. I assume today will be similar to what I did with the adults. I'm in for a surprise. We start with team challenges, but the morning leads up to a daunting experience—involving a telephone pole.

There are two regulation poles. Maybe twenty-five feet tall and seven inches in diameter. A few feet from the top, they're connected by a crossbeam. One pole has spikes for footholds. It's not dangerous, as before climbing the pole, each person

Chapter 25

dons a harness with safety ropes. Everyone will be belayed down. There's no danger of killing yourself. There's only the fear—fear of heights, which I definitely have, compounded by fear of looking like a cowardly fool in front of your peers, or in my case, a bunch of eleven-year-olds.

Everyone on the ground is supposed to cheer on each youngster as he or she climbs the pole. If someone gets halfway up and freezes, refusing to do anything but climb down, that's fine, and the group shouts and whistles. But as the designated boss here, I can't chicken out halfway up, can I?

The kids climb to the top, step out onto the crossbeam, and fall backwards. The staff person at the end of the rope returns them to the ground safely. Some of the kids do more. They climb up the pole, skip the crossbeam, and step out on top of the pole—both feet on the seven-inch diameter top. Then they pivot and jump—yes jump—onto a trapeze that hangs from another structure a few feet away. I tip my hat to those brave athletes. When my turn arrives, I'm feeling ill.

I climb the pole. No problem, as long as I don't look down. Near the top, I stop. I grab the crown of the pole with my hands, eyeing the crossbeam next to me. The facilitator below, ready to use her ropes to help me down, calls to me in a soft, encouraging voice, "Ma'am, you've got to step out onto the beam."

A glance towards the ground confirms they're all watching. I step out on the beam, still clutching the telephone pole for dear life. Then I freeze. My heart races, my stomach is in my throat, and I can't let go of the pole.

Still patient, she calls up to me, "Ma'am, you've got to let go and step away from the pole. Then just fall backwards and I've got you."

"Easy for you to say," I yell back at her. I imagine the kids whispering below about what a wuss I am. They're actually cheering me on.

213

"You can do it Ms. Walker! Just let go! Come on! Go for it!"

They probably wish the chubby VP would hurry up so they can get their turns.

The counselor tries again, with more insistence, "You've got to let go and step away from the pole."

It's too late for climbing back down. I take a breath. I let go, and in one move, turn and fall backwards. Before I can scream, I arrive on the ground, safe and sound. The kids and teachers cheer. I feel like throwing up but summon a smile from somewhere. It's over! I survived! Another daunting task accomplished by sheer will. Perhaps I modeled something for the other scaredy-cats in the group. Is there anything we educators won't do for kids?

LESSON #12: YOU CAN OVERCOME CHALLENGES!

I HAVE BARELY SEEN AMY, the school counselor, in recent weeks. For a change, I invite her out to lunch at the end of the student lunch period. It's a treat for both of us to escape the school grounds, even though I'll be wondering the whole time what I might be missing.

We drive the half mile into town and settle into a private corner booth at my favorite café. It's nearly empty after one o'clock. The waitress takes our order and leaves us to chat.

"So, Amy, anyone we need to talk about?"

"Yeah, but first, how are things with John Carlson?"

"He hasn't pressed me too much about the dinner thing. He did tell me he'd like a referral for counseling. "

"Really? When did he tell you that?"

"A few weeks ago. We went out for a drink after an awful parent conference—"

"You went out with him?" Her rising tone confirms she thinks that was a bad idea.

Chapter 25

"Just for one drink. Yeah, I know I shouldn't have encouraged him in any way."

"Well, if he wants a referral, he can talk to me himself."

I can't argue with that.

Amy updates me on students she is seeing. "Abby has been coming to group, but I think she's moving again."

Abby is the girl who stole a gift back in December. I answer, "Too bad, she seems to have settled in here—she hasn't been back in my office. Nor has Madeline, for ages." Madeline, the bus seat graffiti artist.

Amy continues. "I hooked up Madeline and her mom with private counseling. Having them go together is helping. And I'm including Janelle in a group."

Our salads arrive and we dig in.

"Remember the Greens?" I ask. "You referred the parents for counseling."

"Oh, yeah. How is Jimmy doing?"

"Not great," I answer. "His classroom behavior has improved, but he does a minimum of work. He's still misbehaving outside of class, and I suspect the mom has little control. The last time I talked to her, she sounded exhausted."

"I'll give her a call," says Amy. "Sometimes these issues take a long time to improve—longer than one eighth-grade year."

"Thanks, Amy."

Amy says between bites, "I want to talk about Antonio. His attendance has fallen again, and I think he's scared about the transition to high school."

"That's interesting." I reach in my bag for my notebook. "What do you think it's about?" Most eighth-graders are excited about moving on to the very cool, more adult world of high school. As far as I know, Antonio is still living with his uncle, but he has missed the last two weekly check-ins with me.

215

Amy responds, "It's going to be harder academically. And their School Resource Officer will be on his case if he cuts."

I think out loud, "Maybe I could take him on a field trip over there before the end of the year."

"Great idea," she says.

I write it down for future reference. I need my notes to remember everything and everyone. The next couple of months are going to fly by. Spring break, testing, final evaluations, graduation—a whirlwind of activity. It's hard to believe I started at Hamilton just eight months ago. It's beginning to feel like home.

CHAPTER TWENTY-SIX:
APRIL, NOT IN PARIS

THE PACE OF SCHOOL LIFE ACCELERATES. students' hormones are abuzz and they're hyper because spring break is just around the corner. Teachers are equally excited about a week off. Founder's Day essays are pouring in. Kids want to talk to me about it every day when I'm patrolling during lunch.

"Ms. Walker, have you read my essay?"

"No, the English teachers will read them first. They'll give me their favorites to choose from. Do you want to tell me what you wrote?"

"I wrote about wanting to be in the Air Force someday."

"Great," I answer and offer a smile of encouragement. Not quite what I'm looking for, but I appreciate the student's enthusiasm.

A boy follows me around for ten minutes, begging, "Please choose me, please choose me!" He laughs at himself; the friends following him are cracking up.

I recognize this as entertainment, so I smile and simply answer, "We'll see."

A week before break, I get a puzzling phone message from the district office. Dr. José Padilla, the Human Resources Assistant Superintendent, would like to meet with me. Oh, dear. Could Carlson have reported my friendship with Derek? Am I getting fired? Has a parent sued? I arrange an appointment for late in the day on a Thursday. I'm getting a tension headache

217

as I drive to the district office. Plastering a smile on my face, I tell myself nothing I've done merits firing. Dr. Padilla stands behind his desk and smiles broadly. My hyperventilating slows.

Sitting down, he removes his reading glasses and invites me to sit across from him.

I sit, plop my bag on the floor, and make an effort to hold eye contact.

"So, Cynthia, how's it going at Hamilton?"

"Uh, just fine. It's a busy time of year."

"And what's it like working for John?" He picks up his pen.

"What do you mean?"

"Well, I know this is a bit unusual. I've heard a lot of good things about the difference you are making, but I'm also hearing concerns about John."

Oh my God, I'm being asked to rat on my boss. Do I feign ignorance to protect him or spill my voluminous beans?

I look down at my intertwined fingers. "Um...well...I don't see him a lot."

"Because he isn't there?" He readies his yellow pad.

I look up. Might as well get it over with. "Yes, often I...can't find him."

"And does his secretary know his whereabouts?"

"She usually says he's off campus, or at home."

"I see." Padilla is scribbling. My insides churn. Will Carlson find out about this chat?

"Cynthia, these complaints will be shared with the board. But the source will remain confidential. Do you want to add anything else?"

"Dr. Padilla, this is very uncomfortable for me. It's part of my job to get along with John. But I do want to ask you something...well, am I breaking a district rule if I date a Hamilton teacher?"

"There's no official policy. If a relationship causes a scandal,

218

Chapter 26

the school community may lose confidence, and that's a problem. Say, if the participants are married to others. If two single people form a relationship and are discreet, there's no reason for concern. Has John—"

"One of the single men has become my good friend...and John is...holding it over my head, I guess you could say. "

"I see. Are you evaluating this teacher, by chance?"

"Yes."

"I suggest you transfer the evaluation task to John, to avoid any suggestion of impropriety." His tone is soothing. Does he appreciate my honesty? "But please call me if anything else comes up."

As I take a deep breath of relief, a light bulb goes off in my head. Maybe I can get something else out of this meeting. "I have one more question. How does the district handle employees who may have an alcohol problem?"

"May I ask whom you're concerned about?"

"Ginny Stein. I don't know that she's intoxicated in the classroom, but there's this smell and she once admitted to a party the night before that hadn't worn off yet."

"Glad you're telling me. I've heard her name mentioned before. This is one of the things John has not been willing to address. But we have a staff member who, through the teachers' union, helps employees who have a problem. I'll ask him to contact her. Thanks. And keep up the good work."

"Thanks." We rise and shake hands. Relieved it's over, I escape. I'm free of Carlson's threat to report me but must ask him to complete Derek's evaluation. Will he find out about this *tête-à-tête* with Padilla? And what will happen to Ginny?

I could obsess over this visit, but I must prepare the teachers for testing, which begins immediately after spring break. I need to make them understand that the directions are to be read verbatim, the times are to be followed as prescribed, and there

219

are no exceptions.

We'll be testing for a week with high security. They'll check out test booklets from a locked closet every day and, after counting carefully, return them in the afternoon. At the end of testing, I must verify the number of booklets in each plastic bag and seal them, writing my signature over the seal. If any seal is broken or any materials go missing, embarrassing consequences could follow.

Not everyone accepts test protocols as the holy grail. At my urging, Carlson actually talks at a staff meeting about their importance.

"We don't want our school to be embarrassed like some schools were last year," he says. "And we don't want there to be grounds for accusing anyone of cheating, so do what she says."

That's the most support he's given me to date. My last test advice to the teachers before the break: "Remember, you may give no other examples than what are in the written directions. If kids ask questions, you can only repeat the words you have been given."

FRIDAY MORNING BEFORE VACATION, I remember to see Antonio to talk about high school. I ask Gaby to call him in.

"That boy skipping school again?" she asks and shakes her head.

"He's still one of my favorites," I answer. His grades have improved, but that's only part of the story. I haven't seen him lately and I need to find out what's going on.

He saunters in with a straight face. "Did I do something?"

"I don't know, did you?" My smile conveys I'm joking. "Antonio, I just wanted to check in. Your attendance has been slipping...and you haven't been coming to see me at our usual time."

His face melts into a sly smile. "Yeah, I'm having trouble waking up in the morning." He's looking at me with those

Chapter 26

beautiful brown eyes, serious, but relaxed. It's taken a long time, but there is some trust between us.

"Are you still at your uncle's?"

"No, I'm back at my grandma's."

"And staying up too late?"

"Yeah." He hangs his head. "Ten o'clock bedtime, right?"

"See, you know what to do. How's your mom?"

"She left. I don't know where she is. But my aunt lives with us now. She's a good cook." His smile comes easier than when we first met.

"Amy thinks you're worried about high school. Is that true?"

"Maybe."

"How would you like to go on a field trip with me, just us, to the high school? You could meet a counselor and see the campus."

"Wow, yeah, I guess."

I rise and squeeze his shoulder. "After testing, I'll set it up. Oh, and make sure you're here for all the testing days. You need to show us what you know, so you'll get correctly placed at high school, OK?"

"OK," he answers, still smiling.

SPRING BREAK IS FINALLY HERE. Even without Derek, who will be in New York with his buddies, I'm thrilled to have a whole week to relax and see my parents. And to worry about what I'll say if Carlson asks about my chat with HR.

Flying to my parents' place in Florida uses a whole day of my week off. My mom has planned a full week—lunch out, church, and always, grocery shopping at different markets. The heat, humidity, and constant buzzing of cicadas make me think I'm in a horror film and something terrible is about to happen. It's boring, but a pleasure to be without meetings, misbehaving kids, and crappy bosses. It's nice to be adored by the people I'm with night and day. I stay close to the air conditioning, watch

221

TV, and read chick lit.

I tell them a bit about Derek. They must worry about me still being single, but are too smart to nag me about marriage and grandchildren.

"He's a great guy. I really like him, but the working-together thing is full of possible land mines."

My dad, with a long history in corporate business, doesn't mince words. "Well, you have to make your choices, don't you?"

"Yeah. I decided it was worth the risk of heartache, break-up, or getting fired. Makes me look pretty stupid."

"Or maybe in love?" Mom asks.

I can only grin in response. I miss my frequent chats with Derek, but he's off the grid in the mountains of New York.

The week flies by and soon I'm on my way back to California. Derek saw his buddies and went backpacking. Definitely not my thing. I'm OK hiking for a few hours, but more than that would require the availability of a restaurant and a bathroom on the trail. He calls me Sunday night before school resumes.

"How was Disney World? Did you drink a lot of orange juice?"

"It was more like being the assistant in assisted living…and I don't drink orange juice. And the mountains?"

"Gorgeous. Wildflowers everywhere. Wished you were there."

"Aw. So, are we ready for tomorrow?"

"I guess you're wound up about testing, right?"

"You bet. Today I wish I were still in the classroom, where I only had to worry about one set of tests."

The alarm goes off at six o'clock. I'm wired for the first day, even though testing doesn't start until afternoon. Some people think that right after a vacation, the kids will be too sleepy the first day. In reality, they'll be too sleepy every morning.

Chapter 26

After checking messages and emails, I start counting out tests, with Gaby's help. Sticky notes identify each teacher's stack. I've printed up an instruction sheet to remind them about the answer sheets and practice questions, and to be sure to follow directions. They'll be doing two tests today.

Gaby stays in the office during lunch, for security reasons, while teachers pick up their materials. When I come back in from lunch duty—no fights, hallelujah—there is one stack still there: Ginny Stein. I ask Gaby to deliver it to her and remind Ginny to turn in her materials at the end of the day.

I walk through classrooms to make sure everyone is following directions. A few kids have books or papers out, so I whisper to them to clear their desks. I retreat to the office for a few moments of quiet. There are some nice aspects to state testing after all.

When the final bell rings, I make an all-call announcement, reminding the teachers to return their test materials. They come in one at a time. We count test booklets in their presence and mark numbers on a chart. We'll go through this ritual every day. Pretty crazy, but those are the rules.

Ginny Stein tries to drop off her stack and leave.

"Wait, Ginny, I have to count them."

She grimaces but waits. "Thirty-one, thirty-two. Ginny, there are supposed to be thirty-three. Did you count them before coming down here?"

She gives me a look that says, "Count them? Me?"

I count again. Still one short. "Ginny, we have to find the last booklet."

"I had the kids pass them in," she says.

"Let's go back to your room."

I drag her back to the classroom and after looking on her desk and the counters, we open each student desk until we find the missing test. The student apparently stuffed it in

223

there without following directions. Or perhaps there were no directions.

"Tomorrow, Ginny, I suggest you walk around and collect the test from each student." Some people are so dense.

"OK," she says.

The next couple of days go by just fine. Even Ginny follows instructions. On the last morning of testing, Carlson calls me on the phone from his office.

"Cynthia, I just heard from a parent that Dunning was helping the kids with the answers."

"Oh my God. Do you want to talk to him?"

"No, you're in charge of testing—you do it. But let me know what you find out."

I go immediately to Dunning's class. The room is silent; the kids are working on the test while Dunning circulates. Everything looks fine, but something weird is scrawled on the board. Dunning teaches social studies and the item on the board looks like a math word problem. I whisper in his ear to see me at the end of the day.

At three o'clock, Dunning traipses into the main office and stops at Gaby's desk with his test booklets under his arm. I count them and ask him to step into my office.

"What's up?" he asks. Since he has been working with Derek, he no longer acts nervous when talking to me.

"George, what was the word problem I saw on your board earlier?"

"Hmmm..." He has to think about it. "Oh, yeah, I was trying to show them how to eliminate the obviously wrong answers to a multiple-choice question."

"Great, if that was outside of testing. But was that a test item you were using?"

"It was in the practice section, so I thought it was OK."

"Good grief, no, it's not OK. Remember when I told you to

Chapter 26

stick to the script in your manual?"

"I was just trying to give them their best shot."

"Did you answer any questions they had?"

"I might have. If someone doesn't understand the directions, it's got to be OK to help them."

"But it's not, George. I'm going to have to report this. And tomorrow, be sure you only say what's in the manual."

"Okey dokey." He doesn't seem concerned. *There's* the difference between teachers and administrators. The former have the luxury of thinking only about what is good for their students; the latter have to look at the bigger picture—the district, the state, the U.S. Department of Education.

I call the testing coordinator at the district, who assures me it's not the end of the world, as long as Dunning wasn't giving answers, and tells me to send him a written report, which he will forward to the state. I write and send the report, then call the parent who phoned in the concern. I thank her profusely, explain that no answers were given out, and assure her the matter has been dealt with. Naturally, Carlson is already gone for the day. I leave him a note. Just another day at school!

WHILE I'VE BEEN RUNNING AROUND the school focused on testing, I've had an image in my mind of the stack of Founder's Day finalist essays sitting on my desk all week. Eighty-three students submitted essays telling why they are proud of their town and their country. The English teachers, bless them, spent their prep time reading and rating the essays. They've presented me with the best, allowing me to choose the winner.

I finally sit down to give the five essays my full attention and find all of them compelling. One boy lost his dad in a military accident and wants to honor him. Another kid has proud family roots in town that go back over a hundred years. But the essay that really gets to me is from Janelle Owusu. She writes about racial discrimination—being made fun of because of her skin color and African heritage. Despite hardships they have had to overcome, her immigrant parents have taught her that all citizens—those born in America and naturalized immigrants—should be proud, contributing members of society. Janelle also mentions honoring her brother, who died so tragically. I need a tissue before I finish reading. What a great group of kids. This age group may get a bad rap, but they have their altruistic side. Even the troubled ones have compassionate moments.

To make a fuss over this special group of kids, I call them in, tell them they're finalists, and invite them out to lunch in a few days. They choose the place—McDonald's, of course. I don't take kids out often, as they usually would rather hang out with their friends. The permission slips are a bother, and my car only holds three passengers. I do the paperwork and ask one of the English teachers to join us; with her driving, there will be room for everyone.

The day arrives and the finalists munch burgers and fries while I speak.

"I'm so proud of all of you. Each of your stories is worthy of a special award. We'll honor you at the next assembly."

They're chowing down, but look up with anticipation.

"And," I add, "the newspaper has promised to print all of your essays after the parade."

They've stopped eating now, because they know what's coming.

"You all will walk in the parade next to the float, but only one person can be the Grand Marshal, and that person is... Janelle."

Janelle puts her hand over her mouth in surprise.

This lovely young woman has been through so much in her eighth-grade year. "Janelle, your essay will mean a lot to students and parents. When you lead the parade, it will be a

226

Chapter 26

tribute to you, your school, your brother's dreams, and all the immigrant families in our community."

She smiles broadly. The others, despite their disappointment, reach out for high fives and the two sitting on either side give her hugs.

"Awesome, Janelle."

"You go, girl."

Janelle beams at me and at her competitors. "Thanks, guys."

CHAPTER TWENTY-SEVEN
HOORAY FOR MAY

SIX MORE WEEKS. I FEEL THE FAMILIAR SLIDE TO the end of the year. The same slide I felt as a student long ago—excitement mixed with dismay, anticipating the break from structure and friends. I felt it as a teacher too—the countdown to summer vacation.

Kids get restless in May. Teachers become irritable unless they've learned the magic remedy of relaxing their expectations. With the hard work behind them, they can review concepts and skills with games and hands-on projects the students enjoy. The pressure is off.

Hamilton has several evening activities approaching: an orchestra performance, parent meetings, and a dance. Of course, Carlson leaves most of it to me. Teachers can choose their extra duty assignments; I have no choice.

First up is the Founders Day parade. Derek offers to accompany me. I want to take pictures for Hamilton to post, so I'm going to have to jog next to the float. I put on my athletic shoes and check my Nikon battery. We find a place near the start of the parade and join the crowd. The Owusus are surrounded by Hamilton folks—parents and scores of kids who have come to watch Janelle and the finalists. She looks sporty in her gold Tigers tee shirt and hat, black pants, and athletic shoes. She flits from one group of kids to the next, perhaps releasing nervous energy.

The Grand Marshal's float is a truck with a long bed, decorated like a farm, to reflect the town's agricultural roots. There are rows of grapevines in barrels, corn stalks, a scarecrow, hay bales, and hundreds of sunflowers. Along the sides of the truck bed, a gold and black banner reads "Hamilton Middle School." My heart swells with pride. School may be tough. Administration may be daunting. But these moments make it all worthwhile.

It's a sunny morning, but the air feels cool and fresh. Just before nine, a Rotarian with a bullhorn tells the float participants to get in place. Janelle climbs up on the flatbed and the other finalists position themselves next to the float. The parade begins, and I need to move if I'm going to snap photos. Walking on the sidewalk, I try not to trip over the crowd. I leave Derek behind, pointing and clicking at the same time. A dozen steps into it, I trip and land in the street, twisting my ankle. The float continues down the block. Derek finds me sitting on the curb, my ankle already turning purple. He grabs my arm to help me up. A few of the Hamilton folks come over to see if I'm OK.

"No worries," I say. "At least I got some pictures." Derek helps me to the car, carefully positioning me to slide in without stepping on the injured ankle. He gets me home and settled on my couch with a bag of ice and makes me a sandwich for lunch, so I won't have to get up.

"Is there anything else I can do?" he asks.

"Thanks so much. I'll be fine."

"Call me if you need anything. I'll be at home reading student papers." The serious look on his face says he cares. I blow him a kiss as he goes out the door.

In the morning, I hobble around to make breakfast. There's no chance I'll go hungry. Retrieving the Sunday paper from the porch, I find Janelle on the front page, with a nice article about the essay contest and the text of her winning piece. Tomorrow

230

Chapter 27

we'll put up a bulletin board to memorialize the event.

I limp into the office on Monday. The campus buzzes with talk of the parade and Janelle. For today, she's the most popular girl at school. Another Hamilton success story, thanks to the VP.

Once seated in my office, I remember to call the high school about Antonio. He could have seen the campus during their spring open house, but that's not something he would do on his own. I phone the ninth-grade counselor, Jim Nelder, who understands this is a special case. Counselors often go the extra mile to help a kid. We set up a visit for the following week.

On a Friday morning, I drive Antonio to the high school. We arrive near the end of their morning break, so he sees the teens milling about with their snacks, deep into their social life.

I show him the gym, cafeteria, and little theater. He stuffs his hands in his pockets, but his smile shows he's pleased. The campus must look very grown up and sophisticated. We find the counseling office and I'm left to study my phone while Jim takes Antonio into a few classrooms and through the library and technology center. When they return fifteen minutes later, Antonio is beaming. Jim has told him about their program to help ninth-graders adjust and has signed him up for a counseling group. I hope this sticks. Antonio is a gem. He just needs nurturing.

I HAVE ONLY SEEN DEREK for an occasional weekend dinner, as he's been out hiking most Saturdays and Sundays. I have my sore ankle as an excuse, but I'm happy to see him in the evening, after he's built more muscles and I've slept in and done laundry. He'll be helping me supervise a weeknight orchestra concert, so I suggest we go out for an early dinner. We claim a corner booth and order wine. We'll suck on breath mints before returning to campus.

231

My thoughts are stuck in the quicksand of my job. "I want you to know you've made a big difference with Dunning." The guy who started the year with paper airplanes zipping around his room now controls the class most of the time and offers more engaging lessons.

"Thanks, there was a lot of room for improvement." He's demolishing his salad.

I put down my glass. "But you enjoyed it, right?"

He looks up from his food. "Yeah, it was kind of fun."

"Have you thought more about taking administrative classes?"

"Uh, I looked at the university catalog online, but that's as far as I got."

"Well, I don't mean to be a broken record. But you'd be a great administrator."

He smiles and teases me. "Hey, is this my evaluation conference?"

"Sorry, I'm a little preoccupied." I push my salad around the plate.

"Just kidding," and he reaches over the food to squeeze my hand.

"I've got to take a Saturday to do the final evals."

"Back to Occidental?" He raises his eyebrows. I can see the wheels churning. Occidental was where he met me on a Sunday in January for our first date.

"Not necessarily."

Could we spend a whole weekend together? Not a bad idea.

He continues, "A buddy of mine has a beach house he's not using right now. He's doing renovations. Then he'll put it back on the rental market."

"Renovations?" I visualize a place with no electricity or running water.

"Yeah, mostly on the exterior. I've seen pictures. It's very livable."

Chapter 27

"The beach sounds great...where is it?" Newfound energy bubbles up.

"Dillon Beach." My mouth hangs open, not spilling my dinner, I hope. Dillon is one of my favorite spots on the northern California coast: no town to speak of, one grocery store, one tiny restaurant, and a mile-long strip of sand overlooking Tomales Bay and the Pacific. The modern houses that perch on the hill above the beach feature fantastic ocean views.

"That would be awesome. Will he give us a good deal?"

"He's my bud, it's free."

"Then I'm in. You just have to promise to let me work on Saturday."

"*No problema.*"

"And, by the way, I'm asking Carlson to finish your evaluation—on advice from HR."

"Fine. That probably means it won't happen."

We plan our outing for the next weekend. Two nights and days with Derek is just what I need, even if I have work to do. The school year is winding down. Maybe I'm ready to relax. Our relationship has progressed slowly, due to my worries, but perhaps the time is right to take the next step. I've never before started an intimate relationship with someone who is a trusted friend. It feels both exciting and safe.

MEANWHILE, THE NUMBER of behavior referrals ratchets up. I deal with some marijuana on campus, fighting between boys who like the same girl, and frisky behavior taking place out of sight of the lunch supervisors. One day after school while I'm monitoring the kids still waiting for their bus to arrive, a breathless parent comes up to me.

"Ms. Walker, there's a kid across the street in the park with a big knife."

I hobble over there and sure enough there's Jimmy Green slipping a hunting knife into his backpack. Too late. The handful of kids hanging out tries to gather 'round. I take Jimmy's elbow and lead him away.

"What's going on, Jimmy?"

"Aw, I didn't do anything." He looks down at the ground and clutches the backpack in both arms. He knows it's against the law to bring a knife to school.

"I saw the knife. Why are you still in the park?"

"Waiting for my mom."

"Come with me."

I walk Jimmy across the street to the office, call his mother, and proceed to find out exactly what happened. He admits he brought the knife, but says he was only using it to cut lemons from a tree. He sits across from me, bent over with his head in his hands.

"Jimmy, it doesn't matter. You know it's instant suspension for having a knife. Why did you bring it?"

"To cut lemons." Yeah, right.

I confiscate the large folding knife and fill out the suspension form. When Mrs. Green arrives, I advise her we will be in touch about a possible expulsion hearing. She's teary-eyed while leaving, but her tight eyes and flared nostrils suggest it's more than disappointment or embarrassment. Perhaps she's angry at her son. He has made progress this year, but he still finds a way to break all the rules. Maybe she's finally motivated to take charge.

I spend a whole day interviewing the student witnesses, getting a statement from the parent, taking photos of the knife, and reporting to the district person in charge of expulsions. There will be a hearing before the end of the school year. Jimmy may not return to campus, but will do independent study for the remaining weeks. He will miss out on all the end-of-year activities—including the dance and graduation. What a disaster for him and his family.

Chapter 27

THE BEACH WEEKEND FINALLY ARRIVES. I gather my files and laptop and skip my usual sleep shirt, throwing a lacy, short nightgown into my bag. Derek and I drive to Dillon Beach on Friday evening, stopping in Petaluma for dinner.

Over burgers, I ask, "So how many bedrooms does this place have?" I'm imagining a huge vacation home with five or six bedrooms. As the words leave my mouth, it's clear Derek is thinking of something other than the grandeur of the house.

"It has three. No worries—you can have your own."

"Maybe I won't need it," I answer. Hint, hint, Derek. It's May. The birds are singing, my heart is aglow, and I shaved my legs!

His free hand stays on my knee for the rest of the drive.

The house perches high on a hill above the beach, with expansive views of Tomales Point and the ocean. Derek has the key, but after we open the door and go back to the car to unload, we realize he left the key inside and the front door has closed behind us, locking us out. I can't blame him. Who has a rental house with a door that locks automatically?

We put our stuff back into the car and discuss what to do.

"I'll call Dean. Maybe there's another way to get in," he says. He makes the call, but Dean doesn't pick up. He leaves a message. We walk around the house checking the windows and doors. They're all locked from the inside. It's starting to get dark.

"Damn." Derek scowls. "I'm so sorry."

"Not your fault," I say and put my arm around him. "We can always sleep in the car." We both laugh. Some romantic weekend this is starting out to be.

"At least we had dinner," Derek says.

We sit in the car for a while and then he suggests, "Dean told me not to use the garage. Maybe we should try getting in that way."

235

"But don't you think the inside door to the house is locked?"

"You never know." He takes a flashlight from the glove box and exits the car. The garage door squeaks open. Soon I hear several loud bangs and then Derek is holding the front door open, with a big grin on his face. Very proud of himself.

"My hero," I announce, as I grab an armful of our stuff and take it inside.

"I had to break the lock on the inside door, but I'm happy to pay for the repair."

Our weekend is getting off to a rough start, but Derek ignites the pile of logs in the fireplace and we cuddle up to listen to music—no TV on site. After a while, I go into the closest bedroom and change into my nightgown. It's more sheer than I thought. The look on Derek's face when I reappear is priceless.

"Hmm...is there a message in this choice of sleepwear?" he asks.

"Well, the year is almost over. The testing is done. Carlson can go to hell."

He laughs and puts his arm around me, as I nestle into his body heat. He answers, "I like those words, Ms. Walker."

"I'm so glad we don't have to sleep in the car," I say. I start unbuttoning his shirt and he puts his hand on my cheek to draw me in for a kiss. After a few minutes, Derek stands and takes my hand, leading me to the bedroom, where we fall on the bed, giggling like kids.

"I hope this is worth the wait," I whisper, as Derek gets up to wriggle out of his clothes. He rejoins me, pressing his warm body against mine. Skin against skin is utterly delicious. My hands find the muscles on his back and I'm pretty sure neither of us is going to be disappointed.

I sleep like the satisfied person I am, lulled by the sound of waves and the soft breath of my sweetheart by my side. In the morning, while the coffee brews, we hit the grocery store and

236

Chapter 27

stop to admire the nearby pirate statue. It's a strange monument for this spot that isn't much of a town, but could have been a pirate hangout long ago, when pirates were active on the San Francisco coast. Since Derek and I were both pirates for Halloween, there's something magical about spending our first night together in a place overseen by this giant bronze guy with sword in the air.

Back at the house, we cook a breakfast of eggs and bacon, toast and fruit. Then Derek takes off to explore the beach and dunes, and I get going on the evaluations. Since I have the mid-year ones to work from and only a few more observations to add to my final comments, it's easier than the last time. I struggle with Dunning's, making it clear that he has improved. I give him a satisfactory rating but make a couple of suggestions for things he should work on.

Ginny Stein is another matter. I have no choice but to mark *Unsatisfactory*. I have to document all the suggestions I have given and her inability or unwillingness to try them. The unsatisfactory rating means she'll be evaluated again next year. If she still doesn't improve, a case could be made for firing her. What a sad situation. I don't look forward to sharing my comments with her. And I wonder what HR has done with the information I gave them about her drinking.

Derek returns at midday, sunburned and hungry. He brings a collection of shells and rocks and presents me with the prettiest ones.

"I'm finished!" I announce. "Let's make sandwiches."

We pack a picnic and drive down to the beach. We find a good place to spread out our blanket and set up the umbrella I found in the house. I insist on slathering sunscreen on Derek's now familiar back. There are a fair number of couples, families, and dogs roaming the beach. We're eating and sipping our beers when I notice some activity behind us on the sand. People in costume.

"Look, Derek."

We both stand. Up near the parking lot there's a group of eight people dressed as pirates. Dark pants, white shirts, tri-corner hats. They seem to be acting out a play. They carry muskets and have what looks like a treasure chest. In two groups, they appear to be fighting over the loot.

"What the...?" Derek mutters.

I stare in awe. The others on the beach aren't paying attention. There's no one filming them, no photographic equipment in sight. The playacting continues for about ten minutes and then the pirates take their treasure, get into two cars, and drive off.

"What do you think?" I ask. "Did we imagine that?"

His response says it all: "From one pirate to another, shiver me timbers! Isn't life great?"

We finish our lunch, take a lazy beach nap, and return to the house to work on dinner.

Derek cooks a steak on the barbecue while we sip wine and watch pelicans soaring over the ocean and diving for their dinners. Digging into the juicy meat and the salad I made, I ask, "What are you doing this summer?" OK, I blew my cool by bringing it up first, but I really want to know.

"I was thinking about that too. I don't have plans. Do you want to take a trip together?"

"As long as it's not backpacking, I'd love to."

He smiles.

I continue, "Cheap hotels are OK with me, as long as there's a bed. And I have to be back by the beginning of August, unless I get fired." I laugh, but seriously, who knows what will happen during the next few weeks.

"Mexico? New Orleans? Paris?"

"Wow, that's what I call an open mind. I'd love to go to

Chapter 27

Europe with you."

We have another blissful evening, but I toss and turn thinking about the possibilities. Derek and I kissing on the *Pont des Arts* in front of all the locks. Derek and I watching the glistening Seine from the *bateaux mouches*. Climbing the Eiffel Tower. Drinking French cider and eating crêpes at a street café. I didn't study French for nothing. We linger in bed until midmorning.

By the time we're dressed, we've decided to go to Paris. We'll leave the last week in June. We've looked online at several reasonable Airbnbs. A week in Paris and then we'll rent a car and drive into the countryside for another week, returning home just after Bastille Day. And just like that, the future seems bright. I have a boyfriend whom I adore, and he appears to feel the same. If only I could be sure of my career.

BACK AT SCHOOL, I ASK GABY to schedule the final evaluation conferences. I write Carlson a note, asking him to complete Derek's evaluation. I attach copies of the mid-year review and thorough notes about the observations I have done since then. All Carlson has to do is meet with Derek and sign on the dotted line. To my surprise, Carlson leaves me a note telling me that he wants to do *my* evaluation. I can't believe it. I'm still worried that he knows I talked to HR about him. I show up at the appointed time, late afternoon after most people have left campus.

"Have a seat," he says. I sit.

My evaluation form, with the goals I wrote at the beginning of the year, is in front of him. He has added nothing to it.

"So how do you think your year has gone?" His face is serious, focused on me.

"It's been challenging...and I love it." Challenging? As in doing it all with no guidance or feedback, yeah. All the fires, figurative and real, that I have put out on my own. Kids on the roof, Sheldon's heart attack, trips to the emergency room, child abuse, difficult teachers and parents, all on my own.

"And this request for me to finish Simons's evaluation? What's that about? Do you think that lets you off the hook?"

"Yes, John. I asked José Padilla about any impropriety in me seeing Derek and this was his recommendation."

"I see, you talked to HR."

"I had no choice, John. I value this job, but I also value my relationship with Derek. Now I know it's OK."

He looks down at the desk, covers his face with his hands, and rubs his forehead. Then, still not looking at me, he directs his attention to the evaluation form in front of him.

"All right, let's do this. You and I don't always agree, and I wish you were closer to our wonderful parents...and to me." He looks up at me with what I can only identify as longing. "But you've stayed on top of things with the kids and the teachers. I'm satisfied."

"Thanks." I can't think of anything else to say. Other than *thanks for nothing*. He scrawls one lousy, illegible sentence on the form and finalizes it with his equally illegible signature. He hands it to me to sign, then gives me my copy. Glancing at it, I think I can make out the word *excellent*. Great leadership, boss.

"There's one more thing," he says, sitting back in his chair with his hands crossed on his big belly.

Oh, God. What else?

"It's about Ginny Stein—she's going to retire. Gave me a letter in writing, so you don't need to finish her evaluation."

"Wow, that's good news. It wasn't going to be a good one."

"I think she knows that. Good work, Cynthia."

I leave his office with mixed feelings. Glad that I helped Ginny decide to retire, and that my evaluation is finished, but disappointed in the amount of thought and time Carlson put into it—that is, none. Why would I have expected anything else? No talk about next year, but he can't fire me now.

240

Chapter 27

THE LAST DAYS OF SCHOOL are here. Even though Derek teaches seventh-graders, I ask him to join me at the eighth-grade graduation dance the Friday before the last week. He knows many of the kids and it will be a treat for me to have him there. My evaluation done, I'm no longer worried about being seen with Derek.

"Sure," he says to my request. "Save the last dance for me."

How sweet. "If we're not too busy monitoring the couples on the dance floor," I answer.

The dance begins at seven o'clock. The sky is still light, but by the time things wind down it will be dark. The parents have transformed the gym into a ballroom, with gold and black streamers, balloons, and paper lanterns. A strobe light is in place and the DJ's equipment waits on the stage. The kids have been advised to dress up a bit, but not too much. We don't want floor-length gowns and high heels or tuxedos. They're outside, waiting to go into the gym. The boys wear nice pants and shirts with collars; the girls are in cocktail dresses or dressy pants outfits. There are a few couples, a few corsages, but for the most part the kids arrive in groups.

One of the eighth-grade teachers is stationed at the entrance, using my list to check kids in. Those with major offenses in the last few weeks are excluded. I walk over to see how it's going.

She's put one boy, who should not be here, to the side. I greet him. "Jonathon, don't you remember me telling you after that fight that you could not attend the dance?"

He looks down at the ground, his mouth twisted.

"Does your mother know you're here?"

"No," he says.

"Then come with me and we'll call her." He shuffles after me to the office. I phone the mother. She apologizes and says she's on her way.

"Look, Jonathon, I'm sorry, but we follow the rules.

241

I hope missing this dance will help you to remember there are consequences the next time you're about to lose your temper."

He remains silent and miserable. When the mother pulls up, I walk him out to the car.

The dance is now in full swing, the music at ear-splitting volume. Most of the eighth-grade class has shown up. After nine years of school with kids from the neighborhood, school life is about to change. They'll soon be in high school with youngsters from the other middle school. Ninth grade will bring increased responsibilities for schoolwork and expectations for more mature behavior. Grades will be recorded in the all-important GPA. They'll face the challenges and joys of dating. Before they leave high school, they'll make decisions that will affect the rest of their lives: college or not, careers, leaving home. Whether or not they know it, this last week is an important passage. My heart bursts with emotion, wishing them success and happiness as they move on...but I still have to get them through this evening and one more week of school.

We have a chaperone at each exit, so nobody can slip out unobserved. They have to remain with us until the dance ends at nine o'clock. I start my surveillance of the girls' bathrooms. I wave at Derek across the room. He will patrol the boys' bathrooms.

The DJ plays Katy Perry's "California Gurls," followed by a rap I've never heard. More kids dance than I remember in the fall. By dancing, I mean jumping in time to the music. Others stand in clusters, talking and laughing. Some already surround the table covered with homemade brownies, chips, candy, and bottles of soda. A dad with a camera stands on one side of the room by a balloon arch. He takes photos of kids, groups, and couples, that will be shared on social media. What a great party. The painful memory of my own awkward middle school years is fading fast.

Chapter 27

The DJ starts a series of Beatles songs and I have to dance. Derek comes over as I'm swaying to the music, snapping my fingers and singing along to "Twist and Shout."

"Come on," he says, and grabs my hand, taking me out into the middle of the dance floor. I'm sure the kids think we look pretty silly doing our old-fashioned kind of dancing, but they're smiling. After a couple of songs, we go back to supervising.

I watch one couple with concern, as they are in a close embrace and his mouth seems to be angling for her neck. I walk up to them and tap him on the shoulder.

"Give it a rest."

The boy looks at me like I must be mistaken but straightens himself up and puts a little distance between them. She smiles. Another fifteen minutes of this and the DJ announces the last dance, Taylor Swift's "Love Story." I throw all caution to the wind and put my arms around Derek for a nice slow dance. A little Romeo and Juliet magic can't hurt. Some of the kids laugh or make comments. I don't care.

"Way to go, Mr. Simons."

"Hey, not too close!"

We both ignore it. After all, in a week this group of kids will be history.

CHAPTER TWENTY-EIGHT
EVERYONE GRADUATES

GRADUATION IS SCHEDULED FOR THE LAST DAY OF the school year. And guess whose job it is to organize it? You got it. Why would I expect otherwise? I start by talking to the parent club, as I've heard they plan most of the day. Fantastic—I don't have to do it all myself.

The day will begin with an outdoor breakfast for the kids—pancakes cooked by the dads. The parent club also decorates the gym for the ceremony at eleven o'clock and organizes a short celebration afterwards featuring cake and punch. After the reception, parents will take their graduates home.

My job is to lead the ceremony, print a program, and work with the teachers. They'll prep the kids to line up outside the gym, march in an orderly fashion to their appointed seats, and walk across the stage when it's their turn. Bert Sheldon will set up the microphone and speakers, and we'll be ready to go.

I follow the program format from last year: pledge to the flag, songs by the choir, speeches by two students selected by their peers, and a message from one of the teachers—who will likely say this is the best eighth-grade class he's ever had. Then the students will be called up to receive graduation certificates from their teachers, with administration standing by to shake their sweaty hands. I've been to enough of these to know what to do.

The teachers are on top of the details, including once again instructing the students on what to wear—or rather, what not to wear. Seriously, we have to tell the kids again no tuxedos, no long or low-cut dresses or high heels, and please, no limos. This is middle school, not Hollywood.

The last week features a bevy of fun events: softball games, field trips to local pools, and Bert Sheldon's annual Water Combat. I've heard that just before the end of the day before graduation, the eighth-grade teachers take their kids out on the field and have a blast getting each other soaking wet.

I would not have a problem with Water Combat, except that earlier in the year, the school board outlawed toy guns at school for any reason. So, if you want to put on a play that involves a gun, you're stuck. Likewise for water guns. Everyone got the message. When I arrive on Thursday morning and see the stockpile of watery weapons outside the eighth-grade homerooms, I cringe.

What can I do? Confiscate the water guns? Wring Sheldon's neck? His colleagues were probably too intimidated to remind him of the new rule. They could have limited the event to water balloons or found some other method of delivering the goods. How about pails? But no, Sheldon's traditions are more important than anything else.

Should I talk to Carlson? Wait, the guy who never makes any decision that could upset parents? Do I dare tell the eighth-grade classes I'm canceling the event? It's not their fault. I decide to let it go. Nobody is going to think a purple plastic gun shooting water is dangerous. They'll be on the school grounds with teacher supervision. With some difficulty, I put my dedication to rules aside. I'll make sure the teachers get the message for next year.

I watch the water fight from a hundred yards away where it's safe and dry. The kids shriek with joy. When all the water has

Chapter 28

been discharged, the teachers are just as wet as the kids. They traipse back into their classrooms, laughing and dripping. The floors will need to be mopped. When the kids have gone home, I find the eighth-grade teachers with Sheldon in his room. He has changed his clothes. The others are still wet, drying their hair with towels. They're comparing notes like they might after a sports outing.

Sheldon says, "I really got Thompson good. He didn't know what hit him." The others laugh, until they see me wearing my serious face.

"Guys, are you aware that you broke a district rule today?"

Sheldon gives me a puzzled look. "Huh?"

I can't keep my voice down. "No toy guns, remember?"

The other teachers, towels around their necks, look down at their flip flops. Sheldon stares right back at me.

"No, I guess I didn't think it applied to Water Combat."

"Well, it does. I couldn't bring myself to cancel at the last minute but find some other way to do this in the future."

The quiet ones respond immediately. "We're so sorry, we wondered, but—"

Sheldon looks me in the eyes. "Sure, Cynthia. I'm sorry to be such a pain."

"Bert, I love your creativity, but does everything have to be such a damn show?" I turn and walk out, regretting losing my cool, but I'm done with Sheldon's antics. Too bad I already completed his evaluation.

EVERYTHING IS SET FOR GRADUATION, and although there are clouds in the sky, there is no prediction of rain. The breakfast goes on as planned. At morning break, the teachers assure me their students are appropriately dressed and ready. Parents have decorated the gym with gold and black streamers and balloons. On the stage, potted pink azaleas sit in front of the microphone. Folding chairs for the students are set up facing the podium. Several tables in the back, covered with gold tablecloths, hold bowls of red punch, homemade cookies, and cupcakes. Families are arriving and finding seats in the bleachers.

Gaby rings me on my cell phone to tell me Mrs. Green is on the line in the office. What now? Jimmy is not allowed to be on school grounds after having a knife. He's doing independent study in order to finish the year. Gaby transfers the call to the locker room phone.

"Hi, Ms. Walker, how are you?"

I suspect this is going nowhere good. "I'm fine, what can I do for you?"

"They told us Jimmy can't return to Hamilton, but don't you think it would be OK for him to graduate with the other kids?"

This is a no-brainer. "No, Ma'am. I'm really sorry, but not returning to Hamilton means not for any reason. That is district policy. The independent study folks will prepare a graduation certificate for him. I'm sorry."

"I hoped you would understand. I'm really sorry too." Click. It's just before eleven o'clock and I need to be on the stage, but now Sharon has a phone call for me.

"John isn't available and it's important—the superintendent," she says.

What now?

"Hi Cynthia, sorry to bother you on the last day, but I need to tell you I had a call from the president of the school board."

"Yes?"

"She was driving by yesterday and saw your students playing with water guns."

My heart leaps to my throat. "Yes, I wasn't aware it was going to happen until the last minute and I didn't think it would be fair to the kids to cancel." It's true but sounds pretty lame.

Chapter 28

"You know the board feels very strongly about this. They expect you or John to write a letter explaining how you will make sure this never happens again."

"I'm so sorry. I've already spoken to the eighth-grade teachers. I'll tell John and work on a letter today. Should it go to you?" I put down the phone feeling somewhat ashamed. On the other hand, maybe it's just bad luck that the board member drove by when she did. I can't do anything about it now.

LESSON #13: ADMIT YOUR MISTAKES, LEARN, AND MOVE ON.

I check to see if the kids are ready. They're lined up outside the gym, looking excited and nervous. Everyone has combed hair and bright eyes. "You look great," I whisper several times as I walk past them. I take my place on the stage next to Carlson, who won't miss an opportunity to soak up credit for the event. He looks subdued and is uncharacteristically quiet. He gives me a quick smile and then continues waving at people in the audience.

I go to the microphone. "Welcome, everyone. We're happy to see so many of you here today to honor our eighth-graders. Please stand for the pledge."

One of the scouts comes to the mic to continue. After the pledge, a recording of "Pomp and Circumstance" plays, and the teachers walk in with their students. Their practice shows. The kids stay in line and know exactly where to sit so they will walk to the stage in the right order. The choir sings a rousing "Unwritten," followed by "I Hope You Dance."

I've read the two student speeches, but it's still inspiring to hear positive words spoken by the girl and boy selected by their classmates:

249

"We'll always remember the special friends we made at Hamilton Middle School."

"The teachers at Hamilton got us to work hard and prepare for what's ahead in high school. We'll miss you but we know the future is bright. Thanks to all the teachers, Mr. Carlson, and Ms. Walker."

Good stuff indeed!

It all goes as planned. Except for the parents in the audience shouting and whistling when their darlings walk across the stage. How are we supposed to teach young people to be courteous when their parents are totally out of control at what should be at least a semi-serious event? "Way to go, Billy Boy!" "Shawna! Shawna! Yay!" Really? Their lack of decorum is annoying, but I'm learning to save my rants for battles that can be won.

When the certificates have all been handed out, the audience cheers and the graduates move towards the refreshments. The kids find their parents, many of whom have brought flowers or balloons. The sweat of almost two hundred kids now oils my palms. I wipe them on my skirt and head into the crowd. Overflowing with bittersweet emotion, I smile, greet parents, and pose with kids for pictures.

I see Janelle and her family, and the girl beckons me. "Dad, take my picture with Ms. Walker."

We smile for the camera and the parents thank me. Mrs. Owusu says, "We're going to miss you next year, Ms. Walker. With all those students at the high school, I don't know if an administrator will have time for our Janelle...or her parents." She gives me a warm smile.

"Well, as you know, they have more counselors there, so Janelle, you speak up if you need assistance with anything." Janelle tears up and gives me a hug and I move on, a little teary-eyed myself.

Chapter 28

Next is Antonio. He's looking sharp, dressed up in a suit jacket, with a woman I presume is his aunt. "Hey buddy, you look handsome."

He grins and turns red. I guess I'm just meant to embarrass this young man. "I made it," he says.

"Yes, and you're ready for high school. I think they're even ready for you." I turn to the aunt, "Cynthia Walker."

"Thanks for looking out for our Antonio," she says. "The whole family is grateful. It's been a difficult year."

"It's my job," I answer, "but I must admit, in my first year of administration, I'll remember Antonio fondly...come back and visit me, Antonio."

"OK," he says. I grab him and give him a good hug. Now I definitely need a tissue.

I move on, ready to head back to the office, when one of the teachers rushes over and turns me towards the abandoned stage. There is Jimmy Green, wearing dark pants and dress shoes with a collared shirt. Mrs. Green coaxes him to walk across the stage so she can take a picture. She hands him a piece of paper, I guess to pretend it's his certificate. He looks mortified but walks out on the stage.

Rockets go off in my head. The nerve of this parent! I could make a scene and escort them off campus. But nobody can deter a mama bear who has her mind set. I turn back towards the office. Poor Jimmy. He and his family have a long way to go.

I check in at the office and then turn my attention to the sixth- and seventh-graders, who have another half hour of class before their early dismissal. The usual classroom parties are underway. I poke my head into a few classrooms and get invited in. Students eagerly present me with a cupcake or a cookie they baked. I carry my haul back to the office to share with Gaby.

The final bell rings. With a mix of elation and sadness,

251

I position myself out front. The kids dash off, arms full of projects, gym clothes that need washing, and food. Many stop to say goodbye. Some want a hug and I'm happy to comply. As much as the end of the year provides a welcome break, I'll miss their youthful humor and special world view. Maybe even their pranks. "See you next year," they say. I'm not quite ready to think about that.

I return to the office, physically and emotionally drained. Kicking my shoes under the desk, I lean back in my chair. I draft a letter to the superintendent about the water guns and email it to John.

Tomorrow, we'll have an early staff meeting. It will focus on probable assignments for the coming year, congratulating those retiring, and thanking everyone for their hard work. For a change, I have nothing to prepare. After the meeting, the teachers will have time to settle their classrooms. Then there's a staff party at a nearby winery. Lunch will be catered, and wine will flow. I'm looking forward to it. And in a couple of weeks Derek and I will be off to France.

Derek stops in the office on his way out. His arms are full of gifts from students and leftover food from his class party. He looks at the cupcakes lined up on my desk.

"Guess you don't need any more?"

I shake my head wearily. "I don't think so."

"Good day?" he asks.

"Great day. You?"

"It's always a pleasure to see them growing up. This seventh grade was a good group. I don't think they'll give you too much trouble next year."

I can only smile at this lovely man, who enjoys kids as much as I do. If I hadn't stuck my neck out to try administration, I would not have met Derek. I have confidence and new skills that I might never have developed if I'd stayed in the classroom.

Chapter 28

Beyond the curriculum goals, this VP job requires tough love, consistency, the ability to deal with regular crises, and a commitment to the welfare of students and staff. One year down, many more to go, I hope.

I'm in bed by eight o'clock and sleep straight through until morning. I dress casually in jeans and tennies—no kids or parents to impress today, and it's no longer necessary to prove my competence to the staff. I walk to the library where there's a platter of donuts and the coffee machine is going strong. Settling into a chair, I chat with teachers and wait for Carlson. He arrives ten minutes late. Nobody cares.

"OK, everyone, have a seat," he says. People gradually move into chairs around the table and stop talking.

"I have a big announcement," he says and glances at me across the table with an expression that makes me think he must be feeling ill. "You are a great group, and it has been my pleasure to lead all of you...but due to health reasons, I will be retiring."

It's so quiet, everyone can hear me gasp. He goes on talking about how many years he's been here and all the wonderful things he has accomplished, but I don't hear any of the details. Is this a result of my visit to HR? Have others on the staff complained about him? Is there really a health issue or is that just an excuse? Is this retirement voluntary or has he been pushed out? I come back into consciousness. I search for Derek on the other side of the table. He looks at me and raises his eyebrows. I can't respond in front of everyone. Not a problem since I've been struck mute and expressionless.

"The district will let you know who will be replacing me—well, nobody can *replace* me, right?" He laughs but nobody else makes a sound. He continues, "But never fear, you'll have a new leader before you return in August. So, Cynthia, do you want to talk about the other retirees?"

253

This is not part of the plan, but since I know who's retiring, I thank them. Ginny Stein looks happier than I've ever seen her.

I pass out a sheet with the tentative assignments for the coming year. "Remember, folks, this can change. And we have some hiring to do..." I stop there. "See you all at the winery at noon."

I remain glued to my seat. Teachers go over to Carlson and shake his hand and speak to him. I know many of them are thinking the next principal can't get any worse. They slowly proceed out of the library. Derek walks over and gives my shoulder a squeeze.

"See you in a bit," he says and departs.

John and I are alone.

Still immobile, I say, "I'm sorry."

"No, you're not...or if you are, you won't be for long. Let's call it a day." He rises and walks out. Should I be surprised he didn't tell me about this? Disappointed he didn't confide in me? Does he know HR asked me about him?

I sit there alone for a few minutes. Why do I feel bad? This guy has been tormenting me for a whole school year. Offering no guidance. Ordering me around. Begging me to like him. Touching me. Threatening me. I certainly will not miss him. I guess it's just natural to feel empathy for someone who is in pain.

A new principal will probably be a good thing, but I've been doing so much on my own, it will be an enormous change to take direction from someone else. I walk back to my office and check my messages. I find a voicemail from José Padilla at HR. "Cynthia, would you give me a call before you leave today? Thanks."

Now what? I can't take one more surprise. Maybe he wants to know how John's announcement went. I dial the number.

254

Chapter 28

The secretary puts me through.

"Cynthia, thanks for returning my call."

"Sure."

"John made his announcement?"

"Yes, I'm still digesting it."

"Well, here's more for you to think about. It needs to go through the board for approval, but the superintendent and I agree that you've done such a great job running Hamilton, you should be the next principal."

"Uh?" I'm stunned.

"I know you've just been there a year, but we have confidence that you know how to manage the school. And you'll be able to select a new vice principal to carry on under your guidance."

"I—I don't know what to say...thank you."

"You need to keep this to yourself until after the board acts, which will be next week."

"Do you know about the water gun incident? Maybe the board—"

"Cynthia, I'm aware, but that doesn't change anything. Congratulations. I'll be in touch about hiring a new VP."

"Thanks..." he has already hung up. I am truly in shock. Am I up to this? Well, like he said, I've already been doing most of the job. I'll have to get up to speed on budgets...and, God, am I going to be able to work with gum-chewing Sharon? But wow...this is unbelievably good news.

I finish cleaning up my desk, read and respond to a few emails, and find a place to store all the discipline referrals for the year. My new VP will not have to do it all, I promise. Gaby has left already. I'll see her tomorrow, as there is still a week to work.

I need to talk to Derek. He can keep a secret. A little before noon I walk out on a cloud. The strained feeling around my

255

mouth must be from the smile that has been plastered on for the last hour.

I drive to the winery and look for Derek. "How was graduation?" he asks. "Want to visit the cave?"

He pauses, raises an eyebrow, then goes on. "What are you so happy about?"

I take his arm and walk him around the building away from the picnic area, until nobody can see us. "You're not going to believe this." I hold out my hand for a handshake. He takes it, a puzzled look on his face. I continue, "Derek Simons, meet the new principal of Hamilton Middle School."

"What? Really? Wow!" Derek releases my hand and gives me a bear hug. "You are awesome, Cynthia Walker. You'll be a great principal. Tell me more."

"Later," I say. "We'd better get back to the party, but you can't tell a soul until after the board acts."

Derek salutes. "Yes, Ma'am. Understood."

I float through the rest of the day. Once home, I'm so excited, I don't know what to do first. Call my parents? Tell Erica? Or maybe I should wait. Something weird could happen to mess it up. That would be embarrassing. I'll wait.

The last days of my contract fly by—I'm numb to most everything. I give Gaby a potted plant and a box of chocolates to thank her for a great year. "Are you going somewhere?" she asks.

"Not far," I say, with a silly grin. She probably thinks I'm talking about Paris.

Once the support staff is gone for the year, Carlson and I have three more days to work. A few teachers wander in and out, organizing their rooms and replenishing copies of student worksheets for the coming year. I have no idea if Carlson knows about my impending promotion and I surely don't want to be the one to tell him. On the next to last afternoon as I'm on my

Chapter 28

way out the door at the end of the day, he stops me.

"Cynthia, can you give me a minute?"

"OK." I can hardly deny him a simple request at this stage of the game.

He has a bottle of scotch open on his desk. He follows my eyes. "Want some? Can't get you to go out with me, so I thought maybe we could have a drink here."

"No, thanks."

We sit on the sofa.

"I just want to thank you, Cynthia."

"That's not—"

"No, I want to do this. I know I wasn't much help this year. What with my health problems and my marriage...I wasn't firing on all cylinders, if you know what I mean."

"Well...I learned a lot."

"And you'll make a great principal, Cynthia." My eyes open wide. "Yeah," he continues. "I know, in fact, I recommended it when they asked."

"Oh...thank you." Once again, I don't know what to say.

That night, the board acts and I'm notified by phone that it's official. I ring my parents and friends. The newspaper calls to interview me. Teachers call with congratulations. I'm still on a cloud.

On my last day as VP, Carlson presents me with his desk sign that reads *Principal*, along with an expensive bottle of Pinot Noir. "That's the one you like, right? To help you celebrate."

I still don't know why he's leaving, but it's not my place to ask and I'm touched by the gift.

* * * * *

HERE WE ARE LOOKING OUT ON THE SEINE from the *Pont des Arts*, one of the bridges covered with lovers' padlocks. "Should we add one, *Cherie?*" asks Derek.

257

"Seems silly to me, *Mon Amour.* Waste of a good lock." Besides practicing our French, we've hit the museums and the gardens, climbed the *Tour Eiffel,* and tasted *escargots, macarons,* and a variety of wines. Despite my unwillingness to declare my love with a padlock, this has been the most romantic week of my life.

Derek puts an arm around me and we lean on the railing, watching the sun set on the river and the sparkling City of Light. "What a year," I say.

"The best," he answers.

I can't disagree.

LESSON #14: ABOVE ALL, FOLLOW YOUR HEART!

Acknowledgements

The writing world is a true village. Many friends read this book throughout its development. I especially want to thank those who tackled the earliest stages: Gretchen Hayes, Kathy Martin, Jane Rowland, Vreni Rau, and Marcie Miller—all talented educators. Paul Moser helped me navigate the minefield of editors. My patient critique group members read the novel with a minimum of suffering, a half-chapter at a time. Amber Starfire, Sarita Lopez, Marilyn Campbell, Barbara Toboni, John Petraglia, Jim Mc Donald, Geoffrey Leigh, Marianne Lyon, and Judy Baker, your input is always transformative.

About the Author

Lenore Hirsch enjoyed thirty-one years as a California teacher and school administrator at elementary and middle schools. Since retirement, she has written columns and features for the Napa Valley Register, blogs about her dogs and Napa restaurants, and has published poetry, memoir, short stories, food and travel pieces. In 2013 she released *My Leash on Life, Foxy's View of the World from a Foot Off the Ground* . The doggie memoir was followed in 2018 by a collection of poetry, *Leavings*, and *Laugh and Live, Advice for Aging Boomers*, humorous essays about aging. Contact her through www.lenorehirsch.com or lenorehirsch@att.net.

Printed in Great Britain
by Amazon